THE YOUNG

WORLD

BY

CHRIS WEITZ

www.atombooks.net

ATOM

First published in the United States in 2014 by Little, Brown and Company,
a division of Hachette Book Group
First published in Great Britain in 2014 by Atom

A CIP catalogue record for this book
is available from the British Library.

ISBN 978-0-349-00193-7

Printed and bound in Great Britain by
Clays Ltd, St Ives plc

Papers used by Atom are from well-managed forests
and other responsible sources.

MIX
Paper from
responsible sources
FSC
www.fsc.org FSC® C104740

Atom
An imprint of
Little, Brown Book Group
100 Victoria Embankment
London EC4Y 0DY

An Hachette UK Company
www.hachette.co.uk

www.atombooks.net

For Mercedes, Sebastian, and Paolo

Hope I die before I get old.

—old song

JEFFERSON

IT'S ANOTHER GORGEOUS SPRING DAY after the fall of civilization. I'm doing my rounds, following the path that winds through Washington Square Park like a warped infinity sign. I pass the tables where old men used to play chess, now Brainbox's open-air workshop. Then the fountain, witness to innumerable first dates, proffers of marijuana, and shrieking aquatic sallies of children. Now it's the tribe's reservoir, covered with tarps to keep out pigeon feces and algae-encouraging sunshine.

The statue of Garibaldi, or Gary Baldy, as we call him, is festooned with plastic leis, Mardi Gras beads, retro rappers' bling. The trophies of scavenging expeditions into the badlands outside the walls. The doomed quarters: Broadway, Houston, the shooting galleries of the West Village. Taped to the pedestal, mementos of the dead. Snaps of moms, dads, little brothers and sisters, lost pets. What Mom used to call "real pictures," to distinguish them from digital files. Hard copies are where it's at now that millions and millions of memories are lost in the cloud. An ocean of ones and zeros signifying nothing.

Through the stone arch with Washington (Founder of Our Country Washington, not my big brother Washington) on horseback, you can see all the way up Fifth to the Empire State Building. Smoke still issues from the highest floors. Kids say that's where he lives, the Old Man, the one adult who survived What Happened. Kids say a lot of shit.

Where there used to be grass and flowers, swing sets and dog runs, there are rows and rows of vegetables. Frank is bitching out a work party. And they take it. Yesterday's country mouse is today's savior. Frank grew up on a farm, and he's the only one among us who knows how to grow stuff. Without him, we'd all have rickets or scurvy or something else we'd never have worried about Before.

A foraging party comes in by the Thompson Street gate. Some canned food, some siphoned gas for the generators. A little red Honda 2000i 2k Jenny putters away, charging up walkie batteries and other essentials. Plus the occasional indulgence, an iPod or a Game Boy, if you can persuade BB to let you plug in.

Leaves hiss in the wind and jump to their deaths from high branches. A gust blows in from the north, presenting a bouquet of burning plastic and rotting flesh.

My walkie coughs.

"We've got company coming south on Fifth. Over."

It's Donna, on the other side of the park. I set off at a jog.

"How far away?" I ask. And, when there's no response, I

wonder if I didn't press down the Talk button properly. But then her voice pops up again.

"You didn't say *over*," says Donna. "Over."

"Jesus, Donna, over? Okay? Over, over. How many and how far away? *Over.*"

"They're halfway between Ninth and Eighth. About ten of them. Heavily armed. Over."

"They're not ours?"

Pause.

"*Over?*"

"They're not ours."

Donna can see practically straight down from her perch outside the walls, high up in a building on Eighth. I can make out the end of her rifle barrel projecting from a window.

"You didn't say *over*," I say.

"Oopsies. Over. You want me to shoot? They're right under me now, but I'll have a clear shot once they get past. Over."

"Do. *Not*. Shoot. Over."

"Fine, it's your funeral. Let me know if you want me to kill 'em. Over."

It's time to raise the alarm.

Near each entrance to the park, bolted onto a tree, is an old-fashioned winding Klaxon. God knows where Brainbox found them. I turn the handle, the inertia slowing me and worrying my tendons. The whine starts slow and low and, as the gears catch, turns into a scream out of hell.

As I turn the handle, I think about calories: how much heat I'm expending, how much I've taken in today. When you don't put in more than you burn, you start to die. I think, uselessly, about burgers and fries and cinnamon buns. Historical delicacies, unthinkable luxuries.

Sixty seconds later, our firing positions are bristling.

Six guns, a good part of our arsenal, point down Fifth Avenue from the slits in the armored school bus blocking the street. Plus Donna's sniper rifle behind them. The doors of the buildings approaching the barricade were boarded up months ago, and the street cleared as a free-fire zone.

Wash has joined the party. I'm looking for him to take the lead. But Generalissimo Washington just shrugs. *Your turn, little brother.*

"They're heavily armed," I say. As in, *this is no time for practice.*

"Then you better have a plan," says Wash.

Fine. I shoulder my AR-15 and scuttle into the school bus.

Its stuffed leatherette cushions are slashed to pieces. The walls are tagged with gallows humor:

PARTY AT MY HOUSE TONIGHT! PARENTS DEAD.

"Fuck the world." —me "No, fuck you!" —the world

Remember! Today is the first day of the rest of the end of everything.

I walk past the kids in the firing line. And I notice that even when the world has gone to hell, people still have a sense of fashion. The looting opportunities in our particular neck of the woods have made for some pretty eclectic looks. Prada overcoats with military insignia, peasant dresses cinched with ammo belts. This guy Jack even went full-on transvestite. It's not like his folks are gonna kick him out. And nobody else is going to quarrel with him. The guy is six feet tall and built like the proverbial brick shithouse.

Note to self: It would be nice to have a brick shithouse.

I remember reading somewhere that the guys in Napoleon's army who did all the dangerous recon missions got kind of flashy and dressed up in all sorts of swag. They called them the advance guard, or the *avant-garde*.

That puts me in mind of these books by Patrick O'Brian, with the lines of men ready by their cannons on the gun decks, and that movie they made with the Australian guy, and I think of saying something like, *Steady, lads. Await the order*, but that sounds lame, so instead I just pat them on the back or give them a slap on the butt, like we're getting ready for the big game.

"Hey!" one of the gunners responds when I pat her on the behind. It's that girl Carolyn, the blond who used to be kind of a fashionista before What Happened. Whoops. Even after the apocalypse, girls don't like to get slapped on the butt.

"Sorry," I say. "Totally nonsexual." I try to say it in a cool, devil-may-care kind of way.

She gives me a look like, *You're damn right it's nonsexual,* but I don't have time to explain. I shimmy into the observation post that Brainbox built in the front passenger seat.

There are ten of them, like Donna said; she has a good eye. All of them male, I think. Getting on in years, maybe sixteen or seventeen. They're in green camouflage, which is totally useless in the city. Their suits are festooned with all these military ribbons and medals and crap. Each one has some sort of school crest over his heart. And little skull patches lined up on their shoulders, like the miniature flags on old fighter planes.

There's a guy hefting one of those chunky machine guns, the kind with the feeder belt of bullets. A BAR? Wash knows what that's called. And I'm worried about the flamethrower another guy has, which, as I'm watching, he ignites with an old Zippo lighter.

Bandoliers of grenades, grappling hooks, the works. AR-15s like mine. They must have hit an armory.

"Whaddya want?" I shout. Aggressive, but not too showy. The way Wash would do it.

"I want to talk to the boss," says one of the strangers, a blond kid, seventeen maybe, blue eyes, cheekbones. Quarterback type. Type I wouldn't like back before It Happened. Type I don't like even more now.

Everybody in the bus waits for Wash to say something. But Wash has left me high and dry here. Thanks, brother.

I return my mouth to the speaking tube. Ow. Gotta get Brainbox to cushion the mouth hole.

"I'm the boss."

"You're kinda young for the boss," says Cheekbones. Our eyes meet through the ballistic glass.

"I'm the boss, okay? What do you want?"

But Cheekbones doesn't want to just get to the point. He bows, then starts intoning a speech like he's wandered in from *Game of Thrones*.

"Greetings to the Washington Square Clan from the Uptown Confederacy. We seek to parley."

One of the kids on our firing line titters, and I think they hear it, because they look at one another like they were expecting some sort of ceremonial response.

"*Parley* means—" says Cheekbones.

"I know what *parley* means," I say. "You could just say you want to talk."

"Fine. We want to *talk*, okay? We want to talk business."

They pull something forward on a leash.

It's a pig. Not a curly-tailed, kid's-book-cute pig, but a big, stinky porker.

Meat protein.

Who knows how they got it here from Uptown, through miles of hostile territory. They *are* looking kind of knocked around, and one of them seems to have a bullet wound; at any rate, his arm is in a sling and the blood is still bright red. A recent scrap, maybe up by Union Square. I heard gunfire this morning. But then I hear gunfire every morning.

"Okay. I'm assuming the pig is not your boyfriend, so that's what we're 'parleying' about?"

Cheekbones doesn't like me, but he's here to get things done, so he says, "Yeah, smart-ass, that's what we're here to trade."

"Okay. I'm a reasonable man. What do you want for it?"

Now he starts talking it up. "This is a prize pig from the Hansen farm upstate. One hundred percent USDA Grade-A Fancy, certified organic."

"You are aware," I say, "that there is no USDA anymore and that eating organic is the least of our concerns."

"Whatever. Its brother tasted good."

I look over at Frank. He shrugs. "Looks tasty. Nice and plump."

"Okay," I shout to Cheekbones. "Looks a little scrawny, but we might be able to trade. What do you want for it?"

And here's where things get really weird, because the guy says:

"Two girls."

There's a pause, or what my textese friends would describe as a WTF moment.

"Repeat, please?"

Cheekbones goes back into Tolkien mode and enunciates. "We will trade the pig for two females."

Your SAT word of the day is *nonplussed*.

"You mean human females?" I ask, and the guy shrugs like

it's the most natural thing in the world: Yeah, two girls for a pig. What's the big deal?

Donna comes over the walkie-talkie. "Jefferson? What's he want? I can't hear. Over."

Thinking it best not to tell our trigger-happy feminist sniper that these sociopaths want to trade pigs for girls (at a pretty unflattering rate of exchange, for that matter), I don't answer.

"Helllooooo? What's going on there? Over."

"I'm handling it, Donna, thank you very much. Over."

But *how* am I handling it? I can't say exactly. The girls on the firing line are looking at me.

I clear my throat. "Um, jeez, fellas, what the hell are you talking about? I mean, I'm sorry if you're feeling kind of lonely, but—"

"We've got plenty of girls. We just want more," says a big guy among the Uptowners, who has a lacrosse stick with a grenade in it. Why, *why*, has the whole world gone all Mad Max on me? Cheekbones stares him down, like he doesn't want anybody else talking.

"My colleague is right," he says. "We've got plenty of girls, we've got plenty of food, we've got plenty of everything uptown—electricity, running water, whatever they want. I don't know, makeup and shit. Look."

Cheekbones eyeballs the one girl in their group, a pretty, angry-looking blond. She steps, or is pushed, forward.

"Tell them about Uptown," he says to her. "Tell the girls they have nothing to worry about."

But she doesn't say anything. I look closer, and maybe it's the word *makeup* that did it, but I can't help noticing that she's got a bit of flesh-tone makeup on the left side of her face, which is where you'd hit somebody if you're right-handed.

I don't like it. Not even if there were girls in our group who wanted to leave. I wouldn't send them with these fascists, and I sure as hell wouldn't trade a person for a pig, no matter how much I miss bacon.

"Can I please just shoot that bitch?" says Carolyn, and I realize she's talking about the Uptowner girl, and I think, *Why does Carolyn want to take it out on* her? I'm not sure I'm ever going to understand the way girls think.

Anyway, she pulls back the slide on her rifle, and they hear it out there, and there's a whole lot of weapon-cocking and magazine-jamming and safety-take-offing from the Uptowners, who get down on their knees and bellies and point their guns right at our firing holes, and I think, *Their assault rifles are going to go right through the side of this bus, through the reinforced plates, and we are all going to die.*

"This is *Donna*. Ov—" I turn off the walkie.

Where is Wash? He is nowhere to be seen. He's left this one entirely to Number Two Son.

Then Frank shouts, "You think we playin' *Call of Duty* here? You think we in multiplayer mode? Over Wi-Fi or some shit? You all gonna get shot up and just *respawn* someplace? Ain't no Xbox up in here. Ain't *no respawn*. So chill the fuck out."

He's right. There's no respawn for anybody except the rats. There's no end to them. Kill one and up pops another.

"Bridge to nowhere," I say, the phrase coming to me from sometime in my childhood. In the silence of people getting ready to shoot one another, it has a certain ring.

"What?" says Cheekbones.

"Thanks, but no thanks," I shout. "Be on your way now, O *Confederacy of Uptown*."

"We'll go to the Fishermen," shouts Cheekbones. Bargaining.

The Fishermen live down on South Street and, as memory serves, bunk in an old tall ship, USS *Peking*. I think they'd rather be called "the Pirates," but hey.

"Tell them hi. Enjoy the sashimi."

But they just lie there. They actually look glad of the rest. That's when I realize they're not taking their business elsewhere. They don't have a plan B. This pig must go. This is too bad, because if they're out of options, so are we.

"We can *take* what we need," says Cheekbones.

Don't show any weakness. Wash says that a predator has to think about whether he'll get hurt taking down his prey, even if he knows he'll win.

"No, you can't. Good day to you and Porky."

I see them muttering among themselves—

And I see lacrosse guy reach for the ring on his grenade—

And—

A shot.

People like to say stuff like, "A shot rang out," but there's nothing melodic about it. It's percussive. *POCK!* It erases all your senses for a moment, not the least because your instinct is to squeeze your eyes shut and try to find the nearest hole in the ground.

I shout into the walkie. "Donna, I said don't shoot!"

"I didn't do it, Jefferson. Over."

Everybody is frozen—our people, their people. Then suddenly, everybody is shouting at one another, like they used to do on TV and in movies, with all kinds of threats and cursing, but none of our people are hit, and for that matter, none of them look hit, either.

The pig.

Its eyes roll upward with what I have to say is perfect comic timing. As if to inspect the new hole in its head. It falls like a hinge and *THUMPS* onto its side, legs twitching.

"Hold your fire!" I shout as my guys (and girls) grip their rifle stocks and take aim.

A couple of the Uptowners grab hold of the pig's legs and try to shift it, but the thing was heavy when it was alive, and *dead* weight is even heavier. It just doesn't want to cooperate. The dead demonstrate a startling indifference.

With all the trouble it took them to get it downtown, there is practically no way they're going to get that pig back to where it came from, its blood calling out to wild dogs every step of the way.

That must be what Wash had in mind.

My big brother. He stands on top of the wall, tall and handsome, in plain sight of the Uptowners, who now have every one of their guns trained on him.

"Go ahead," says Wash. "Tomorrow's my eighteenth birthday."

I've been trying not to think about it. But he's right. Soon enough...no respawn. So he's daring them to shoot him.

And he didn't even say good-bye. It's selfish, but that's what I think. *He didn't even say good-bye.*

Wash stands there on top of the wall like a statue, backlit, greeting the future.

Cheekbones, who looks like he really, *really* wants to shoot Wash dead, lowers his gun and smiles.

"Nah," he says. "I'm not going to do you any favors. Enjoy the Sickness."

The Uptowners are arguing among themselves. Some of them want to storm the gates, and the rest just want to get the hell out of here. Cheekbones finally gets them to shut up, and they withdraw, crabwalking and flashing the muzzles of their guns around in a move they seem to have stolen from a video game.

"This isn't over," shouts Cheekbones.

"Good," says Wash. "Come on back with some baked beans."

After an hour or so, when we've made sure the Uptowners are genuinely gone and not using the pig as bait to snipe at us, we drag it in, chasing away the rats.

DONNA

A LOT OF BOOKS YOU READ, the author thinks it's cool to have an "unreliable narrator." To keep you guessing and to acknowledge that there are no absolutes, and everything is relative, or whatever. Which I think is kind of lame. So—just so you know—I am going to be a *reliable* narrator. Like, totally. You can trust me.

First thing about me, I'm not beautiful. If you're wondering how to picture me in your head, don't picture, like, some movie star or something.

Maybe the girl next door. Except that it's a little different in New York, because we don't live in houses; we live all stacked up in apartment buildings. I remember every time I saw a TV show about the suburbs, where people, like, played on their lawns and bicycled around, I thought it was so *exotic*.

So—the girl next floor? Whatever. Point is, don't go nuts. A character actress. The pixieish, wacky best friend, not the one with the legs and the boobs and the perfect teeth.

I mean, I don't think I'm a troll, either. It's just, even with the new end-of-civilization meal plan, I'm not totally happy with my body. Maybe it's the lack of protein. I probably should not be worrying about this. Life is too short.

Ha-ha. Life is too short.

My dad used to say that. I used to call him Dad to annoy him because he wanted me to call him Hal, which isn't that weird, because it was his real name, but come *on*, it's not the sixties, and my calling him Hal wasn't going to make him any younger. Nope, those girls he wanted to have sex with were still—how to put it?— young enough to be his daughters. *Uch.*

Well, you're dead, *Harold*, and so is Mom and every other fucking adult. Talk about the ultimate flake-out. And the little kids. All the little kids. Charlie.

So there's a *few* things that I'm bummed at my parents about. The fact that they named me after Madonna—not, like, the mother of Jesus but the one who sang "Vogue." *Dude.*

But am I gonna change it? Nah. Everybody's changing their name, because they figure, why not? It's like, "Hi, my name is Katniss."—"I'm Threeyoncé."—"Call me Ishmael." Forget it. I want to keep *some* things from Before, even if they're lame.

Yeah, so, (Ma)Donna's problem, nutritionally speaking, is that protein is hard to find. Carbs? Sure. You'd be pretty shocked how long that shitty nonorganic bread, that wonder-of-wonders bread, *keeps* before blue fuzz starts growing on it. Sometimes the rats get to it first.

So what do we eat? The rats. Which, kind of, means we're eating the bread anyway, right? I mean, the rats ate the bread; we ate them.

And what else do the rats eat? Before we eat them? Well, let's not get into that.

We did a whole lot of corpse burning back in the day. Cleansing by fire, Wash called it. Said some dudes called the Zoroastrians used to do it. Yes, I spelled that right. I may not be all SAT-wordy like Wash and Jeff, but no way are they gonna lord it over me, knowing bonus words and shit.

Cleansing by fire! Those were some good times. Douse a bandanna in Chanel No. 5, put on some sassy pink North Face gloves, and heave-ho! Make a big pile of bodies and try not to use too much gasoline and try not to lose the lunch you didn't have enough of.

Not enough hands or time to get rid of all the bodies, though. And they're still out there, millions of them, slowly turning into mulch, pulsing with maggots. It has been a banner year for carrion eaters.

Hope I didn't spoil your appetite. 'Cause when Porky Pig goes down, and those fools from wherever take off, I'm all, *barbecue*! And as soon as I get relieved from lookout duty (I may act totally slack, but the fact is I'm such a good girl. If only my teachers had known!), I'm down in the Square, nipping at Frank's heels. He orders a bunch of our peeps to tie up the carcass by the back legs and hoist it on a tree branch, and I'm all, pulled-pork sandwich, please! Pork chop, trotters, snout, whatever, and I am doing a little happy dance, but then—

Then I see Jefferson, and he sees me, and he does not look happy, and I remember Wash—he was standing up there in front of all those guns like a jackass, and I realize, one-two-three, oh, I get it, that's why...that's why Jefferson is looking so bummed. Then I feel like an asshole.

See, when you're hungry, it's your stomach thinking. Like, your stomach actually *thinking*. I heard somewhere that your stomach has as many serotonin receptors as your brain. So we're like those dinosaurs with two brains. We're like dinosaurs in other ways, too. For instance, we're going extinct.

Charlie's favorite dinosaur was stegosaurus. He had a stuffed one he called Spike.

Stop it.

So I realize that Wash was trying to commit suicide by cop— that's what they used to call it, when some dumbshit would decide life just wasn't worth living (this was when life *was* worth living, mind you) and would come at the cops with his gun blazing and force them to take him out....

Or he just *really* wanted a McRib sandwich and thought, *What the hell, it's worth a shot.*

I'm kind of curious about that, so I go to Wash, who's standing by the tree where they're hauling up the pig. He's securing the rope with a trucker hitch to a bent piece of rebar sunk in the ground.

Wash always leads by example. The officer corps of the Pocky. (That's my cute name for the apocalypse. It's also the name for those yummy Japanese candy sticks.) I inquire after his reasoning, diplomatically.

"So what the fuck was that, dude?"

He keeps tying his fancy knot.

Wash: "What was what?"

Me: "Uh…I don't know…lemme *see*…the part where you stand in front of a bunch of douche bags with guns and dare them to blow your brains out?"

Wash cinches off the knot and shrugs. Stands up and looks me in the eye finally.

Me: "People need a leader." It doesn't sound quite right, coming out of my mouth. Not the sort of thing I say. But it's true.

Wash: "They're going to have to find a new one soon, anyway."

And then he walks off. Which, by the way, you should never do to someone who, you know, you almost did, you know, with. It's just rude.

So I'm pretty pissed. But then he turns around and smiles and says, "Oh, you're invited to my birthday barbecue. Tonight. The theme is…" He thinks.

Me: "Post-apocalyptic?"

He laughs.

Wash: "*Pre*-apocalyptic. We'll pretend to tweet each other. We'll talk about the new iPhone they're not coming out with. Snapchat."

Me: "We'll ask if we look fat in this. Download ringtones."

Wash: "Yeah. It'll be awesome."

And he walks off again. But not so fast! Little brother Jeff is right there in his face, follows him and pushes him. They square off. Wash and Jeff. Now, *there* were some parents to have. Name their kids Washington and Jefferson. I bet they were all, "Son, it's time you learned about the Golden Rule," and sailing weekends and scaling fish or whatever, not asking you where you get your herb 'cause their dealer just got arrested.

Whatever.

I can't hear what they're arguing about, but it's a doozy. Wash is trying to hug Jeff, like, "It's okay," and Jeff is clearly *not* okay, and I wouldn't be, either, I guess. Finally Wash sort of wrestle-hugs Jeff, and I look away, because boys hate it when people see them expressing emotion.

Compartmentalizing. That's what Wash called it. You put your feelings here in this compartment, and you put your mind in another compartment. And I said to him, looking up from where my head was resting on his chest, "How big a box is your heart in?" and he looked at me and didn't say anything, and that's when I kind of figured this was not going to be love among the ruins for Donna and Wash.

Frank is chewing people out, saying, "Where is the tarp and the bucket?" Because he plans to catch all the blood to make blood sausage with the intestine casings, which a couple of years ago would have made me want to hurl but now makes me even hungrier.

Rrrrrip! goes Frank's knife down the center of the pig's stomach, and—*plop!*—he reaches inside the rib cage with the knife and his whole hand, and he makes a cut, and the whole of the pig's insides neatly flop out onto the tarp, like this is one of Brainbox's machines and he's just pulled out the restraining bolt or something, and "Catch the blood!" goes Frank, and all his helpers are in there catching the blood in buckets. I decide to head for home, not because I'm too grossed out but because I'm too hungry.

Home isn't far—25 Washington Square North, a cute little four-story walk-up with a green door. Prime real estate, but it's a buyer's market.

There's only a couple hundred of us here in the Square. Pretty much everybody has a sweet pad, except Brainbox, who lives in the library. I mean literally *lives* in the Bobst Library.

I like it on the north side of the Square—not far from my sniping position, good light. Six bedrooms. Yeah, I moved up in the world.

I've decorated in End-Times Eclectic. A looted Eames chair here, a milk crate there, with a wooden piece or two I saved from the winter bonfires. And let's not forget the rattraps. Did you know that "yakitori" is an anagram of "ick—I try rat"? Well, not exactly. But you get the idea.

I check my Impatients on the first floor. Did I mention I'm the tribal doctor? Yeah. My mom was a nurse. She used to take me to the ER when she didn't have babysitters, which is maybe why I can handle the assorted bumps, bruises, and projecting bones of the Pocky.

I look at Eddie Hendrix's knee. The swelling is down. He'll be up and about in a while, but the pull test tells me that his ACL is gone and that the tibia is going to keep popping out every now and then. At least, that's what my old *Merck Manual* says. Back in the day, they could fix it with a bone graft from the patella, even an allograft from a cadaver. Now? An Ace bandage if you're lucky. Serves him right for risking his life playing a game of hoops outside the walls.

Duddie is getting better, too. I can't tell whether it was strep until somebody makes another hospital run, but about 60 percent of us have it just hanging out in our throats in a little streptococcus party, waiting to come out. I wanted him up here to keep him from infecting anybody else. And he's not bad-looking.

After the nursey stuff is done, I head up for some reading. I'm working toward my degree in pre-apocalyptic social structures from the University of Donna. Currently, I'm catching up on *Us Weekly* from 2011.

My bedroom is my favorite room in the house. Because there is not one motherfucking piece of my past in it. A lot of girls, they've plastered their walls with pictures of their family, the stuff they used to do, Disneyland, ponies, friends (yay!), parties, whatever. Fine. Have yourself a big old group grope with your ghosts. I suppose it beats some of the boys' rooms, full of porn. Top relationship tip, fellas? There is nothing quite like a tacked-up picture of a spread vajay-jay over the bed to end a date on just the wrong note.

Dusk comes on pretty fast, and it's time to light the candles.

Some people really resent the lack of electricity, the dearth of modern comforts, appliances, hot showers, all that stuff we used to take for granted.

I'm one of those people.

I'm tired of this full-on urban camping experience. I'm not gonna pretend that candlelight is romantic, like, *Oh it's so great to read by. In a way we've gained so much. You don't know what you have until it's gone.* OKAY, I GET IT. I want central heating. I want TV. I want a *hair dryer.* So sue me.

The darkness coming in is like death in slow motion. It's like What Happened, every night.

But a wonderful smell comes through the window....

Pig.

And I'm down the stairs and out the door, and I'm promising to bring plates back for my Impatients. I'm promising them slaw, country biscuits, pecan pie, all kinds of crap.

Okay, so Washington Square *does* look pretty great by firelight. All the lamppost torches are lit. They're dotted over our ten acres of purgatory, painting everything near them yellow and red. The light—well, it may not be bright, but it breathes oxygen like we do. It's alive.

The paths are marked out by solar garden lights from Target. They suck for illumination, but they keep you from tripping over the runner beans. And I skip—I'm actually skipping to the middle of the Square with my doggy bowl. Runners are already heading out to the sniper positions with food for the lookouts. Everybody else is forming an orderly line, and there, spitted on a push-up bar and roasting on a repurposed bench-press stand Brainbox must have rummaged up somewhere, turned by hand over a fire of smashed library chairs, is the piggy.

We all read *Lord of the Flies* in what—sixth grade? So we know that you've got to cook the pig through or you'll get sick.

Frank throws some hefty slabs of belly into a tray. "Cover 'em in salt," he says. I have seen the future, and it is bacon.

There's all these old chairs and couches out in the Square. They get moldy when the rain comes, but they're dry and comfy now. You can lie back on them and see the stars. With the wind in the right direction, blowing the smoke from the Uptown fires away, you can see the stars like you were out in the country. Look at those stars that don't care for you.

There's a guitar going—Jack Toomey, thank God, not Jo, who only plays Beatles songs. Some beers scrounged from somewhere. 'Cause the grown-ups are away, you know. Other kids are smoking weed from the rooftop patches. Up there it grows like—well, like a weed. Wash banned hard drugs and hard liquor, which makes sense. Gotta stay frosty, or people will jump you and cut your throat.

Brainbox spares some of his precious gas for one of his precious generators. He calls them Jennies. We gave each one a name—Jenny Jones, Jenny Craig, J-Lo, Jenny Agutter, who was in some movie about Australia Jeff likes. So tonight Jennie Honda Garth is showing us a Blu-ray movie projected onto a bed cloth strung between two trees.

It's our tribal favorite, *Star Wars Episode IV: A New Hope*. Which is confusing, because it's basically episode one, but whatever.

A lot of girls don't get *Star Wars*, or all they know about it is they want to be Princess Leia on Halloween, the part where she looks all hoochie mama in the golden bikini. Me, when I was little I wanted to be Han Solo. Dude was a certified badass. *And* a drug smuggler. I mean, those hidden compartments on the *Millennium Falcon* weren't for pirated lightsabers.

I ask Jefferson who he'd be, and he says, "Luke, of course." Of course.

Me: "I think you're more the C-3PO type." He blushes.

Jefferson and I have been engaged in friendly trench warfare since we were in kindergarten. I make fun of him for being too proper. He's, like, the Guy Who Talks in Complete Sentences. He gives me shit for swearing too much and saying *like* all the time.

Which, yeah? But here's the thing. Everybody thinks that *like* is just a sort of junk word, empty calories or whatever? But my theory is that it's totally unfairly maligned.

Look at metaphors and similes. They're, like, the press darlings of language. Can't write poetry without 'em. And what's a metaphor? It's just saying that one thing is *like* another. In fact, you could say that whenever people talk, they're just making comparisons. This is good, this is bad, subject-verb-predicate. That's why *like* is such a useful word. It means that what you're saying isn't *exactly* the deal. It's *sort of* the deal. It's a linguistically humble means of comparing. It's an acknowledgment that the world is not black and white, and people understand one another only approximately. Know what I'm saying?

Anyway, Brainbox says he'd like to be R2-D2. Which, yeah. A robot who nobody can understand except C-3PO? Yeah.

Jefferson: "Actually, I'm of the opinion that R2-D2 is the real hero of the movie."

Me: "How's that?"

Jefferson: "Well, *he's* transporting the Death Star plans, right? *He* ejects from the rebel blockade runner, then *he* makes sure he gets bought by Luke, then *he* escapes and finds Obi-Wan. *He* fixes the hyperdrive. In the end, he gets shot up by Darth Vader, but he still survives. Really he's the most self-actualized character in the entire story."

Me: "You are so Threepio."

Jefferson keeps sighing and tsk-tsking at the movie for some reason, and he throws a rock at the screen when the green guy tries to shoot Han Solo in the bar. The galaxy far, far away ripples. I don't even ask.

Instead my mind wanders back to a place I don't want it to go. Like an addict looking for a fix.

It's two years ago, and the Sickness has just hit.

Mom has been working nonstop at the hospital, trying to stem the flow of patients. But Charlie has got it now, and she's at home. She's barely able to care for herself—she's got It. It seems like every adult in the city has It. The TV is always on, chattering away like a lunatic in the living room. It says that the Sickness is spreading all over the US, and the first case has been reported in Europe.

Mom is throwing up someplace. Charlie's fever is spiking incredibly high.

"Am I gonna die?" Charlie asks me, his voice on the edge of tears.

"No, honey, you're not going to die." I'm mopping his forehead as I'm lying to him. I don't know why I'm alive and unaffected while he's sick. "Do you want some more water?"

"No," he says in his little voice. "I want you to snuggle with me. Will you snuggle with me until I feel comfy?"

I nod, and more tears come. I lie down on his bed and hug him to me.

"I'm afraid to go to sleep. I'm afraid I'll never wake up again."

So am I. But I say, "You'll be fine, honey. You'll get better. Go to sleep now. Get some rest." And I hold him as he falls asleep for the last time.

JEFFERSON

EVEN THROUGH the temporal-spatial distortion of hyperspace, the death throes of the planet Alderaan strike the aged Jedi. He totters and sits. Luke asks him what's wrong.

"I felt a great disturbance in the Force, as if millions of voices suddenly cried out in terror, and were suddenly silenced. I fear something terrible has happened."

You said it.

Brainbox won't let me watch the movie and eat in peace. He's dead set on some damn fool crusade.

"That's pretty far, dude," I say.

"What's pretty far?" asks Donna, who returns from scrounging for extra scraps of pork under the guise of cleaning people's plates for them.

"The main branch," says Brainbox.

"Of what?"

"The public library."

"With the lions?"

"Yes."

Brainbox doesn't meet Donna's eyes. Instead, he does what he always does, which is turn the little crank on his plastic emergency radio and twiddle around between stations, which are nothing but static anyway, because everybody's dead.

"Have you read all the books at the Bobst *already?*" Donna asks.

"Think about it, Donna," says Brainbox. "How could I read all the books at the Bobst? They have over a million ti—"

I crash in on Brainbox's pedantry before it drowns us. "Brainbox found an abstract."

"Like, as opposed to a concrete?"

"An abstract is a summary of a scientific paper," says Brainbox.

"Uh-huh. Awesome?"

"Brainbox thinks it has something to do with What Happened," I say.

"Oh, *that*," says Donna.

"There's only an abstract listing at the Bobst. And, of course, the computers are dead. So I need to go to the main branch to find out what the whole article says."

"Tell her what the abstract's about," I say.

"It's called 'The Risk of Wexelblatt Effects in Enilikoskotonic Agents.'"

Donna acts excited. "Why didn't you say that in the first place!"

Brainbox doesn't know what to do with this. There's really no point being ironic around him.

"Two hours, there and back," I say.

"Uh, no thanks," says Donna. "I heard the library was haunted."

"Where'd you hear that?"

"I don't know," Donna says. "Around."

"There's no such thing as ghosts," I say.

"Whatever." Then she adds, "Just Google it, dude." This is a popular catchphrase in the tribal lingo. You say it when you realize how little you know and how much you thought you knew before teh internetz up and died.

"Tell her what *enilikoskotonic* means, BB."

"It means 'adult-killing.' "

"It killed the little kids, too."

Brainbox shrugs.

Donna doesn't say anything, but I can tell from her expression that it shakes her up a little. I'm kind of an expert in Donna's facial expressions.

She doesn't know it, but I love looking at her.

His point made, Brainbox goes back to playing with the windup radio. He turns the little crank, then floats the dial up and down. Static.

Wash shows up. He's wearing a tuxedo, and he must have gone to the trouble of boiling some water, because he's had a shave.

He intends to celebrate his eighteenth in style.

There's cheering, the guitar rolls into "Happy Birthday," and everybody sings. But it's kind of halfhearted. That song has a sting in its tail. Nobody has the bad taste to sing "and many more" at the end.

The whole place goes dead at that, realizing that there probably won't be any more.

So I get up and I shout, "AND MANY MORE!"

And the guitar gets strummed back to life, and the song starts up again. But people are singing it for real now, that same old crappy song, belting it out. And suddenly everybody is hugging. And people are crying. Peter is hugging Wash, and everybody is all around him, and he's making sure he hugs them all, the ones he knows best, the ones he knows least, the ones he loves, the ones he doesn't.

He goes over to Donna and looks in her eyes, and it's *good-bye, I don't want to be alone.* I mean, he doesn't say it, but I *know.* He hugs Brainbox, and I see *good-bye, I'm sorry I can't protect you anymore,* and he comes to me, and I see *good-bye, I know you don't want it to be, but it's good-bye, little brother, good-bye.*

And it's good-bye, good-bye, *good-bye.* Good-bye, my friends, I love you; good-bye, I'm sorry I didn't know you better; good-bye, I'm sorry you'll die soon, too; good-bye, maybe there's hope for you; good-bye, good-bye, good-bye.

DONNA

I WISH THAT I didn't have to help Wash die.

Don't get me wrong. I'm not squeamish or anything. In the first place, I'm pretty much used to people buying the farm, and besides, I've seen the gnarliest stuff you can imagine with Mom at the ER.

It's that Washington and I had this *thing*.

I sort of kind of thought I was in love with him for, like, ten minutes. And he sort of kind of was interested until I wouldn't go all the way.

Here's when we get to the part that I haven't mentioned yet? Because people get totally prejudiced by this? But I'm sort of kind of a virgin. Not, like, totally. Not, like, Goody Two-Shoes or anything. Like, I've done *some* stuff, but…yeah.

It was just…when It Happened, suddenly everybody was hooking up all over the place. I mean, things were very NC-17 verging on X. When your life expectancy falls below the drinking age, you kind of have an incentive to live it up. Make hay while the sun shines. Car-pay the diem. Gather ye rosebuds while ye may. YOLO. Etc. Who cares about STDs? Who cares about rehab? Who cares about reputations?

That's for people with *futures*. And you can imagine what happened when people realized they couldn't get pregnant. For a while it was total Sodom-and-Gomorrahville.

So—doing it was the thing to do. Like, even more than Before. But I guess I'm just not much of a follower.

I mean, basically I had lost everything. What did I have left to keep?

Which is odd, because my parents were *sooo* not religious or anything. My mom told me more than I ever wanted to know about the birds and the bees and stuff. It was like, *ugh, spare me the Latin names for everything.* And it's not like I felt I was keeping myself for anything or anyone. Just...

So once Washington realized that he wasn't getting any hot stuff, he lost interest, and I felt like a total moron. I was never able to tell Jefferson. I know he doesn't have those kinds of feelings for me—I mean, I'm totally not his type—but all the same, for some reason, I felt like it would hurt our friendship. And *that's* something else I have that I don't want to lose.

Anyway, the suckiest thing about being tribal doctor isn't setting broken bones and hearing the muffled *crunch-crunch* through the flesh; it isn't having to tell someone there's no more pain medication because all the morphine and oxycodone and fentanyl have been hoovered up by junkies.

It's watching people you know die from the Sickness.

Everybody thinks they know what dying looks like, because they've seen it on TV and in the movies. Like, some guy gets shot, and there's just enough time for his buddies to say, "You're gonna be fine! Stay with me! Chopper's on the way!" And then the guy will say something really cool and poignant, and then he'll log out.

So not the deal.

Generally, when somebody falls off a roof or gets shot or contracts cholera from some dirty water, they take a LONG time to die, and they're screaming and moaning the whole time, and the smartest thing they can think of to say is, *It hurts so much!* over and over again. And you're not thinking, *Don't you die on me!* but *God, I hope she kicks it soon.* And they're all, *Help me! Help me! I don't want to die! It hurts! Kill me!* Which, yes, is contradictory, but, you know, as Walt Whitman said, "Do I contradict myself? So what? Life is complicated as a mofo."

So—Washington starts showing symptoms, like, right on his birthday. This is odd, because the age thing is not some *rule.* Some people knock off around eighteen, some earlier, some later. You really never know. It has something to do with hormones. Something *we* have and little kids and adults don't; that's what protects you. But we must be hosts, because when you reach maturity, the stuff kicks in. *Physical* maturity, I mean. If you didn't die until you reached *emotional* maturity, dudes would be living forever.

Maybe Wash had been hanging on until his eighteenth, waiting for little bro Jefferson to grow up. But the day after the party, he starts coughing. And he knows the deal. Checks in to the infirmary. I give him his own room—a nice clean one overlooking the Square.

Wash: "Go find Jefferson, will you?"

Well, you can't refuse a dying man, but I wish you could.

Jefferson is at the north gate, talking to Brainbox about wiring something for sound. I don't even have to say anything, thank God. When he sees my face, he knows.

He drops what he's doing and walks up to me. I give him a hug. *Give* him a hug? He gives me a hug. We exchange one. We share one.

Grief cuts you open. Our nerves are poking out of our flesh and twining around each other like fighting octopi.

And for some reason, I remember a time in kindergarten. Jeff is holding my hand, and I say, "Yes, I will marry you. Let's go play!"

Well, that was then.

He's forcing himself not to cry during the walk to the infirmary, which, *why*? What the hell is it with boys? Their heads must be all backed up with tears. Dumbshits. I love me a good weep. Let those toxins out.

When they see each other, it's like, "Hey."—"Hey." Like they're just *hanging out*. I try to leave, but Wash calls me back. Jefferson looks like he's glad I'm there, too. Wash holds my hand, and then Jefferson takes my other hand, and it's, like, *awk*ward! But, oh well. I'm in for the ride.

Wash is still in the coherent stage. Once they start babbling, the end is near. The sweats are just setting in. "Tell me a story, Jeff," he says.

Jefferson is kind of the resident storyteller. When we got this whole groovy commune/armed compound thing going, people started gathering near the fountain at night. Nobody could stand being on their own. They'd hang out, play music, and shoot the shit. Get baked. Talk a lot about movies and TV, in a pathetic, nostalgic kind of way, like the end of the entertainment industry was the worst thing to come out of all this.

Jefferson usually sat reading a book with a windup flashlight, acting kind of asocial. Every page or so—*zipzipzip!*—he'd wind up his flashlight. Then Brainbox would have a go on his radio. It was the two of them, cranking away.

One night somebody asked him to read aloud, and then it became kind of a thing, and then somebody asked him to tell the story of a movie—just to, kind of, dramatize it.

And the thing was, he was *good*. Once he got going, he'd do different voices, he'd comment on parts of the story, he'd twist things around so you never totally knew what was going to happen. Eventually people asked him to make up his *own* stories. So every night, he would tell one. Kind of like the stories parents make up for their kids, but more grown-up. "The Dude Who Played *Diablo* With the Devil," "The Phantom Subway Stop," "The Garage That Ate Bands," that sort of thing.

Once I saw him looking all preoccupied, and I asked him what was up, and he said, "I'm working on tonight's story." Thing is, people were just fiending for anything familiar and non-end-of-the-world-ish. He didn't have to try so hard. We were like four-year-olds at bedtime. But Jeff started to take some pride in it.

Jeff: "I don't have a story."

Wash: "Last chance." And Jeff looks as if a wave of misery has smacked him in the face.

He starts telling Wash a story about this guy Sid Arthur, who grows up super rich. His parents want to give him the perfect childhood, so they, like, keep him indoors and turn off the TV, and he's not allowed to know about all the lame shit that goes on in the world.

One day, he's in the maid's room and he sees TV for the first time. It's some detective show, and a dude's been murdered. He's never even *heard* of death before, and it blows his mind.

Sid decides to go out into the world and find out about all the stuff he's been missing. This is a major downer, and after a while, Sid wishes he hadn't seen all the homeless people and the beat-downs and the old folks in retirement homes and whatnot, but it's too late. There's no "undo" command for life. So he ends up sitting for days on end under a tree in the park, and he figures out that the reason everything is such a drag is that people are totally obsessed with hanging on to what they have—cool stuff and good feelings and youth and even life itself. Sid realizes that it's all bullshit, and then for some reason, he gets totally blissed out.

I have absolutely no idea what this means, but Wash nods and laughs. I have a sense that Jefferson is riffing on some story they already know. Maybe it comes from the Asian mojo side of them. They're, like, half Japanese, which, by the way, is part of what made Wash so majorly hot. Best-of-both-worlds-type situation.

Jefferson isn't as much of a babe. I mean, he's cute. I guess I just never think of him that way.

The first convulsions hit, and it's not gonna be long till the crazy talk starts and then the coma sets in. Wash knows what's coming, and he tells Jeff it's time to say bye, but Jefferson won't leave.

I go catch some sleep. I leave Jeff and Wash together. When I leave, I finally hear Jeff cry, those horrible I-can't-breathe, little-kid tears.

Wash didn't want a funeral, but naturally people gather around the fountain that night. Everybody with their candles and their lanterns and their plastic rave blinkies. It's kind of nice that people would use up their precious blinky batteries, crack those glow sticks and let them burn out. Everybody's wearing their best gear. Dior dresses with combat boots, sharp suits with band patches on them, basketball shirts with Native American beads, sabers, handmade spears, bolt-action rifles with craft-knit slings. People have painted tears coming from their eyes. Black armbands and *Wash* graffiti on their jackets. Somebody has even unearthed a varsity jacket with a big purple *W* on it.

I have to admit I kind of *like* us, I mean our tribe. Especially when you compare it with a bunch of creeps like the Uptowners. We definitely let our freak flags fly. It would have been cool if everybody had felt so free-spirited *before* the end of the world, but better late than never, I guess.

We've been through the funeral routine before, of course. Somebody gets accepted into the big university in the sky every few weeks.

Usually we try to just forget about it. Around here we try *not* to think about the future. And we try to delete the past.

But Wash was different. Without him, we'd be a bunch of cliques and floaters. We'd be dead. So they sit around, they swap stories about him, they say "I can't believe it." The mood starts to feel like despair. I even hear somebody talking about heading out on their own. Wash would hate this. Wash would stop this.

Jefferson seems like he gets the way people are feeling. He steps onto the edge of the fountain and calls for quiet.

JEFFERSON

EVERYBODY'S LOOKING AT ME. I'm wearing Wash's hand-me-down authority until they realize it doesn't fit. "Listen," I say. "I get the feeling that everybody's thinking about what happens now. Maybe you're scared. Well, I'm scared, too."

Okay, everybody's listening. Now what? I'm not used to making speeches. So I decide to think about it like I'm just telling a story. Everybody likes a story.

"Wash felt the same way about all of you as he did about me. You were his family." Oh crap, don't cry now.

"Before he died, he said I should tell you all this: He wanted to make sure that we stuck together, no matter what. He wanted to make sure that we did everything we could to help each other. He was proud that we'd managed to pull together a life on the edge of this...this chaos and darkness. He wanted me to tell you to love each other and protect each other." I can't think of anything else, so I just say, "That's it."

I hop off the edge of the fountain. And the moment I do, I

hear somebody say, "Jefferson for generalissimo!" That's the title Wash chose when they voted him in. He thought it was funny.

Everybody applauds; everybody joins in. Popular acclaim. My election is seconded and thirded and fourthed and down the line. A landslide for Wash's little brother. Like the divine right of kings is back in style.

This isn't what I had in mind. Telling people what to do isn't my thing. I don't want to call the shots. All I wanted was to give people a little backbone, maybe make them think twice about bailing on the tribe. It wasn't a political speech or anything. But then I realize there's no difference between talking and politics when there are so few of us.

See, direct democracy is kind of unavoidable when you're all huddled together in a five-hundred-by-one-thousand-foot rectangle.

Not that there's much to vote *about*. People can kind of agree on everything important. Guard the gates. Get food. Dig latrines.

Wash says this is—*said* this is—about "the Hierarchy of Needs." He said we didn't have time to argue about the usual crap, like whether it's cool to gay-marry somebody or whatever, because we were too busy trying to eat. We're from three different schools—the rich kids from the Learning Center, the poor Catholic kids from Loyola, and the gay kids from Stonewall—but we don't give each other much hassle. Thank you, Hierarchy of Needs.

What else is keeping us together? We don't even have a constitution. Life, liberty, and the pursuit of happiness? We're still working on the first one.

Here's our domestic policy: Just chill.

Here's our foreign policy: Go fuck yourself.

So I don't want to run the show. The show sucks. The show is gonna close. "New York, New York" is playing while people file out of the stadium.

I don't know. Maybe it's time to take control. Maybe it's time to do something big. Maybe I should tell Donna how I feel.

Maybe tomorrow.

It's been a while since I realized that I was in love with Donna. When I did, it seemed like I always had been in love with her, and that everybody else who had taken up my emotional time had been a smoke screen, channel surfing, Web browsing.

It just seemed too *obvious* to fall for the girl I'd known since nursery school. So I didn't do anything about it.

And then she had a thing for my dead brother.

I guess he felt the same way about her. This is what Washington really said, when Donna left us alone.

"It's all over, Jeff."

I didn't know what to say.

"We're running out of medicine," he said. "We're running out of food. We're running out of ammo.

"Listen to me. These people are finished. You've got to get out of here. You and Donna, take all the ammo and take all the food you can. Save yourselves. Anybody stands in your way, kill them."

Maybe he was right.

Maybe he was just losing it.

So I didn't tell everybody what he actually said. Everybody likes a good story.

Brainbox doesn't drop the library idea. That's his way. He was always talking Washington into these expeditions.

He'd show up all overheated and tell Wash, "I've located some deep-cycle batteries in Chinatown, we can use them to power the blahbity-blahs, and I can replace the paper filters if I have the right acid bath." Then they'd bushwhack down to Canal Street, Wash the brawn and Brainbox the—well, you get it.

Before It Happened, nobody really gave BB much credit. Everybody treated him like an embarrassment. I mean, the kid was president of the Robotics Club. (He was also its only member.) But it turned out the things that made BB a social pariah before What Happened were things we *needed* after. People were pretty stoked when he used something called Arduino to make a wooden platform that rotated everybody's little solar chargers to face the sun all day. That way they could still listen to their iPods. They appreciated that he knew how to make heaters with nothing but wood, black paint, and mirrors. He was the only one who could keep generators running or rig a spider box. Whatever that is.

So BB shows up at my place. He absently twiddles the crank

on his radio as he looks at my bookshelves. My castle walls against insanity.

"You've got a lot of fiction," he says.

"So?"

"So it's all made-up stories about made-up people."

"And?"

"*And* that means it's all lies. It can't be verified."

"It can't be *quantified*," I say. "There's a difference."

Not to Brainbox, I guess.

"Why are you wearing black?" he asks me.

"No reason," I say. Then, "I don't know. Mourning."

"Oh. I thought it was to trap sunlight for heat."

"No," I say.

"So have you thought about the abstract?"

"Yeah, I have."

"And?"

"If we find out what you need..."

"Yeah?" says Brainbox.

"What can you do about it? Will it actually make a difference?"

"Maybe," says Brainbox. "Maybe not."

"Let me put it this way, BB. The Sickness killed my parents, and it killed my brother. I want revenge. Can you do that? Can you kill it?"

"I can try," says Brainbox.

Good enough for me.

I have dreams about the Sickness. Sometimes it takes a human shape. A figure wearing a hazmat suit, with nothing inside but a blinding white light.

I know that I have turned the Sickness into a person because it is so hard to grasp the idea of something as tiny as a microbe defeating us. And it was hard to understand how something that started as a rumor, a throwaway item, blotted out everything else within the space of a few months. It has only been two years since a man reported to Lenox Hill Hospital complaining of chest pains. Within a day, the entire hospital was riddled with the Sickness, and the reconstructed line of Patient Zero's movements through the city was like a wound bleeding infection all over the map. As soon as he had been identified, another popped up, then another and another, until it was clear that containment was hopeless.

As the Sickness worked its way out from New York, up and down the East Coast, across the country to California, it was impossible not to see It as something gigantic—a single entity with a purpose of its own. Whereas in fact, it was a virus, an exponential host of scraps of life so fractured, we were told, that it was hardly life at all.

Eventually nothing explained it, and nothing defeated it. Not the CDC or prayer or quarantine or emergency sessions of Congress or martial law. And one by one, the Internet, then TV, then radio winked out, and in their place came hysteria. By the time we were isolated, the West Coast, Canada, and South America were in the throes, and the first cases had been reported in Europe and China. A month later, all the adults in New York were gone, and the children, too.

Mom hung in for a long time, and I think she would have been around longer if my dad had still been alive. It wasn't that she believed she would join him—except in some totally conceptual sort of way—but I think she saw less reason to hang around at the party. She told me and Wash that she didn't feel so bad for herself, since she'd lived a good life. But her heart was breaking for us.

When I thought about how many times I'd wished my parents would just *leave me alone*, I felt sick.

Chiquita is waiting in the cloisters at the entrance to the old NYU School of Law.

She's a Ford F-150 pickup truck with bulletproof glass, metal reinforcement, and tires filled with silicone so they can't go flat or get shot out. All thanks to Brainbox and Wash.

There's a patchy mold of insignia, stencils, and graffiti on the side. DAYS SINCE LAST ACCIDENT: 0...COME GET SOME...IF YOU CAN READ THIS, YOU'RE DEAD. Saint Christopher, bobblehead Buddhas, and hula girls on the dash. Cans of siphoned gas in the back.

Generalissimo gets the keys. Which means she's my ride.

Brainbox takes the tarp off the swivel-mounted M2 and eyes its works. We found the M2 one day when we were sweeping through the Village for anything useful. The nut who owned it must have been planning to shoot up the neighborhood, but he never got his chance.

For the rest of our armament, we've borrowed some guns off the day watch. This leaves the tribe a little light on weaponry.

There just aren't enough guns to go around in New York Failed State. Private ownership was low in the city, and except for Dad, who was a veteran and a gun owner, I didn't know anybody in my school who had access to a firearm.

The first thing Wash had us do when we formed the tribe was raid the Sixth Precinct. You'd be surprised what you can find at your local police station. When the cops made a bust, they were in no hurry to let go of the guns they seized. The uniformed guys and the detectives couldn't use them, but the SWAT teams could. We found various makes of AR-15, AKs, Ruger M77s, even a Barrett M82 sniper rifle that could put a hole in a wall from a mile away. But it wasn't enough.

Because guns don't kill people; people kill people—but guns definitely help people kill people better.

"Hey!" I hear. "Hello-oh?" It's Donna, jogging around some tomato plants. "Where are you going?"

"Road trip," I say.

"That abstract thing?"

"Yeah."

46

"I'm coming with." Not like she's asking.

I weigh my concern for her safety against the appeal of being near her. The crush wins.

"Fine, hop in."

"Back in ten." She bounces off again.

I go through my backpack. Two-liter CamelBak filled with clean water. Check. Two cans of tuna, two cans of green beans, a Leatherman Multi-tool, a packet of beef jerky (teriyaki-style), a Milky Way, a blanket, a Smith & Wesson twenty-one-inch collapsible baton, two boxes of 55-grain rounds for the AR-15, three extra 30-round mags, my ancestral *wakizashi* short sword.

Road trip.

DONNA

ONE OF THE MORE BOGUS of the bogosities of our unnetworked times is that you have to actually go see somebody in the flesh if you want to talk to them. I mean, I really took for granted that if you wanted to speak to somebody you could just text them and be, like, "Wasuuuupppp?" or "Heyyyy" (people thought it was rude if you didn't expend the thumb energy to add extra letters). I have to, like, *hoof it* over to Peter's place.

He lives in the old apartment building on the west side of the park. It used to be fancy. Some poor dude had to wear a goofy uniform and wait around to open the door for people all day. Now the bulbs and glass panels in the marquee awning are all smashed, and the foyer is like an ocean full of trash islands—a Garbagelapagos.

You take the back stairs to go up, since the elevator doesn't work. There's a rope you slide your hand along to lead you up in the dark, and you can tell by the number of knots what floor you're on.

Peter's pied-à-terre, as he calls it, is on the second floor. Pretty prime location.

It takes him a while to answer the door. He must have been getting his beauty rest.

The interior of the pied-à-terre is done up like a giant Facebook page. Like, he's painted a giant blue stripe all the way around the walls. There's a big picture of him above a bunch of tabs, and then pictures of his "friends." When he doesn't have a real picture, he's drawn one. I'm a stick figure with spiky brown lines sticking out of her head and two little apple boobs.

His "status," which is on a shingle that he changes from time to time, is currently **pensive**.

I go to the wall, which serves as his "timeline," and write, *Can you cover for me today? I'm going on a road trip with Jefferson.*

Peter: "Eff that, bitch. I'm coming with. Unless it's, like, a *date* or something."

Me: "Uh, *no*."

Peter: "Why not? I always liked Jefferson better than Wash. Wash was too butch for you. Jefferson's a total NILF."

Me: "I'm guessing the first word in that is *nerd*?"

Peter: "Uh-huh."

Me: "Gross."

Peter is my best friend in the tribe. I sort of never fit in with the other girls at my school, not even my besties, and Peter, well, he never fit in with anybody. Not even the kids at Stonewall.

For one thing, he's African American, which kind of ups the rarity factor vis-à-vis gay dudes. For another, he's Christian—I didn't know that was even allowed.

"For real?" I asked him when he told me.

"Jesus is my homeboy," he said.

And, you know how gay dudes are supposed to be all neat and persnickety? Not so much. It's like a teen girl and her brother are living in the same room.

He holds up two knapsacks. "My Little Pony for that Harajuku look, or should I go all macho and Fjällräven?"

Me: "The second one, if you don't want to get us shot."

Peter: "You're paranoid."

Me: "Yeah, I'm totally overreacting to all those armed mobs. You really want to go outside the walls?"

Peter: "*Yes*. I'm dying of boredom. I've gotta get out. *Meet* some people. Only time I ever leave is to look for, like, dried garbanzo beans and beef jerky. Bo-ring."

Peter's always complaining about meeting people. He says the apocalypse wrecked his love life.

Me: "This is not a girls' night out. It's, like, a very serious mission or something. To the library."

Peter: "We have a library."

Me: "Jefferson wants to go to a bigger library."

Peter: "Didn't know he was a size queen. Fine, let's go to the library. Who knows what'll happen on the way?" He sets the scene. "Pablo didn't know he had such desires in him until the day he saw the dashing stranger's eyes over the stinking heap of rubble. But when he saw him through the smoke of the burning tires, his heart leaped like a feral cat."

Me: "Nice. Do you think we can convince Jefferson to go to the Bazaar?"

I've heard that there's a market in the old Grand Central. I've kind of been dying to check it out.

Peter: "I don't think I have much sway with him. You, on the other hand—"

Me: "Shut up. I'm not his type."

Peter: "Please. There aren't enough people left to have 'types' anymore."

There's a piece of rebar with a duct-tape handle leaning against the corner. He hefts it in his left hand while he adjusts his status:

Out kicking ass

JEFFERSON

I GO:

Namu butsu
Yo butsu u in
Yo butsu u en
Buppō sō en
Jō raku ga jō
Chō nen kanzeon
Bo nen kanzeon
Nen nen jū shin ki
Nen nen fu ri shin.

You could call it a Buddhist "Our Father." Except it's not addressed to a father, but Kanzeon, aka Kuan Yin, aka the Bodhisattva of Compassion.

Don't get me wrong—I'm not some kind of Zen Holy Roller. It's just that, of all the stuff people have managed to think up as opposed to "it all means nothing," Buddhism makes the most sense to me. And it just happens to be what I grew up with.

Dad said he used to chant it on patrol in Italy during World War II. As you can tell from that, he was an oldie. Seventy-three when Mom had me. She met him when she was writing a book about the 442nd Regimental Combat Team, the most decorated American unit in World War II. They were a bunch of kids whose families were interned in camps because of their Japanese ancestry. So they went and kicked ass all over Italy and Germany. Took it out on the fascists abroad instead of the ones at home.

Anyhow, I guess you could say Mom got really, really involved in her subject.

They got to work making East and West meet, raising a litter of scholar-soldiers.

Wash got the soldier part. He'd just applied to West Point when the first cases of the Sickness started showing up on TV. Me? I guess I got the scholar part. For what it was worth.

Going outside is a roll of the dice. Sometimes it's a cakewalk. Go, snag some food or medicine, and hightail it home. Sometimes you don't *get* home. There're banditos, wild dogs, toxic smoke, flash fires. Randoms who've gone nuts and don't care anymore. Berserkers, rageaholics, rapeaholics. I've even heard of kids who murder people for fun.

Why?

Why not?

Those two questions pretty much sum things up these days: a big WHY? and, right next to it, a big WHY NOT?

Wash would've had everybody do a weapons check, so I do, too. While they're going through their stuff, I do a people check. We've got:

Brainbox (evil genius)

Donna (slightly unhinged girl-power chick)

Peter (gay Christian adrenaline junkie)

And me (nerd philosopher king)

Not exactly the Fellowship of the Ring, but not too shabby, either, when you think about it. I can't say the selection committee did such a great job at the Council of Elrond. *Four hobbits?* Seriously? Out of *nine* people? I know it all worked out, but—questionable management.

I'd rather drive out in silence, but I'm voted down. So I insist on choosing the music. I really don't want to die to a Nicki Minaj track.

The Big-Ass Speakers, sucking strength from the engine, pound out Buju Banton's "Ring the Alarm." The whole car rattles to a sleng-teng rhythm. Oh, Divine Internal Combustion! We hardly knew ye!

We go out the east gate, down Washington Place. I'm driving; Brainbox is shotgun (literally). Peter, in back with Donna, is manning the .50 cal.

On post, Ingrid snaps a sharp salute before closing the gate. Frank is there, too, looking pissed off not to be going, but he's the best guy to be in charge. Who knows if I'll make it back. From this point, we're out to sea. I watch the Square recede in the mirror.

The first few blocks are inside our scavenging radius. Every abandoned taxi and garbage Dumpster and looted storefront is familiar. All the same, I have to go slowly, maneuvering the slalom course of junked cars and detritus. Of course, I want to blast through here like the Master Chief, but these days you don't get points for acting cool. Sometimes you just get dead.

Scaffolding exoskeletons, the tattered purple banners of New York University. Chinese food menus, takeout napkins, traffic cones, mangled bikes chained to posts, garbage cans rolling on their sides. Bone-dry, busted-open fire hydrants.

As I drive through, I think, *You sucker.*

I bought it hook, line, and sinker. I thought the filmy walls of the bubble were solid rock. Woke up to the buzzing of a clock fed with electricity from coal burned on Long Island. Rinsed my mouth with water from the Catskills. For breakfast, eggs from Vermont, bread from a bakery factory in California. Butter from Iceland. Coffee from Colombia. Mangoes from the Philippines. I bounced my voice off a satellite in geosynchronous orbit. A bus powered by million-year-old plants and microorganisms took me where I needed to go. People impersonating imaginary characters clamored to entertain me on liquid crystal boxes.

I saw no reason this shouldn't continue.

Sucker.

There are no bodies for the first few blocks. We burned them all in the early days to make a disease-and-critter-free zone.

For the most part, people had done their dying inside.

At first, they flooded the hospitals. Later, when they realized that nothing could be done for them, they grew ashamed of being sick and hid. We'd treated death like a dirty little secret for so long we had no way to face it in the open. We crawled back to our dens and turned on CNN and Fox News and died in front of the television.

Foot light on the gas pedal, I scan the street for anything new. There's the empty police van, there's the abandoned Tesla, the door still open. The Mercs and the Beemers and Toyotas, Lexi, Hondas, Fords, Chryslers, GMCs, Caddies. All the gas tanks are empty. The hoods are open and spray-painted with symbols. B means the battery's been stripped; G means the gas has been siphoned.

We roll past the hulled and festering halal kebab stand. Window boxes, strangely raucous with flowers, as if in celebration.

Dog crap everywhere. Flies rioting and rocketing through the middle air.

At the crosswalk of Washington Place and Mercer, someone has spray-painted REVELATION 2:4 on the ground.

The writing continues, I HAVE SOMEWHAT AGAINST THEE, BECAUSE but then trails off, the writer having run out of paint, or time, or interest.

Peter finishes the thought. "I have somewhat against thee, because thou hast left thy first love."

I puzzle over this. Is the "I" God? What "first love"?

At the corner, I stop short and lean out to scope Broadway.

"Did I ever tell you that you drive like my grandma?" says Donna. I ignore her. The way I see it, we're on a little boat approaching some nasty rapids.

The low ridgelines of the old shirtwaist factories and walk-ups of Broadway are empty. No movement in the broken windows. Out here, up until the territory of the Drummers, it's mostly animals and randoms. Small groups that don't last long and aren't likely to tangle with us.

A pack of dogs keeps its distance to the south.

"*Must Have Clothing*," says Donna, reading a store awning. "Ha-ha, too true. LOL."

I hate when kids speak in textese. If you want to Laugh Out Loud, just laugh. If you're really gonna Roll on the Floor Laughing, well, there's the floor.

I also find gallows humor kind of tired. Every storefront, every bit of advertising, every artifact of What Was seems ridiculous now. Le Basket. The Vitamin Shoppe. The Body Shop. You just want to shout, "Don't you know what's coming?"

And yet, as I drive on the sidewalk up Broadway, we can't help but recite the names.

"*American Apparel*," says Donna.

"*Superdry*," says Peter.

"*McDonald's*," says Donna.

"*Foot Locker*," says Brainbox.

It's hard to believe that all this crap actually mattered and that these words moved something in us. Now we repeat them like we're conjuring ancestors. Like stores were a thousand shrines to little deities, and they're still demanding tribute. Like they're the thousand names of our dead god.

"I want a number four meal with a Coke," I say. It just pops out.

"I'll buy," says Peter. Then, "I was a vegetarian until the apocalypse. Very hard to maintain these days. Now I'm an omnivore. I eat omni."

"And omni eats us," says Donna.

We keep worming our way northward.

"You know SeeThrough is following us, right?" Peter says.

I've been noticing a little form flitting to and from cover behind us.

"Those dogs are gonna get her," says Peter. The pack is following, sniffing the air and calculating the odds.

I put Chiquita into park and hop out, scanning for shooters in the buildings around us.

Somebody small ducks behind a taxi.

Peter says, "I thought she was, like, a ninja or something."

"Ninjas are Japanese," I say. "She's Chinese. She thinks she's Shaolin."

SeeThrough got her name because she wanted everybody to call her Sifu. That's Mandarin for "teacher." Her dad taught kung fu and tai chi at my school. Did I mention that the Learning Center was kind of hippie-dippy? Anyway, she figured she got to inherit the title.

Except she's barely five feet tall and thin as a greyhound. Hence, SeeThrough.

"Come out," says Peter. "I did," he adds to himself.

She pokes her head up as if she's just amazed that we saw her. I motion her over.

"Look," I say. "Thank you for wanting to help. But you're too...what's the word...small."

"You don't know me." Her face is set.

"I would love to get to know you better. When we get back. In the meanwhile, we're gonna take you home."

"No," says SeeThrough. "I can help."

Seeing that the reasonable approach has failed, I put my hand on her shoulder to turn her around. I'm annoyed that we'll have to double back with her.

Suddenly SeeThrough has my wrist in her hand, and she bends my fingers back, and the pain is a shrill, unbearable piping in my brain. I stumble, and she kicks my leg out from under me. Then she hits me in the windpipe with her little fingers puckered into a sort of claw.

I spend a while learning how to breathe again.

"Damn, sister," says Peter.

"I can help," says SeeThrough.

Donna pulls me up. She's trying not to laugh.

I bend over and hold my finger up for attention.

"Welcome aboard," I say.

So we've got our hobbit.

DONNA

AT ASTOR we pass Peter's old school, Stonewall. It was a high school for gay and lesbian and transgender kids, the ones who got nothing but shit at "normal" schools.

Peter: "Dear old Alma Mother."

Me: "What was it like?"

Peter: "Oh, it was just *gay gay gay* all the time. AP Interior Decorating, then Musical Theater, then Disco for third period. Then the dykes would go to shop class." He pauses. "Nah, it was just like regular school. Except nobody gave you shit. Well, not for being gay, anyway. Sometimes you got shit for not being gay *enough*."

Me: "But…it's better now, right? I mean, nobody has, like, the *leisure* to be homophobic."

Peter: "Yeah. Hooray. I always said the world would end before people let us be."

I decide to change the subject, so I say, "Hey, did they ever make you read that story 'By the Waters of Babylon'?"

Jefferson: "Is that the one about this kid in the future who finds this mysterious place, and it's New York after the Third World War?"

SeeThrough: "Yeah. We just read that. I mean, Before, you know. It was fun."

Me: "Best apocalypse? *The Road Warrior.*"

Jefferson: "You're just a raggedy man."

Peter: "I always liked zombies. But I only like the slow ones. When they start running, it gets too stressful."

Me: "How about *Logan's Run*? This is kind of like *Logan's Run*. I saw it on Netflix. Everything's great, except people get killed when they turn thirty."

Peter: "Thirty? That's *old.*"

SeeThrough: "I like it when kids get special powers. Like telekinesis."

Me: "I know. This apocalypse sucks. It smells terrible, and we don't have magical powers or *anything* cool, like hoverboards and stuff." I shout into the cab, "How come you can't make hoverboards, Brainbox?"

Brainbox: "The laws of physics."

Me: "Aw, you suck."

Brainbox: "I don't suck." He's offended.

Me: "Take it easy, Brainbox. I'm just kidding. It's a joke. *Sarcasm.* Like, reverse talking. I was saying what I *didn't* mean."

Brainbox wipes his face the way he does. Like he's not really wiping it, he's hiding it. Like the exercise of squeezing meaning out of what people say is tiring for him.

The streets are quiet all the way up to Grace Church, where the road jogs left. Peter bangs on the hood of the cab, and Jeff stops the truck.

Peter: "I'm gonna put in a good word for us with the Big Guy."

Jefferson: "We can't afford the time."

Peter: "Aw. C'mon. We're doing great. No zombie attacks or anything."

Me: "Who says God is even paying attention? Or, like, exists?"

Peter: "Can't hurt. Pascal's gambit. If you believe in God and you're wrong, you're dead anyway so you won't know. If you believe in God and you're right, jackpot!"

Jefferson: "All right."

Peter: "Thank you, boss. Won't be but a moment." He hands me his rebar club and hops down from the truck bed.

The church doors are big, wooden, and closed. Somebody has painted some Latin words on the front:

QUEM QUAERITIS IN SEPULCHRO,

O CHRISTICOLAE?

Peter walks over to the doors of the church and opens them.

As he does, everyone realizes that something horrible has happened. A stench breathes out of the church—less like a smell than a feeling, like a slap.

Through the crack of the open doors, I can see piles of people. The pews full, the aisles full, corpses collapsed against one another so tightly they're still standing up. Like they all bum-rushed the consulate of heaven and never got their papers.

Peter bends over and starts to throw up. The rest of us are just frozen.

I jump down from the truck and, with Jefferson's help, heave the door shut.

Nobody knows what to say. I mean, sure, we've seen stuff like this before. In this world, if you keep your eyes open, you are going to see some terrible things. Whole families dead at the dinner table, like that Norman Rockwell Thanksgiving thing gone wrong. Adults curled up in their elderly parents' laps. Once I found a yoga center where they just, like, unrolled their mats and yoga'ed their way to the end of the world.

Talk about corpse pose.

But this has really gotten to Peter. And I don't know how to deal with his existential crisis. Like, all I can think of is to point to the store across the street and say, "Look, Peter—that store's called Lucky Wang!"

He sits there on the curb, staring at nothing.

Then Jefferson reaches out awkwardly and puts his hand on Peter's shoulder. He sits down next to him.

Peter: "I used to think maybe he forgot about us. Lost us in his pocket. But now I feel like he threw us away. As far as he could."

I think that from the way he's saying it, he means He, with a capital *H*.

Jefferson smiles. "Pascal's gambit, man. Let's see how it ends up."

Peter nods slowly, takes a deep breath, and gets up.

Back in the boat.

Terrific omen, I think, and I wish I were back in my crib reading old *People*s. But then—there was the letter.

Wash left this envelope for me. Might as well have said, *Not to be opened until I die*. Jesus, it was all messed up, like he wrote it with the wrong hand? But the gist of it was, stay with Jefferson. Take care of him. *Love him*. Well, what's that supposed to mean? That's not something you can just do. I mean, I *do* love him. I have since we were about five. But, you know, there's love and there's Love.

Isn't there?

Anyway, I've got his back. That's what matters.

JEFFERSON

I'D LIKE TO AVOID UNION SQUARE, but the side streets from Tenth to Thirteenth are blocked with cars and decomposing bodies and fallen buildings from the West Side fire. The downside of taking Chiquita is that you need a clear path. Maybe we could sweep west and avoid the Union, but I wouldn't want us to get out of the car in tight streets that could be hard to fight our way out of.

Union is *usually* cool.

When it all came down and the lights went out, lots of people gathered in the square. Hopeful kumbaya stuff. Candles and joints and vegetarian casseroles. A bunch of drummers showed up and started playing. There were conga players from Spanish Harlem, rock guys from the East Village, buskers hammering on upturned plastic paint buckets. The circle got bigger and bigger as the Sickness got worse, like the city was trying to show it had a pulse.

People came from all around to join in. I mean, even people

with no rhythm at all. They drummed and drummed, like they were trying to scare away evil spirits. They kept going, and when things broke down and they got sick, they just slumped over their drums and died.

The drumming has never stopped in the Union. Now that the cars and trucks are gone, the nights are so quiet, except for the barking and the occasional scream—you can hear it down in Washington Square when the wind is the right way. Some people think it's creepy. The-natives-are-getting-restless creepy.

Me, I kind of like it. I even entertain this funny superstition that when the drumming stops, it'll mean that the end of the world is really here.

Still, I wouldn't drive through Union Square unless I had to. There are people we don't know there. And people mean risk.

The drumming gets louder as we approach. We roll past New York Costumes (a popular scavenging spot for swag), Zen Grill, DVD SALE! (mostly porn), Lifestyle Salon.

"Remember *lifestyles*?" I say to Brainbox. "I have to remember to get a lifestyle when things settle down."

Brainbox doesn't have that thing that makes him feel he needs to reply to stuff you say. Instead, he says, "Good chess section."

He's talking about the Strand, which rolls past us on the right—18 MILES OF BOOKS, according to a banner flapping loose of its pinions.

The Empire State Building hoves into view over the broccoli-like profusion of trees in the park as the drumming gets louder. I wonder if the Old Man can see me.

It's hard not to get swept up in it, the syncopation of a hundred different percussion pieces. Brainbox taps a beat on his door; I can hear Donna slapping her hands on the cab roof. Maybe they drummed like this in the streets of Rome when *their* whole empire thing went to shit.

DONNA

BACK IN THE DAYS before the poopoo hit the fan, we had this thing—the social contract? The basic idea was, let's be cool to each other, because things get too messy otherwise. It wasn't heaven on earth. It was just the easiest way to get through the day. It worked even if you would never see somebody again. Even if they weren't going to blast you. So it was all "please," and "thank you," and "excuse me." First person to raise her hand gets the cab. That sort of crap.

Well, the social contract kind of got put on hold.

End result? You really never know what you're getting into with strangers. Hence—some butterflies as we rock up to Union Square.

I see a crowd of Drummers on the steps by the round metal kiosk that looks like a safari hat. They see us, too. One of them, a white dude with long, ratty dreads, pauses and then starts up a new beat on the biggest drum of all—some kind of big-ass Japanese one hanging from a scaffold, the kind those guys in diapers used to play. Jefferson would know the name. *BOOM. BOOM. BOOM.* The other drums fall silent for a second as everybody checks us out.

Now, me, I'm all for Being Yourself and whatnot, but the Drummers kind of schiz me out. Like, they drum more than they talk. Like, they're saying something to each other I can't understand.

Also they look like the Hacky Sack Players From Hell. All hippie hipster chic that they let rot off their bodies. Smoking up all the time so their eyes are yellow and red like pool balls. I can see a dozen little huddles around bowls and bongs.

So I lean on the cab and smile, but at the same time, my finger's on the trigger of the M2, like, "Hey, guys! Groovy! Check out my .50-caliber!"

When we take a right and start to round the square, I see more and more feral, wild-eyed types leaning against the masonry walls of the park.

They're scoping us out as the beat thickens again, a complicated pitter-patter that sounds as if it's saying something different from before.

Me: "Keep your eyes open, Peter."

Peter smiles and nods while waving at the crowd and tapping his metal bar against the side.

SeeThrough shows nothing but her eyes above the level of the cargo bed.

About halfway up the east side of the square, they start backing away. Which seems like a good thing, except...it isn't.

The way is blocked by a burned-out van that wasn't there a moment ago.

I see gun barrels peeking over the low park walls.

The drumming changes again.

Me: "You see this, Jeff?"

Jeff: "Got it."

He throttles up and swerves Chiquita over a median that divides the blocked roadway from a clear one over to the right.

Just as he does that, the drumming stops.

And the gunfire starts.

Pop-pop-pop, small-arms fire from the park that slams into the reinforced side of the truck like falling apples on a tin roof. Peter and I hit the deck. Rocks clang off the wheels. Arrows whistle through the air.

I open up with the M2, which *CHUG-CHUG-CHUG*s rounds into the park. The rounds are so powerful that the gun almost jumps out of my hands. I see the top of a tree fall off and a mailbox spin up into the air, disgorging letters that were stranded in the Sickness.

The cab jolts upward and then down again—we're momentarily airborne as it bounces down from the median. SeeThrough is thrown over the back door and out of the truck.

Peter grabs her wrist before she hits the road. She's so light that he pulls her in with one hand. He holds his rebar in the other hand, flailing away at the Drummer who surges up to the tailgate, out of my arc of fire.

We're on the eastern roadway now, blocked from the square by a line of bushes, but faces and guns peer out from Babies "R" Us, and soon we're taking fire from the ruins of a mural of anthropomorphic ants carrying slices of watermelon away from a picnic.

I hose down Babies "R" Us with the .50-cal, tearing chunks out of the stone pilasters and bringing what's left of the plate glass falling onto the Drummer gunners. Brass casings are raining around us, hitting the bed with a *Ping! Ping! Ping!* When one of them lands on my skin, it burns.

Then Peter gets hit.

He groans and crumples to the cargo bed, holding the side of his head, which runs with blood.

Meanwhile, we're attacked from above.

People on the rooftops are throwing bricks, glass, toys, anything.

A baby bottle hits the hood, and fire spills out.

Make that a baby-bottle Molotov cocktail.

Jefferson hits the brakes and the truck starts to fishtail. Brainbox leans out of his window and calmly, methodically spritzes the fire with an extinguisher.

"Get us out of here!" I shout to Jefferson, and he manages to straighten the fishtailing truck and gun it. Chiquita leaps forward, parting a surging mass of Drummers.

Just like that, we're out, and the Drummers don't take up the pursuit. We've squirted free of the crowd, past the W hotel and a CVS on Park Avenue South.

I leave the M2 alone and try to get as much pressure as I can on the side of Peter's head to stop the bleeding. My own blood is sluicing through my veins—*poom poom poom*. And I think, what with the rattle of the guns, and the purring of the engine, and the tinkling of the shell casings, and the beating of my heart, the drumming never stopped.

JEFFERSON

AT TWENTIETH there's an old Duane Reade that doesn't look too cracked out, and I stop Chiquita. We keep Peter in the cab with Donna while SeeThrough and Brainbox go in to get what she needs for him.

There's a ragged wound where half of Peter's right ear has been shot off. Donna is clamping it in one hand, and it looks like the bleeding has stopped. She's washed it in Betadine and applied some Neosporin from her bag.

Peter is taking it pretty well. When he's not wincing in pain, he's laughing. "I can totally make the one-eared look work," he says.

I take a walk around Chiquita and check the damage. A bunch of holes in the body panels. The tires took some shots, too. It's a good thing Brainbox pumped so much silicone into them. The driver's window is shattered, and a lopsided .22 bullet drops from the upholstery when I wiggle the rearview mirror. A few inches from finding my skull.

The paint job is burned off the hood, and the nipple of a baby bottle has melted onto it.

There's a doll by my feet, and in her backpack, an unexploded M-80 whose fuse extinguished on the way down toward us. Dora the Suicide Bomber.

I clear out a bunch of shell casings from the cab and check the ammo on the M2. Donna sure went to town. Another session like that, and we're all out.

Things look safe for now, so I head into the Duane Reade in case SeeThrough and Brainbox need my help.

The place is a catastrophe, of course. Every drugstore got mobbed during the Sickness. At first they tried to maintain order with rent-a-cops, and there were fights, so you can usually find a body or two dead from gunshot wounds or blunt-force trauma. I scoot past a skeleton clutching a broken NyQuil bottle.

When the Sickness passed, the looting began. The medicine aisles and pharmacies were picked over for anything narcotic. Forget about finding OxyContin or Robitussin. Some enterprising souls even started little Manhattan meth labs, so there's no Sudafed around, either.

I wade through the undergrowth of items scooped from the shelves and dismissed. Diapers, toothbrushes, laxatives, insoles, dog collars, heartburn relief, condoms, reading glasses, floss, lipstick, eco-friendly cutting boards. *Stuff.*

SeeThrough and Brainbox are nowhere to be found.

I heave myself up onto the counter and find the pill-dispensing machines called Baker Cells. Sometimes they're left alone because scavengers are so desperate and unhinged that they don't think to look there. But that's where pharmacists kept the most commonly prescribed stuff.

I see some chalky orange pills in one of the slots. Adderall.

Adderall was a treatment for ADHD. But kids at school basically used to get it prescribed every time they sneezed. It sharpens your brain for studying, and coincidentally makes you feel like you are the most important person in the universe for about four hours, so...there is a secondary market. I crack open the cell and empty it.

I find some Bactroban on a back shelf, hidden beneath a hill of garbage. I pocket it and head back to Chiquita.

On the way, through a gap in a looted shelf, I catch sight of SeeThrough leaning against the wall. She's crying.

"Did you get hurt?" asks Brainbox, standing there with some packs of batteries in his hands.

"No. I just...I was afraid I'd get left behind."

"But Peter grabbed you," says Brainbox.

"But what if he hadn't?" says SeeThrough. "Would you have come back for me?"

"Well," says Brainbox, "not if you were going to die anyway. I mean, there's no point in everybody getting killed."

"But I'd come back for *you*," says SeeThrough. "For anybody. That's what you're supposed to do."

"Oh," says Brainbox. With no inflection.

My man Brainbox. Smooth.

Was there something going on between them? He's definitely blowing it big-time if that's the case.

I promise myself, the way I do every day, that I'll tell Donna how I feel about her. Soon.

Maybe tomorrow.

No. Today. I'll tell her today. For all I know, there is no tomorrow. I just need to get her alone.

I take the meds out to Donna and Peter.

DONNA

PETER BITCHES AND moans as I fix up his ear. Boys are such wusses. I mean, all those movies they used to make about tough guys. I'd like to see them pass a watermelon through their butt.

Which, you know, is how I've heard the pain of childbirth described.

Not that I'll ever know.

I spritz a little Bactroban on, then—and this is a special Donna touch—Krazy Glue the edges of a torn piece of flesh and cartilage back together. Cover the whole wound with duct tape and, voilà! Homemade wound dressing. That Martha Stewart bitch couldn't do better.

Jefferson is kind of shaken up from our Action Movie Experience down in the Union, so he lets me drive. He keeps eyeballing me, though, like maybe he doesn't trust my driving. I see Peter, SeeThrough, and Brainbox settle into the back. When Brainbox sits next to SeeThrough, she switches sides to get away from him. Wonder what that's all about.

After our throw-down in the Union, I make sure to avoid Gramercy Park and Madison Square. I keep the Empire State Building to my left. Don't want anybody dropping shit on us anymore, especially not from, like, the hundredth floor.

We pass a few randoms. Some zip into the nearest doorway. Some are too far gone for that and just keep walking down the road. One or two even *wave*.

I see a guy talking on a cell phone and then I realize that he's not making a phone call; he's just insane. It used to be the other way around. Like, for a second, I'd think the dude jabbering away at nothing was crazy, then I'd realize he was trading stocks or something, not talking to aliens.

Nowadays phones are like—what did they call them?—phantom limbs. Like, something's been amputated but you can still feel it moving. You'll be talking to somebody, and they'll look down and start rubbing their fingers together. They want to be texting someone, they want to be checking their e-mail, surfing the net, anything other than being fully, totally *there*. It's pathetic.

I thumb the rounded edges of the iPhone in my pocket. There's still a little bit of charge.

We roll past banks; bus stops; humble, ugly little buildings; and grand, proud ones with carved marble doorways and gargoyles peering down. The sun comes out, and I crank up the music, Gnarls Barkley's "Going On." And the way is clear, and the air is warm, and for just a moment, it feels like we could be a bunch of kids out on a lark in Mom's car.

Everybody sings along except for SeeThrough and Brainbox. Whatever is up between them has also united them in gloominess. But the rest of us sing, and for a second, it seems like we actually might be going to a place in the sun.

The library squats on Fifth Avenue, its front stretching all the way from Fortieth to Forty-Second. It's surrounded by glass and sandstone towers raising radio antennas to the sky like they're flipping the bird. The trees in front are all shaggy, and they make the lions look like they're hiding in the foliage, scoping out someone to eat.

But the strange thing is, it's well preserved. In this city full of wreckage, dead technology, and sad, useless stuff, this building is just, like, chilling. The steps are clean of trash and bodies. The flags of New York (the Empire State) and the US (the empire itself) still float from the flagpoles.

I pull Chiquita to a stop.

Jeff: "Somebody's got to stay with the truck."

SeeThrough: "I will."

Me: "You'll need a gun."

She shrugs and climbs up to the .50-cal. Sits on top of the cab, crisscross-applesauce, right next to it.

Me: "You know how to use that?"

SeeThrough: "Do *you*?"

Jefferson: "Okay. Let's keep it simple. We're looking for a copy of the *Journal of Applied Virology*, May 2010."

Me: "Ooh, is that the one with three hundred seventy-two must-have summer looks?"

Jefferson (after a pause to emphasize that he is not amused): "We go in, find out wherever they keep the science periodicals, grab the journal, get out. We check in every half hour here at the main entrance. Everybody, sync your watches."

We all have windups, of course. Mine's a Hello Kitty.

Jeff says we should form teams. I'm about to go with Peter, but he tells Peter to go with Brainbox. Jeff's going with me.

We start up the stone stairs to the front entrance.

There's a statue of a fat, bearded Greek dude sitting on a sphinx to one side. A half-naked chick with a cellulite problem on the other. There's a—what do you call it—plinth? With some more Greek ladies on top of the entrance, which, like the rest of the place, has been made to look like an ancient temple.

Come to think of it, it is an ancient temple.

Three doors underneath tall arches are all padlocked from the outside. Jefferson runs back to the truck and gets a sledgehammer. With a few heavy, echoing thuds, the lock gives way.

You can almost feel the big entrance hall take a breath of air into its lungs. We walk into the stale chamber.

It's all white marble. Crazy quiet, crazy clean. No poop, no blood, no trash. I want to call it peaceful.

But I can't. There's something very strange about the place.

Our steps echo through the vaults and up the big creamy marble staircases.

It's hard to figure out why there's nobody here. A huge building, defensible, plenty of books for fuel, completely abandoned. As we

79

head up the staircase to the next floor, there's not a soul around, not a sound except for us.

The library is haunted.

Don't be ridiculous.

We light our Coleman camping lanterns to make our way. I'm not crazy about the slasher-film vibe this gives everything, throwing these oily shadows on the walls, but it's better than shuffling around in the dark.

Inside our bubble of light, we emerge from the stairwell into a long, wide corridor decorated with gigantic murals above swirly pink marble.

All the paintings are about reading and writing. Moses and the Ten Commandments. Monks with bad hairdos copying books by hand. Some Shakespeare-time dude with a crazy beard showing a page of a book to a rich guy, who's all, "Hmmn," like he's not too sure about the idea. And other people, less legendy. Some guys putting out a newspaper in the twenties or thirties. A couple of girls lying around on the grass with a book. I guess the idea is, "Yay! Reading through the ages!"

And I'm all for it. Back in the day—I mean before the Sickness—when we were addicted to Twitter and Facebook and stuff, we were all about spreading words *sideways*. Like, everybody in the world could know right away that you just took a pee. But we didn't really give a crap about communicating stuff forward, through *time*. The funny thing is that people thought books were so useless, like, Kindle and everything was going to kick their asses. Which, now that I think of it, *Kindle* is kind of a douchey name. Like, *I'm going to* Kindle *a fire with your shitty, old-fashioned books.*

Anyway, when It Happened, all this technology that was supposed to be better at preserving stuff? Totally useless without electricity. All those status updates and tweets and blog entries got erased, or lost or trapped or whatever, when the servers went down. In a way they never really existed—they didn't exist in *real space*. People *freaked out*. Like, twenty years before that, they had never heard of e-mail, and now the Internet was vital to their mental health.

But books—books are handy. You can keep ideas on paper for, like, centuries. And if you want to find stuff out, it's right there. You don't have to grab it out of the air, call it up from some data center in, like, New Jersey.

So books had the last laugh. Nobody is going to know what the hell me and Jeff and the crew did five years from now. Unless Jefferson writes it down in one of his fancy notebooks or there's space aliens who can read things from people's bones or something. But Huck Finn is gonna be chillin' on the Mississippi forever.

We split up. Peter and Brainbox head one way down the corridor, and Jefferson and I go into the Bill Blass Public Catalog Room.

It's a big square chamber with a wooden kiosk in the middle. The walls are lined with thousands of big-ass ledgers.

Jefferson: "This is how you used to find books, before they started using computers. You'd locate the book in one of these big catalogs, then you'd write down the number on a little blue slip. You'd give it to a librarian, and they'd send it to the stacks in a capsule that ran through a pneumatic tube."

Me: "Huh."

Jefferson: "From the Greek *pneuma*, for 'breath.'"

Me: "Huh."

Then he looks embarrassed.

It's really cute sometimes how nerdy he is. He gets all blushy.

He starts slipping catalogs from the shelves but can't find what we're looking for. I gaze around the room and just marvel at how clean the place is. There isn't any dust.

I read somewhere that most dust is actually human skin, so maybe that's why...no humans, no dust.

Jefferson: "Come on." He goes out by the opposite doorway from the one we entered and takes a left. Above the doorway I see an inscription in gold letters:

A GOOD BOOKE IS THE PRECIOUS LIFE-BLOOD
OF A MASTER SPIRIT, IMBALM'D AND TREASUR'D
UP ON PURPOSE TO A LIFE BEYOND LIFE

I follow Jefferson through a little foyer—

And then we're in the most beautiful room I've ever seen.

Imagine a cavern of wood and marble. High, arched windows with metal balconies running beneath. The ceiling is painted like a sky at sunset, pink and gray clouds framed by brown and gold carving. Gigantic chandeliers with circles of lightbulbs suspended from chains like upside-down cakes. Row after row of long tables made of wood the color of honey, with golden lamps on them. In the middle of this super-tall, super-wide space, there's a little hut, like a sort of border crossing between one part and the other.

Me: "Holy shit."

Jefferson: "Shh." (Smiles.) "No swearing in the library."

I smile back.

Then Jefferson stops smiling.

Jefferson: "Um, um, Donna?" (Like he's working up to ask me a big favor or something.)

Me (a little suspiciously, noticing he's acting weird): "What?"

Jefferson: "Well...you know how we've known each other for a really long time?"

Me: "...Yeah?"

Jefferson: "I just. I have something. I want to say." (Looks like something has gone down the wrong pipe.)

Me: "So...like, spit it out."

Jefferson: "Well, it's just." (Coughs.) Then—"Donna, I love you. That is, I'm in love with you. If there's a difference. Anyhow, I've been wanting to say that."

Uh-oh.

JEFFERSON

UH-OH.

When I tell Donna I love her, she just stands there, blinking. Then she looks as if she thinks I'm kidding and she's going to laugh. Then she thinks better of it.

"Really?" she says. Not in an excited way. More in a bemused way, as if I'd said that I like opera.

Then she says, "*Why?*"

This is an eventuality I hadn't planned for. I had prepared myself for her saying *Thanks* or *I don't feel that way about you* or *I love you, but just like a friend* or even, say, a 5 percent chance of her saying *I love you, too* and falling into my arms. But no matter what, I figured she would take my word for it.

Why?

I'd never really thought about that. I mean, you just feel what you feel, don't you? If I had to break it down, I'd say it's because I know her, and she knows me. I'd seen her Before and After, at our best and at our worst, happy and sad and starving and feasting and laughing and fighting, the whole nine. I'd always have her back, and she'd always have mine. I liked talking to her, and I liked thinking about her, and I wanted to hang out with her every day.

But you're not supposed to say boring stuff like that. You're supposed to say things like *You are the fire that burns in my heart forever*, or something like that.

So when she asks why, I just say, "Because."

She wrinkles her brows. Like that wasn't a good enough answer.

"I mean you're, um, a fire in my heart," I add, mumbling.

"A what in your what?"

"Didn't you…you had no idea?" I say.

"Well…I mean, I thought maybe you had the hots for me. I caught you staring at my boobs once or twice, but—guys just do that sort of thing."

Why does she have to take it there? Is she trying to change the subject? Her boobs? I mean, they're beautiful, I mean, as far as I can guess, but not what I was talking about.

It's strange that you can be in love with somebody while hating so many things about them. Like how she doesn't seem to be able to be serious, about anything, ever.

"I'm not 'guys,'" I say.

"But you are a *guy*. You do admit that you have, like, a Y chromosome, right?"

"What does that have to do with anything? Why are you being like this?"

"Like what?" she says.

"Like avoiding the subject. Just...whatever you have to say, just say it." Now I sound like I'm scolding her. I hate the way I'm saying things. This is all going wrong.

"I don't have to say *anything*, do I?" she says.

"Well, it's considered polite to respond in some fashion." I'm getting annoyed, which is a weird place to go from telling somebody you love her. Heartbroken, yes. Pissed off, no.

"Polite? Well, I guess I'm just not a *polite* enough girl for you, then."

This whole conversation is making my head hurt. From what I can tell, she's not crazy about what I said. Or me. If she were, it would've been all over right there. All she has to do is say *I love you, too*. Simple. But instead she's splitting hairs and starting fights.

Except, "not a *polite* enough girl for you" ...that implies that she does think about the possibility of being *a* girl for me, right? Except for certain differences of character? That's promising, right?

We just stand there for a while, staring at each other. I can see her heartbeat in her neck. I want to kiss her. That's maybe what I should do. But she hasn't given me the go-ahead.

Welcome to the suck, as Wash would say.

I'm almost relieved when I hear the booming of the .50-cal from the street outside.

We run toward the noise, out of the reading room, through the catalog room, down the dark stairs.

It's like a conversation. Some tentative *pop-pop-pop*s of small arms, like a suggestion, and then the M2's throaty roar, like somebody trying to put an end to an argument.

But it keeps going on.

Peter arrives in the foyer just as we do. I thumb the safety off the AR-15 and switch to single shot.

I can see her through the fretwork of the brass front doors: SeeThrough's wispy frame is huddled behind the .50-cal. Her legs are off the side of the cab, her feet propped against the open window frame of the driver's seat.

She's choosing her shots carefully. She knows that she doesn't have many bullets to spare.

The Uptowners, the same crew that brought the pig, are scattered behind cover to the south. Some of them are using the frontage of the BCBG Max Azria store on the northeast corner of the street; the others are perched behind a stone railing on the south end of the library plaza. They're popping from cover and taking potshots, afraid of what the .50-cal can do if they get in the open.

SeeThrough's advantage won't last long. She's running out of ammo, and soon enough the Uptowners are going to send somebody around the other side of the library. Then they'll have her flanked.

I have to do something.

The only thing to do is to give up Chiquita and get SeeThrough into the library.

I'm not usually this brave, not brave at all, really. But I got SeeThrough into this. I'm the one who let her come along.

And besides, part of me wants to get wounded. *Picturesquely* wounded, that is, not *seriously* wounded. Just so Donna has some regrets. Not the cleverest way to build up my courage, but I'll take what I can get.

"Cover me," I tell the others. "I'm going to bring her back."

I'm half hoping they'll tell me not to do it, but they nod and smash the noses of their guns through the door glass. Now I *have* to go.

I take a breath and open the door while the others lay down suppressing fire on the Uptowners. The *tack-tack-tack* of our guns keeps them from getting a bead on me.

"SeeThrough!" I shout.

She runs out of bullets just as I'm out the door. A tinny *click-click* resounds along the street. She looks back at me, wide-eyed with fear. One of those frozen moments, the kind people talk about when they describe falling or almost dying. Time seems lazy. Then it hurries along, bringing the crack of guns aimed at SeeThrough and me.

"Get off the truck!" I yell, and then I hit the ground as a bullet breaks a step near my foot. My elbows and knees bang the stone hard, and I suddenly can't catch my breath.

And I see Cheekbones peeking around the edge of the store. He's motioning for his people to rush the truck now that the .50-cal is out. I raise my rifle and position him behind the front sights, take in a breath and let half of it out, and as I'm about to pull the trigger, Cheekbones sees me. *Recognizes* me.

Then a flamethrower vomits fire onto Chiquita and the truck explodes.

It's thunderous, deafening. A shock wave blows my hair back, sends my shot wide, and almost takes the gun out of my grip.

Searing heat from the flames.

Chiquita is a blackened metal skeleton, the fire reaching ten feet high.

I see a couple of the Uptowners, the closest to Chiquita, on the ground, covering their heads. Others are inching their way toward me.

I try to stand up but can't. The message isn't getting through to my arms and legs. My hands can't seem to grip the gun.

Cheekbones looks around the corner.

Takes aim at me. Smiles.

And then the edge of the building above his head explodes into powder, and a steady *rat-tat-tat* from the entrance of the library sends the Uptowners hustling back to cover. I feel myself pulled by the collar of my jacket, dragged up the stone stairs toward the entrance, where Donna is firing. I see Peter's face upside down against a blue sky as he pulls me to safety.

And I think about how we've lost somebody as I black out.

DONNA

JEFFERSON'S EYES ARE rolling back in his head, and I'm afraid I'm going to lose him.

Peter is at the door firing his Glock. I never realized he was so strong. He pulled Jeff up the stairs like a duffel bag.

Peter: "Is he gonna be okay?"

Me: "Yeah." Yeah. Maybe.

This has gone south, and fast. Bushwhacked in the Union and now stuck here, with SeeThrough gone and Jeff out of it.

And Brainbox is nowhere to be seen.

Peter: "They're leaving."

I ease my bag under Jefferson's head and crawl over to the doors.

The Uptowners are bailing. I guess they only wanted the truck. Now that it's up in flames, all the aggro has gone out of them.

I go back to Jefferson. His eyeballs are moving under the eyelids, making the soft skin roll like he's dreaming, like something is cresting the water.

"Dude," I say, "come on."

No response. I lean close to him.

Me: "Wake up, Jeff. Please."

Please don't let it end like this.

A thought flashes through my mind. *Kiss him.* An image. Our lips touching, kindling the spark of life.

Why not?

But before any of that happens, he coughs, rolls over onto his side, and gingerly pushes himself up.

You were close, buddy.

Jefferson: "SeeThrough?"

Nobody talks. Peter wipes tears from his eyes.

Peter: "She's gone, man."

Jefferson squeezes his eyes shut, like he's trying to keep the thought out of his head.

Jefferson: "Where's Brainbox?"

Me: "Don't know."

Jeff picks himself up and looks out the door. The flames from the truck play on his face even though it's still daylight.

He stares at it a long time, like he's hoping SeeThrough is going to come walking out of the wreckage. When he comes back, he looks dead tired.

Jefferson: "Let's eat something. Then we find Brainbox and go home."

Peter: "What about the journal?"

Jefferson: "Fuck the journal."

We circle around our packs and have a quick meal in the foyer. Nobody has much to say.

I think about what Jefferson said in the reading room.

At first I didn't know what to say to him. I thought there was no way he could really love me—I mean, whatever *that* means. If he knew me well enough, he wouldn't. He's all idealistic, and I'm all flawed. Maybe it was just leftover adrenaline from the scrap at the Union.

Besides, seeing him lights-out? Maybe I'm sick, maybe I was supposed to realize how much he meant to me, but—all I could think was that there was no point loving somebody when you know you're going to lose them so soon. Maybe that's cowardly. I don't know.

Jefferson keeps checking to see if the Uptowners are coming back, but there's no sign of them.

Peter: "It's not your fault."

Jefferson: "Whose fault *is* it?"

Me: "She wanted to come."

Jefferson: "And *I* wanted to cure the Sickness. So we're both idiots." Jeff stows the rest of his beef jerky in his bag and gets up.

"Give me that sledgehammer." Jefferson takes it and slips it through the handles of the door, securing it.

Peter: "You don't want to leave somebody behind to guard the entrance?"

Jefferson: "No more leaving anybody behind." He looks for a second like he's going to cry, then just sniffs and starts up the stairs.

I'm expecting—worrying? hoping?—that he'll buddy up with me again. Maybe I could explain the way I acted in the reading room. Maybe. But he wants to go on his own. I'm with Peter.

Me: "Shouldn't we stay together?"

Jefferson shakes off the idea. I think, basically, he doesn't want to be around me.

So we're not looking for the article or paper or whatever. We're looking for Brainbox. We're looking to drag ourselves home.

Epic fail.

We search the ground floor, keeping in touch with Jeff on our walkies. We call out for Brainbox but hear nothing back.

I figure he's staring at a diagram of a molecule or something, so absorbed that he doesn't hear us. I mean, if he didn't hear the fricking firefight, I don't know what's going to catch his attention.

Nada on the second floor. Jefferson, clearing the third, can't find him, either.

"Nothing," says a digitized version of Jefferson's voice through the walkie.

I tell Peter that I'm worried about Jeff.

Peter: "Worried how?"

Me: "Worried like he's losing it."

Peter: "When was the last time you got somebody killed?"

Me: "Uh, never?"

Peter: "Well."

It's dark down here—only the occasional bleed of light from outside when we pass a room with exterior windows.

Without electric lights, your average city building is just a stack of square caves with a few holes in it. *This* place is like a tunnel complex.

Fortunately, I've got a pair of night-vision goggles we scrounged back in the day, when we hit the SWAT lockers at the precinct. A creepy setup with two eyepieces but only one eye stalk projecting out that makes me look like some techno-insect Cyclops. When I look through them, everything seems like the scariest part of a found-footage movie.

Peter has a much less impressive rig, a tiny Petzl headlamp that provides a little normal illumination. Without that, I wouldn't be able to see a thing. The goggles need a little light to work.

Me: "But it wasn't his fault."

Peter: "Tell that to *him*." We keep edging around the walls. "Jefferson's a brooder. He's gonna blame himself."

His last words echo, and on the right, a doorway appears. I see a big room—maybe a hundred feet square—filled with tables, pictures mounted on the walls, dividers running its length. It's hard to tell what the place is for. Through the goggles it's all just shapes of Day-Glo green and band-shirt black.

Me: "Jeff told me he loved me. Hello? Brainbox? You there?"

Peter: *"What?"* I'm blinded for a moment by his headlamp. "Girl! Why didn't you *tell* me?"

Me: "I just did. Turn that light the other way, will you? You're burning my eyes out."

Peter: "And what did you say? What did you do? Did you just *do* him right there?"

Me: "What? No! It wasn't that kind of, like, moment."

Peter: "Girrrl, I *told* you things get interesting when you get out of camp! So?"

I can't really see his face, but if I could, I know one eyebrow or the other would be raised.

Me: "So nothing."

Peter: "You don't love him back?"

Me: "I don't even get that word anymore. I mean, *love* was, like, Before. When you could take people out to dinner and watch movies and get married and have kids and stuff. Love is, like, *forever* stuff. I've got, what, two years to live?"

Peter (practically shouting): "But that's what makes it so *romantic*!" He seems annoyed with me. "Don't you get it? It's the end of the world! That's *exactly* when you fall in love. When else?"

Me: "Wrong. That's exactly when you get desperate and *convince* yourself that you love somebody. Even though you don't know the meaning of the word."

Peter: "Who *cares*? Quit staying on the sidelines. Game's almost over."

Me: "Ooh, sports. You're so butch."

Peter: "Shut up. *The meaning of the word!* The meaning of the word is the word. The meaning of the word is...it's being able to say it. He's obviously nuts about you."

Me: "What?"

Peter: "Ugh, you are such a dizzy bitch. Well, if you're not going to go for it, *I* will."

Me: "He's all yours."

Then I feel a funny little bumping in my chest. Jealousy? Ridiculous.

A man in a white robe is standing in front of us.

I scream—okay, I'll say it, I scream like a *girl*—and step back. Peter has his gun up and shouts at him to stay right there, don't fucking move!

The guy doesn't move. At all. Nobody can be that still.

That's when I realize it's a dummy wearing some kind of robe or something.

There's a badge on the chest—a black *X* on a red background. At first I think it's a costume from one of those superhero movies everybody was into. Then I look up and see the pointy white cowl.

It's a Ku Klux Klan outfit.

Me: "You see this?"

Peter: "Yes. WTF?"

Looking around, I realize that what I thought were tables are actually display cases. We're in some kind of exhibition room. Peter and I fan out, checking what's inside the cases. I find a copy of the Koran, a picture of Malcolm X kneeling on a carpet. He has a nice face.

Peter: "Um, I think I just found the first draft of the Declaration of Independence."

Me: "Ha-ha."

Peter: "No, for real."

Me: "Oh."

Moving on to the next case, I see some wrinkly typewriter paper:

```
April is the cruelest month, breeding
Lilacs out of the dead land, mixing
Memory and desire, stirring
Dull roots with spring rain.
```

And I think, *Yeah, preach, brother.* Life used to be beautiful, and now it sucks. What's the use of stuff growing if it's going to die? And I wonder how this Eliot guy got it so right. But then, the thing about living through the apocalypse is that everything, like, *means something.* It's like when you get dumped, and suddenly every song on the radio is, coincidentally, about you and your stupid breakup.

I think about cracking open the case and snagging the papers for Jefferson. He *likes* long, purposely obscure poems. But it feels wrong, even if the people who put it there are dead.

Peter: "Wow, I've always wanted my own copy of the Gutenberg Bible." He's looking at a heavy book on a stand.

Me: "That's the book in the painting upstairs."

Peter: "Could be worth something on eBay."

We come to the wall at the end, and I see a little cluster of toys in a decorated box.

I recognize them.

I reach out for Peter's hand. "What?" he says, then he seems to understand.

But he can't really. He didn't spend a whole year reading the books to Charlie.

Charlie, my little brother, my little monkey, tucked up in his Lightning McQueen pajamas, warm from the bath, his skin smelling like ripe fruit. His round forehead with a tiny splotched scar from when he ran into the coffee table; his little fingers traveling up and down my back of their own accord as I read him stories from the Hundred Acre Wood. His eyes following the words but not knowing them.

He likes to learn, but he's not sure he wants to read, because he's worried I'll stop reading to him. He's afraid of being alone at night, and he asks for "advice on how to get to sleep." So sometimes I slip into his little bed, infested with stuffed animals and smelling of innocence. His cheeks are pillowy and new. He holds on to me like a drowning sailor and asks silly questions until he starts to drowse.

I tilt the goggles up on my head and adjust to the real light coming from Peter's headlamp. In the case, there is a half circle of stuffed animals, scrubby and matted and loved into threadbareness. Pooh, Eeyore, Tigger, Piglet. The originals. Somebody once told me they were here, but I forgot.

And I am slipping away, washed into the past. Full-throttle hugs with sprinting run-ups. Tickles and kisses and ordinary fears. I want him back. I want to give up and join him in the big dark, find him there and keep him safe.

Peter: "Come on." He pulls me away.

Me: "Why?"

Peter: "Our friends need us."

I wipe my eyes and fit the goggles back into the sockets.

After another half hour of feeling our way around in the dark, we find a door marked SOUTH STACKS. Behind it, there's a staircase leading down.

Below, we discover a whole floor of nothing but metal book-shelves, extending city blocks in either direction. Millions of books, everything anyone ever knew.

Me: "This reminds me of *Resident Evil*."

Peter: "Great. I'm in a video game."

Me (for about the thousandth time): "Brainbox?" Nothing.

Then some scuttling.

Peter: "Did you hear that?"

Me: "No. Yes. Unfortunately."

Me: "Jefferson? Where are you? Over." I hear a squawk, with no distinct words.

Then things are quiet again, and a search of the entire floor shows us nothing—except for another set of stairs, leading down to an identical floor, with more long canyons of bookshelves.

We're on our fourth—maybe fifth—floor of shelves when the scuttling starts up again.

Peter: "Fuck."

Me: "Should we get out of here?"

Peter: "Brainbox! Stop fucking around, man!"

Scuttling from behind us.

Me (on the walkie): "Jefferson?" Maybe he followed us down. There's no reply.

My heart breaks into a sprint. I taste copper.

Something black flashes in front of me, between two stacks. It's moving too quickly to tell what it is.

Me: "Who are you? Next thing I see, I shoot it!"

Something metallic clatters to the ground in front of us. A cylinder that gives off a little *pop*.

We're backing away when it blows up—and my goggles go off the chart, flooding my eyes with light.

I tear them off, but it's too late—my whole field of vision is one big green afterimage. I shout to Peter, but I can't hear anything; I can only feel the cold rasp of the air running over my vocal cords.

I'm deaf and blind.

Something grabs my carbine, and I kick and hit flesh and bone. Someone else has an arm around my neck. I'm hit in the back of the knee and bent to the ground. It feels like five, maybe six, hands on me, pressing my face into the floor, bending my arms behind my back. I scream and bite until a musty cloth sack is pulled over my head. And then I'm raised off the floor. When I struggle, I'm hit in the stomach with something hard. It hurts like hell, and I stop kicking.

I can't hear anything but a buzzing in my ears, I can't see anything, and I don't know which way is up or where I am as I'm carried along.

Okay. Be rational. It was probably an M84 stun grenade. I've got some kind of zip tie around my wrists—I felt the plastic teeth gritting when they tightened it. It's strong as hell. Trying to break it only makes it cut into my skin.

Maybe the Uptowners followed us in—but it doesn't make sense. The place was pitch-dark, and we were completely surprised. No, it was somebody prepared and well stocked. That probably means they knew the terrain, which means...

Somebody lives here.

The library is haunted.

That's why the place is so clean. It's inhabited.

I'm carried up the stairs—I count by the turning, eight landings or four floors—then some jogs right and left, then a long corridor, then another left. Then I feel a thin breeze, and I think I am outside.

I'm lowered into a wooden chair.

My hood is whipped off—and I can see again.

We're back in the reading room. Peter is sitting on my left, trussed up like me.

I read his lips as he shouts, "Can you hear?" I shake my head.

On my right—thank God—is Jefferson, also bound up to a chair with yellow nylon ropes. Our weapons and our packs are nowhere to be seen.

We're being *observed*—that's the word for it—by twenty or so pasty-faced types in bulky clothing. It makes me realize that the library, with all its big rooms and passageways, is actually kind of chilly compared with the outside. Their heads must be cold, though, because each of them has shaved his or her hair off. Not a very appealing look. In fact, I'd say it's downright creepy. The home-brew facial tattoos don't help much, either.

Jefferson is talking to them, but I can't hear what he's saying. My ears are still screwed up.

Whatever he's saying, it had better be good.

JEFFERSON

"HI," I SAY. "My name's Jefferson. What's yours?"

That's the best that I can think of at the moment. The way I see it, there's no point being aggressive, given that I'm tied to a chair.

Peter and Donna seem to be deaf, which would explain the thumping we heard around fifteen minutes ago. Stun grenade.

Looks like we all got some knocks in. One of the Ghosts is hunched over, nursing his kicked crotch. The guy I hit in the face with my rifle isn't around as far as I can tell.

They just stare at us as dusk falls and the light in the high windows turns blue. I've asked them who they are, and I've asked them what they want, but there's nothing doing. They just sit there in their rags and wait.

The markings on their foreheads must mean something. I recognize that they're Greek letters. I'm trying to remember what they mean. I seek out the guy with the A-shaped mark.

"Alpha?" I say.

There's a silence.

Finally, "Yes," he says. It's the first word any of them has spoken. The others look to him.

"That's your name?" I ask.

"It's my new name, yes."

"What happened to your old name?"

"Same thing that happened to everything else," he says. "It's gone."

"Okay...my name is Jefferson. Would I be right in guessing you live here?"

He nods.

"So that means we broke into your place. I'm sorry about that. We didn't know." I try to sound as sympathetic and reasonable as I can.

"Now you do," he says.

"Yeah. Look," I say, "we'd be happy to just get on our way. Just give us our stuff back, and we'll go. We won't tell anybody about you."

Nothing.

"Why did you come here?" says Alpha.

"We were looking for some information," I say.

At the word *information*, all of them kind of nod and hum, like it was a magic word.

"What information?" says Alpha.

"A medical journal," I say. "My friend thought it had something to do with What Happened."

A girl with a kind of funky-shaped *b* painted on her forehead—a *beta*—turns to Alpha and whispers something in his ear. He nods.

"But didn't you know the library is haunted?" says Alpha.

"Yeah," I say. "I can see what people meant. You guys scared the crap out of us."

"In a way," says Alpha, "it *is* haunted. You see, this is all that's left of civilization. This is the biggest repository of information—of wisdom—anywhere in the world. And it's our job to protect it."

"I get it," I say.

"I don't think so," he says. "What happens if we let you go and you tell everybody that the library is just waiting here for somebody to take it over?"

I don't want to know where this train of thought is going. So I just say, "We won't tell anybody. All we want to do is leave."

Beta looks at Alpha, who nods, and then she says, "Was there anyone else with you?" It's the first time any of them except for Alpha has spoken aloud.

"Yes," I say, hoping I've made the right decision. "There's a guy called Brainbox. He's missing."

Alpha nods.

Now he walks toward me, taking a thin knife from a sheath on his hip.

He slips behind me.

"There is one God, and he is Information," he says.

I can feel the edge of his knife in my mind. He is going to cut my throat. I can feel the blood soaking my shirt, the air whistling into my neck....

He saws away the plastic zip-tie handcuffs, and with a *pop*, my hands are free.

DONNA

FINALLY MY HEARING COMES BACK, and hoo boy.

To simplify: The library has been taken over by a bunch of psychos. They've started, like, their own religion, because, hey! That'd be fun!

It seems to have something to do with *information*, which is their favorite word ever. It's all information this and information that. Once you get them started, they can't shut up. They say that even atoms and genes and stuff are information, the way that bits are for a computer. The universe is like a big computer programmed with atoms.

The further away things get from *information*, the worse it gets, according to them. Stuff, like bodies and chairs and tables and whatnot, is a big drag to them. Bodies especially. I think they'd rather be ideas floating around like they're in some kind of sci-fi movie. Creatures of pure energy.

According to them, the Sickness was some kind of punishment from God because information was being locked up or something.

It's a little fuzzy.

The library is kind of like their holy place, and we've violated some taboo by breaking in. Which would be a bummer, except that somehow Jefferson has managed to convince them that we're okay. The fact that these nutburgers like him may be the only thing keeping us alive.

That's the thing about Jefferson—he doesn't like confrontation, so he's really good at getting along. He always wants to seem like a nice guy, with the result that, actually, he does seem like a nice guy.

Which he *is*. He *is* a nice guy. Which is part of the problem.

I remember once before It Happened, we were doing a little strategy session re: his love life.

There was this girl Chloe, of the Blond Angelic brand that he always fell for. Blue eyes, wavy hair, nice rack, the works. This kind of chick always made Jefferson all deer-in-the-headlights. He was utterly incapable of discerning any flaws in them.

The main flaw, in this case, was that she was an idiot.

We had known her since kindergarten. She was always kind of a priss. Like, she would cry if some dirt got on her patent-leather shoes. Once in first grade we were walking to the park in an orderly line and I kicked a puddle, and she said, "Don't! The poor people need to drink from that!"

So, not the brightest bulb.

Worst of all—big-time princess fixation.

I have a theory about the Princess Thing. Basically, my theory is that it doesn't just go away when you realize it's not cool. Since it can't stay outside—like, you can't be thirteen and walk around wearing pink acrylic tutus and carrying a wand anymore (and by the way,

I would have no objection to *that*; if that's your thing, knock yourself out)—it goes *inside*.

It's not a choice; it's a syndrome. All that mental energy that went into dressing up like Cinderella at the ball actually takes over some part of your brain. And then, for the rest of your life, you just figure some dude is going to put a crown on your head and sweep you onto a white charger or whatever. All the haters are gonna grovel in the dust and maybe have their eyes pecked out by birds, like in the Grimms' fairy tales.

If you're not all hot and popular, this leads to misery and depression and a sense of how *cruel* the world is. If you *are* hot and popular, well—watch out. Trouble ahead.

Because there is no dude in the world with a Prince Complex. Nobody to fit together all the jigsaw pieces of your weird conception of the world.

I mean, guys do okay at the beginning. They can, like, take you out somewhere nice, give you flowers, tell you how beautiful you are, blah blah blah. Which—what is *that* all about? Why do guys have to go through all those hoops? Whatever happened to just getting to know somebody and liking them?

Anyway, at some point, the act drops. Which is either (a) when they run out of interest, (b) when they get in your pants, or (c) when they realize they're supposed to keep this up, like, full-time (which often strikes them just after condition (b) has been satisfied).

Did I say that no guy ever has a Prince Complex? Let me modify that. If there ever *was* a guy with a Prince Complex, it was Jefferson.

I don't mean that he geeked out on *Sleeping Beauty* or anything. Just that, unlike anybody else I ever knew, he was totally obsessed with goodness. Like, being honorable, protecting the weak, doing the right thing, etc., etc. Or maybe it'd be better to say he had a Jedi Complex. Like, he saw *Star Wars* when he was seven years old, and it was all, *That's me.* He even has a lightsaber. Well, an ancestral samurai sword. Whatever.

The problem with all this, the Princess Thing and the Jedi Thing, is that—and I can't put too fine a point on this—they are fictional. *They don't exist.* In real life, there are no evil witches, no wise mentors, no fairy godmothers, no evil empires. Everything is shades of gray.

Ugh, I can't believe such a *useful* phrase got hijacked by those fricking books.

Anyway, Jefferson, my Friend Who Is a Boy, had already crushed on everything that looked remotely like a Disney heroine all the way through ninth grade. Finally he turned his attention to the big prize, Princess Chloe.

One day we're hanging out at Café Orlin, which I loved because the coffee was only meh, so it wasn't overrun with hipsters.

Jefferson is all revved up because he took Chloe on a date to the Metropolitan Museum.

Where to begin? First of all, as previously mentioned, Chloe is a nitwit. I can just imagine her clocking all the art. Like a chicken looking at a newspaper. And you can bet Jefferson was dragging her around to his favorites, blathering on about what they *meant* to him, how they *affected* him, working the romantic angle. Like, trying to sex her up with Georgia O'Keeffe paintings. Ugh.

Jeff wasn't faking it, either, the classy artsy bit. This kid would actually *go to the museum on weekends, on his own*. Catch the number six from Astor Place, hoof it to the Met, pay one penny because he objected to the "suggested donation" being so high, and cruise around looking at all the art. I went with him once, but that was enough. It was all so fricking *worthy*. Like, I *get* it. The cultural legacy of man and stuff. But I'd just as soon get all hopped up on caffeine and check out the freaks in the East Village.

"So what happened?" I asked him after the museum date.

Jefferson: "What do you mean, what happened?"

Me: "Like, what did you do? How far did you get?"

Jefferson: "Donna!"

And he gives me this look. As if to say, *How could you possibly think my intentions were* carnal!

Jefferson: "We talked for hours, and there was really a connection."

Me: "Okay, give me some notable quotables."

Jefferson: "Well, she told me I was the nicest guy she knows."

Me: "Oh, boy."

Jefferson: "What?"

Me: "Was that the exact word? *Nicest*?"

Jefferson: "I think so."

Me: "You're screwed. By which I mean, you are not getting screwed."

Jefferson (annoyed): "What do you mean?"

Me: "For a girl like Chloe, saying you're 'nice' is code for 'I will never, ever get it on with you.'"

Jefferson: "*Nice* is positive." But he's already looking a little thrown.

Me: "Look, you've got only one option here, which is the Hail Mary play. You've gotta be all, 'I am not *nice*. You think I am, but I am definitely *not*. I am a stealth badass.' And then you just totally mack out on her. Like, kiss her. And not all gently, either. Grab her."

Jefferson: "Uh, I think that's called *assault*."

Me: "Suit yourself. Probably wouldn't work anyway. *Nice* is like a death sentence."

Jefferson looked crestfallen.

Me: "Look. If it's any consolation, it was all over when you took her to the museum. When you took her on a *date*. That's not how people get together. Not since the nineteen fifties or something. You want to get together with somebody, you make sure you're going to a party they're going to, get sloppy, and freak on her."

Jefferson: "Thanks for the advice."

Me: "She's a moron anyway. You think just because she's pretty she's worth the time of day. She isn't."

Jefferson: "She's more than pretty."

Me: "Okay, fine. I would just—direct my attention elsewhere, if I were you."

Jefferson: "Like *where*?" As if there weren't any other girls in the world.

And for a moment, I thought of just leaning over the table and kissing him. *Like* me, *you moron*. That's how it would happen if we were in a romantic comedy. Except I'd known him too long. I wasn't thinking, *Kiss me, you fool!* I was thinking, *Get your head out of your ass!*

He was too…nice for me. Which maybe said something about me. Like, I had my own problems.

Like, a guy has never told me he loved me before. So maybe I can't believe it. Jeff kind of threw me with that one. Weirdly, though I should have been all gooey, or at least all sentimental, like, *Oh, how sweet*, I acted defensive. Like somebody was trying to tell me what to do. I suppose he kind of was. He was trying to tell me to feel the way he did.

How can I even trust what he's saying? I mean, he wouldn't be trying to trick me, but he might trick himself. Kid is a basket case.

Says the basket case.

Anyhooters, turns out Jefferson got his big chance with Chloe, after It Happened. She joined our tribe and sort of attached herself to him. I don't know if she was still the girl he liked. She'd kind of lost it. Wore too much makeup, dressed like a stripper, spoke in this screechy little-girl voice. But Jeff didn't cut her loose. He was *nice*. He wanted to protect her, I guess.

Then, one day, she stole Jefferson's handgun. Went to the Sephora down on Broadway, what was left of it. Picked out her favorite cosmetics. Gave herself a full-on makeover.

And blew her brains out.

Nice.

This is what I think about while the librarian freaks are taking us back down into the stacks. Weird to be taking a trip down memory lane at that moment, but maybe my mind is protecting itself, cushioning itself in cottony memories.

Meanwhile, Jeff is being all *solicitous*, asking questions, acting interested in their effed-up cult. You can tell that they're feeling kind of flattered. Like, they think they have a potential convert or something. Any moment now, they're going to give him a free personality test.

It helps that we're actually looking for some of their precious information. Like, we didn't come here to steal their food; we came here In Search of Knowledge. That really floats their boat. So they take us down to a special section in the stacks where the periodicals are kept. Because they may be deranged, but they know their Dewey decimal system.

When we find Brainbox, he's just chillin' with a couple of the Info Loonies. They seem to look up to him, like he's dazzled them with his Beautiful Mind. There's a couple of bald girls (I think they're girls— their freaky costumes don't exactly flatter them) bringing him boxes of medical journals. While we were getting handcuffed, beaten to the ground, and generally terrorized, Brainbox was being led through the stacks and assisted in his search for *Disease Weekly*, or whatever it is.

He looks up, and he's all, like, "Hey, where have you guys been?"

By the light of solar-powered lamps, we hunt the information.

JEFFERSON

I UNDERSTAND NOW why people say the library is haunted. Alpha and his tribe may be humoring us for now, but there's something very, very wrong with them.

I used to come here to study before It Happened. It was easier to concentrate when there were all those other people around getting stuff done, or at least not out having a better time than I was.

Mostly the people you saw in the reading room were there for the same reason as me. They had reading to do, and this was a good place for it. They called stuff up from the stacks and checked their e-mail. They came, and they went, and they even interacted with one another occasionally.

Then there were the other ones. Barricaded behind walls of books, they snuffled, picked at themselves, ate lunch out of crinkly plastic bags, and scribbled feverishly in crackling, worn notebooks. If you snuck a glance, you'd see column after column of tiny, precise writing. Sometimes it was words, sometimes numbers, diagrams, proofs. They were unraveling conspiracies, filing griev-ances against the CIA, figuring out the equations that ruled the cosmos. They would already be installed when I arrived, and they'd stay there gulping their sandwiches and writing until the closing announcement came. Halos of stink and madness buzzed about their heads.

Some of them would have been young enough to survive What Happened. Precocious lunatics just waiting to pool their madness and figure everything out.

I'd be lying if I said that Brainbox didn't fit in here. When we tell him SeeThrough is gone, he just stands there and blinks. Then he goes back to searching through boxes of journals.

I shouldn't have been so easily convinced, but I thought Wash would have taken him up on this. And *I* wanted to do something. Strike a blow against death. Get the Sickness back for taking my brother.

I don't know. Maybe I just wanted to get away from the Square, the whole tribe looking to me to make decisions. Maybe I was pretending to lead while I was really hiding.

I watch Brainbox flip through box after box of papers as he mutters to himself. In him, I see those conspiracists. I see the Ghosts.

And then I realize with a turn of my stomach that Brainbox never actually showed me the abstract.

Maybe there is no journal. Maybe there is no article.

Maybe he made it up.

From that point, I start planning our escape.

The Ghosts have taken all our gear, including the weapons. A guy with a *k* tattoo on his forehead has my AR-15, and Alpha has my *wakizashi* tucked into his waistband. The rest of our stuff is scattered through their alphabet.

They don't have any guns of their own, which is strange. I don't understand how they've managed to keep this place without firepower.

Brainbox keeps going through the motions of searching. The Ghosts are standing around, their faces gruesome in the sickly light.

"Brainbox," I say, leaning in to him, "it's okay."

"What's okay?" says Brainbox.

"It's okay if there's no article. I get it."

He looks up at me, his expression blank.

"You wanted to do something. So you made it up. It's okay. I loved Wash, too. But he's gone."

Brainbox smiles. It doesn't look quite right on his face. Then he lets out a cackling laugh.

"Brainbox, *enough*," I say.

But he holds up a crisp cream-colored booklet: the *Journal of Applied Virology*.

It's not like an ordinary magazine. There's no cover photo, just a table of contents right on the front. I can see something about megaloviruses, something about pneumonia, something about toxoplasmosis.

And halfway down, **The Risk of Wexelblatt Effects in Eni-likoskotonic Agents.**

Brainbox lifts it up and shows it around, and the Ghosts start laughing, too, laughing and nodding. See? The information.

When the hilarity dies down, I say to the Ghosts, "I want to thank you all. Thank you for your help. Now it's time for us to go home."

"Oh, no," says Alpha. "You can't go yet." He smiles and takes the journal right out of Brainbox's hand. "We need to celebrate."

They've got our guns. So we'll celebrate.

We're walked back up to the reading room, and on the way, I hear skittering and shuffling again. I wonder how many of them are creeping around the place.

In the reading room, we find one of the tables laid for a feast. The smell of cooking meat perfumes the air. They're using the fine china, the stuff they used to put out back in the day for benefits and weddings. By now night has fallen, the gridwork of high windows holds tiles of blackness, and hundreds of candles make hazy spheres of light. They're using the ornate hutch dividing the reading room in two as a kitchen. Smoke rises and pools in the gloom of the ceiling.

Alpha is at the head of the table, with Brainbox on his right. The rest of us are interspersed among about ten of them, from Beta all the way to—is it Mu? Other Ghosts are shuttling back and forth, bringing food from the makeshift kitchen.

We're all friends now, it seems. Not give-you-back-your-weapons friends, though.

"So," says Alpha, "what will you do now?" He forks some fiddlehead fern, from God knows where, into his mouth.

"We'll go home," I say.

"What about this?" says Alpha, holding up the journal.

"What about it?"

Alpha leafs through the pages. "It would reward study." The guy sounds priggish, like what I imagine Donna thinks I'm like. "Do you know what a Wexelblatt Effect is?"

"No," I say.

Alpha looks at Brainbox, who says, "The unpredictable inter-action of technology and natural phenomena. Like disasters."

I find it strange that Brainbox hadn't told me that before.

"Such as?" I say.

"Hurricane Katrina," says Brainbox. "The way the levees broke. Deepwater Horizon."

"Chernobyl. Fukushima Daiichi," says Alpha, smiling.

"Hurricane Sandy," says Brainbox, and I can see that the gears are turning.

"So What Happened was a Wexelblatt Effect. That's interesting, but I don't see what we can do about it."

Alpha shows the article to Brainbox and points something out. Brainbox looks at it and then up at Alpha. Alpha smiles.

"The Old Man," he says.

"What?" I say. "What about the Old Man?"

Alpha refuses to explain what he's talking about. Instead, he digs into a bowl of strawberries.

"Where did you *get* these?" asks Donna.

"We have our own garden," he says, and gestures toward the windows to the west. "In Bryant Park."

"Yeah, that's weird," I say. "How do you manage that? I can understand how you might be able to hide here in the library. But how are you able to keep people from taking stuff out of the park?"

Alpha smiles. "It's simple," he says. "Fear."

"Fear of what?" says Donna.

Alpha waves his hand dismissively. "Arbitrary distinctions. Taboos."

The other Ghosts laugh.

I don't know how to respond to this. I take a bite of a strawberry. It's absolutely delicious. There's a roast pork smell coming from the kitchen, and now more Ghosts appear, carrying platters.

"Let me tell you more about the information," says Alpha. "Look at all life as a system of information from the ground up," he says as the Ghosts set down the platters. "Quarks make particles, particles make atoms, atoms make cells."

As he keeps talking, he cuts himself a piece of the roast and takes a bite. "That's all that matter is. Information."

Brainbox suddenly looks up at me. "Jefferson," he says, looking concerned, but Alpha keeps talking.

"What are animals? They are matter constructed into functional models by their execution code—C, G, T, A." He swallows. "DNA. When you eat something, it is information eating information."

The smell of the pig infiltrates my mind.

"You ask me how we keep control of the library," continues Alpha. "And I say arbitrary distinctions. What is the difference between an animal and a person? And don't tell me an eternal soul. That can't be verified. What is the difference between flesh and meat? Nothing. It's *noise*. Taboo."

"Jefferson," Brainbox says.

"Most taboos are rooted in the notion of generational continuity. Why is there a taboo against incest? Because closely related DNA patterns are more likely to produce abnormalities when recombined. But if nobody has children, does that matter? You see? *Noise*."

I look down at the slice of roast in front of me.

The roast is an oblong hunk of meat, browned on the edges, sweating pink juice onto the platter. The smell that rises from it is sublime.

My mouth waters as I gag.

"You could say that about other taboos," says Alpha.

Then, a moment before the part that I call "I" can say it, I realize that I am looking at a cooked human thigh.

Alpha says, *"Verily, verily, I say unto you, except ye eat the flesh of the Son of man, and drink his blood, ye have no life in you."*

Peter sees it, too.

"Eat," says Alpha. And the other Ghosts start carving off slices of flesh.

My tribe reads my face. None of us moves.

"*Eat*," says Alpha, raising Peter's pistol out of his robe. He points the gun at Donna's head.

What happens next happens very quickly.

There is a sharp scream and a sickening crack, and one of the Ghosts carrying a serving plate falls over, his arm pointed the wrong way. The carbine he had hanging from his shoulder, Donna's carbine, goes off and the girl, Beta, slumps forward to the table, a precise hole in her head.

SeeThrough emerges from behind the guy whose arm she just broke, holding the carbine. "Let's go," she says.

Alpha points the gun away from Donna and toward SeeThrough. I am already up and running on top of the table, plates clattering around me.

He gets off one shot at SeeThrough before I'm on him, my momentum throwing his chair back and slamming his head into the ground.

Meanwhile, my friends are up, grabbing at weapons, striking out with dinner knives.

I've got the wrist of Alpha's gun hand. He's firing wildly, puncturing the painted sky. But it's not the gun I'm after. With my other hand, I find the pommel of the *wakizashi* and draw it out before he realizes what I'm doing. His left hand flails and slaps against my chest, and he tries to push me away as I jam the point of the blade into his side. It scrapes a rib and then goes deep. I *feel* it go through skin, muscle, and organs. He looks at me and coughs, blood running over his white face.

I've killed before. But not this close-up. The intimacy is sickening.

I yank the sword out. He's still writhing on the ground. I step on his gun hand in case there is any fight left in him, grab the journal from his other hand, and look around for Donna. She's struggling with one of the Ghosts, both of them sprawled over the table.

I hack at the Ghost's neck and he spasms backward, revealing Donna. She looks at me, startled.

We have the advantage now. The Ghosts are retreating toward the kitchen, kept off balance by SeeThrough, who is firing into the dark after them.

I slash away as many of the candles as I can, as Brainbox and Peter start to push the table over for cover.

"No," I shout at them. "We're getting out now!"

I grab an astonished Brainbox by the scruff and throw him toward the door. Peter has retrieved his gun and is firing at anything that isn't us.

We scramble to the catalog room, the Ghosts taking the occasional shot with the stolen guns but missing us in the darkness. Behind us, bullets thud into books, and dead computer monitors explode into dust and smoke.

I tell the others to head for the exit and shove the thick wooden doors between the painted corridor and the catalog room closed. As they make their way down the stairs, I wait. I realize what I have to do to stop the pursuit and give us all time. What to do to keep them from following. I tell myself that it's worth it, that all this blood won't stain me. It's an arbitrary distinction.

Battle not with monsters, lest ye become a monster.

When it's done, I fly down the stairs.

In the entrance hall, everyone is calling for Donna, who has disappeared into the dark opposite the front doors.

As I look up, fearful that the Ghosts will gather their courage and follow, I hear the sound of glass breaking.

Then Donna emerges from the dark, carrying some sort of stuffed animal.

A teddy bear.

DONNA

WE STUMBLE DOWN THE STEPS, joyful, disgusted. We are free. We are alive.

We are changed.

My body and clothes are bloodstained and my heart feels like it is running out of beats as we pass the smoking wreckage of the truck and turn left, heading north up Fifth, avoiding the direction the Uptowners attacked from.

Our bodies are taking us as far from the horror as they need to go. After a few blocks, it's obvious that there will be no pursuit from the library. A pack of dogs keeps pace with us for a while, smelling the blood, but we are looking wilder than them, and they decide they want no part of us.

We get our brains back in front of a short old building, white like a wedding cake. The wrought-iron doors have glass between the grilles. Jefferson tries one, and it swings open. We pile into a marble-floored hallway, a sleek wooden counter at the end.

A hotel.

I catch my breath.

Jefferson, his eyes crazed, calls out into the darkness.

"If anyone's here," he says, "get the fuck out, or we'll fucking kill you!"

Not very nice.

We pile the reception couches against the front door and retreat to the wood-lined bar. We have a drink or two. Nobody has much to say except SeeThrough. She tells us about her escape from the Uptowners, scurrying into a ditch when the truck blew, too scared to move until darkness came. Some major ninja or Shaolin or whatever action to get hold of my gun, throwing down with the Ghosts.

I can't say I wouldn't have just legged it back home before taking on all those freaks. Saving our lives. Girl is a major badass. Brainbox is definitely giving her the eye now. The fish are biting.

It's too late to be out, too dangerous to be at street level. We take the stairs. The second and third floors have been ransacked. We make our way up to the fourth, which is mostly untouched, and after plotting an escape route, we kick open the doors along the corridor.

The rooms are clean; the sheets are crisp and cool. The hotel must have been shut down as the Sickness spread. Midtown was never a place where people lived. They just did their business and moved on.

Everybody gets their own suite.

Mine is done in olive drab and beige: the colors that signaled to out-of-towners that they were staying someplace sophisticated. *Bright colors are so—tacky.*

The minibar is still stocked with candy, preserved by all the sugar. They're stale, but they mean calories, protein and fat and glucose.

There's a xeroxed sheet on the desk detailing the closing of the hotel due to "the recent health situation we are facing," but other than that there's practically no sign of What Happened. Bathrobes are folded on the bed, an orchid is mummified on a table in front of the inky, dead flat-screen. It blurrily reflects me. I don't want to see myself any more clearly right now.

In the bathroom, dimly illuminated by moonlight through the tall windows, I peel my clothes off.

I look like a ghoul. My pale flesh, my boyish chest and hips splotched with blood.

There's a square of perfumed soap still wrapped in paper. I break it open, and then I make sure to throw the wrapper in the little garbage bin under the sink. I want to keep up, for just a little while, the spun-sugar-fragile illusion that, in this one place, things are the way they were.

I hope that the water tower on the roof was full before the power went. I stand under the showerhead and pray. Please, just work. Just a little. Just something. I turn the faucet.

Water streams out cold and clear. There's no boiler working to warm it, no filtration system to clean it, so I keep my mouth closed and shiver, but it runs down my body like a blessing. When I look at the drain, I see dirt and blood from my skin. I scratch and scrape at myself to get rid of the matter, the memory. *The information.*

The bath towels are big and fluffy. I barely have the energy to wipe myself dry.

I rub my hair until it is soft and only a little damp. The towel comes away pink. I fold it so that I can see only white, and hang it back over the rail.

I can't bear to put my clothes back on right now. The gore is still wet. I unfold one of the bathrobes and slip into it. It's like an embrace.

This is one of the times when you're supposed to be "asleep before your head hits the pillow." No such luck. I think of the fear, the blood, the shouting, the gunfire, the flesh on the table.

Sleep is far away. I sit up on the bed. I leave my room and make my way down the hallway in the dark.

I knock lightly on the door of his room. I don't want to wake him if he's asleep.

Jefferson opens the door. His hair is damp. I can tell he's just out of the shower, too. He's got a towel around his midriff and his chest is bare. I'm surprised at the muscles beneath his sleek skin. I guess fighting for your survival will do that.

We glimpse each other in the meat of our bodies.

Jefferson's room is a duplex, with a sleeping loft above windows from floor to ceiling.

Me: "Wow. How can you afford this place?"

Jefferson: (Shrugs.) "There are a lot of vacancies. I got a good deal."

I look down at my feet.

Me: "Listen. If I...can I come in here without it being, like, a big decision?"

Jefferson: "You can do whatever you want. There are no rules."

Me: "I just...I'm afraid I'm going to have nightmares."

Jefferson: "Me too."

He steps away from the door and puts a bathrobe on over his towel. Extra reassurance for me, I suppose.

We sit on the couch. He offers me a sip from a miniature bottle of cognac.

He looks at the window, which is curtained off so nobody from outside can see us.

Jefferson: "Donna, I did something terrible, and I need to tell somebody."

Me: "Okay."

He can't look me in the eye.

Jefferson: "We have to fight sometimes. Kill people, even. That's just...the way things are. But when they were chasing us, in the library...I felt like I had to scare them off."

I look at him as if to say, *Go on.*

Jefferson: "I closed the big wooden doors on the first floor behind us. Then I *waited*. I could have run, but that would mean they would follow. So I waited." He looks at his hands. "I made sure that the first person who pushed through, well...I lined up the stroke...and I cut the way I was taught." He pauses.

Me: "Yeah?"

Jefferson: "I made sure I cut their hands off, Donna. I wanted to keep anybody from coming through, so I made sure I cut their hands off. I heard screaming and then I forced the door shut and then nobody followed. But the hands were still on my side of the door."

Now he looks at me. "They were girl's hands. Delicate, you know? I could tell."

I reach out to take his hand, but he withdraws his—he's looking at my fingers.

Me: "You were trying to save your friends. You *did* save your friends. You did what you had to."

Jefferson: "That's not it. It's what came after. That's a horrible thing to do, isn't it? A disgusting thing. But—Donna, I want you to know me, so I have to tell you—"

Me: "Stop. You don't have to tell me. I know." I touch his chin to make sure that he is looking me in the eye. He kind of shivers. "I know that when you did it, you didn't feel bad; you didn't feel disgusting or evil or wrong. You felt *good*."

Jefferson: "How do you know that?"

Me: "That's how I would feel. They wanted to hurt us. They were...you saw what they were doing."

Jeff nods.

Jefferson: "What's happening to us?"

Me: "I don't know. Maybe there's gonna be time to figure that out later."

Now he takes my hand.

Jefferson: "What I said before?"

I wait.

Jefferson: "Well, I'm not going to take it back. I don't care if that makes things weird. I don't want to *make* you feel weird, but I can't lie."

Me: "I understand. I only…I don't even know what love is anymore. All that stuff is gone. I mean, of course I love you. I love you as a fr—"

Jefferson: "Don't. I don't want to hear it. I'll always be your friend, but I want more."

Me: "I know. Maybe I'm crazy."

Jefferson: "Just—just try, will you? Try to love me if you can."

And like that, we're out of that place we were in, the place where we understand each other. Because you just can't *try* to love someone. I don't know very much about love, but I know that's not how it works. Right?

That's enough for one night, I guess. Jefferson goes up the stairs to the sleeping loft.

I follow him, and when he lies down, I lie down beside him. His back is turned to me. I lay my head against his back.

We just stay there like that.

A couple of minutes later, the others knock and come in, one by one. They lie on the couches and the floor. We fall asleep hearing the sound of one another's breathing, like waves on nearby shores. The tribe rests.

JEFFERSON

I'M UP BEFORE anyone else, when dawn is just a purple bruise on the sky. I look at Donna for a length of time just past Appropriate and just short of Serial Killer.

If we were together, I think, I would know her face this way. The curve of her lips, the swell of her forehead, the contour map of her ear. Unanimated, her spirit away in the dreamlands somewhere, resting in peace, skirting the border of death. Charming me.

But we're not together.

I wonder, with everything that's happening, what the point is to caring about her the way I do. It seems like a silly, useless thing. And I feel embarrassed and alone. And then I tilt the idea another way, and the whole thing shifts. What's the point to anything else? What matters more? As long as I believe in her and me, I'm not lost.

I pull on my clothes.

Downstairs, Brainbox sleeps on the floor, his fingers intertwined with SeeThrough's. That's curious.

I touch him on the shoulder, and his eyes pop open. "Yeah?" he says.

That's Brainbox for you. Quick start-up sequence.

I nod for him to follow me out of the room. I take him next door.

"Brainbox, what were you going to do with that article?"

"It doesn't matter," he says. "We don't have it."

I give him the crumpled, smeared journal I took from Alpha when I killed him.

"Have you looked at it?" he asks, sitting on the couch and flattening it against the coffee table. The blood-stiffened paper crackles.

"No," I say. "I figured I wouldn't understand it anyway."

I follow BB's eyes as they follow the text. They jump ahead, left, ahead at a speed that seems impossible to me. The time between his blinks gets longer as the gears in his mind mesh with the ideas in the article.

"So...what's going on with SeeThrough and you?" I ask.

"I think she likes me."

"Oh! Great, man."

"What do you mean?" asks Brainbox, looking up from the paper for a second.

"Well, I mean...do you feel the same way about her?"

Brainbox blinks. "I don't know. I hadn't thought about it."

Then he turns back to the paper, but as he does, he says, "I guess I had figured I'd always be alone."

He doesn't say it in a self-pitying way. Just matter-of-fact. I don't really know how to respond. So I don't.

"Well," he says after a while, "this is interesting."

"How?"

"Okay. The thing about scientists..." he says. "People don't really understand what they're like. They think it's all standing on the shoulders of giants and working together for the advancement of knowledge. It isn't. It's brutal. They compete with one another for the same resources. They get into feuds. They... *talk shit* about each other."

"You mean they *used* to do that," I say.

Brainbox freezes in place for a moment.

BB's parents were scientists—a biologist and a physicist. They're dead, of course. I worry that I've touched a vulnerable spot.

"Yes. Sorry. They *used* to do that," he continues. "And, if I understand this correctly, it was written by one scientist trying to... what's the expression? *Cock-block* another."

I can't help but laugh at the way BB just deployed that term.

"This is a theoretical paper warning the scientific community about a kind of bioweapon," he continues.

"Like a plague or something?" I say.

Brainbox nods. "Yeah. And as I thought, it has to do with diseases that selectively kill adults."

"But how would they let that kind of information just get out there?" I say. "Wouldn't it be top secret or something?"

Brainbox shrugs. "The *specifics* would be secret, sure. But that doesn't mean that the *idea* would be secret. I mean, the idea of an EMP wasn't a secret. The idea of—"

"Excuse me?" I say.

Brainbox blinks and stops himself, in a characteristic tic, like he's used to people not knowing as much as he does but occasionally forgets and has to take it down a notch.

"An electromagnetic pulse. A weapon that could short out the electrical grid. The government used to worry about that."

"Oh," I say. It's kind of funny, in retrospect, because you didn't need to figure out some superweapon to take out the electrical grid. All you had to do was get rid of the people who knew how to keep it up and running.

"There was a lot of stuff like that," says Brainbox. "EMPs, dirty bombs, orbital weapons platforms. Those *ideas* were public knowledge. Same with bioweapons. So it's not that weird that somebody would write about it. Besides which, this is a specialist publication. You'd be surprised how much stuff was hiding in plain sight. So much…"

"Information," I say.

"Yeah," says Brainbox.

"Okay," I say. "Okay, so this is a guy trying to screw up somebody else's research by saying it's dangerous."

"Yeah. On the surface it looks like an opinion piece, or an essay on scientific ethics, but it feels to me like the stuff my parents used to deal with. They called it *ax grinding*."

"So why pay it any attention?" I ask. "If the writer's just trying to screw somebody else over, isn't the information going to be biased?"

"Yes, except it seems kind of...accurate."

"Accurate like how?" I ask.

"Accurate like what the author describes...what he warned could go wrong..." Brainbox looks up at me. "It's What Happened," he says.

I absorb this for a second. "How do you know?" I ask.

"Here. Look. Steroid hormone-binding proteins. See?" He points to a diagram.

"BB, I don't understand any of this stuff."

"The body produces them during puberty. Once physical maturity sets in, they level off. And little kids don't have them. That explains why the little kids died. They didn't have the proteins to bind with the adult-killing agent and keep it from attacking."

"But why?" I say. "Why would anybody want to kill everybody but keep adolescents alive?"

"Don't know. You'd think it'd be the other way around." Brainbox looks at me. "I think I just made a joke."

"Congratulations," I say. "Still. The question remains."

Brainbox shrugs. "It doesn't matter," he says. "That's the why. The why is less important than the how."

"Because if you know how, you're partway to knowing how to stop it," I say.

"Thank you for catching up," says Brainbox. "I was getting bored."

"But the guy who wrote this paper isn't going to explain the how, is he? I mean, he was just hating on the guy who actually did it."

"Correct. But there is a lead here. The article targets this research being done by a team working at Plum Island."

"Okay. What's that?"

"Plum Island Animal Disease Center," says Brainbox.

"Well, at least that doesn't sound creepy."

"It was creepy. Well, sort of. My dad told me about it once. It was a quarantined research site for work on foot-and-mouth disease. That's not too weird. Foot-and-mouth is just a disease that affects livestock. But they were supposed to have worked on bioweapons, too. Apparently that stopped in 1969. Still, there were always conspiracy theories knocking around about the place."

"Like what?"

"Crazy experiments," he says. "Mutant animals. Bioweapons."

Brainbox saves the kicker for the end. "It says here that the entire facility was placed under the Department of Homeland Security in 2002."

"So?"

"So Homeland Security dealt with immigration and customs, and it makes sense that they kept an eye on diseases that could affect US livestock. But they also handled terrorism."

"Like bioweapons," I say.

"Yeah."

"You think the Sickness could have started there? Like, they found a weapon and tried to disarm it or something?" I feel cold sweat starting from my pores.

Brainbox nods.

"Oh, crap," I say.

"Yeah," says Brainbox. "Oh, crap."

"So"—I'm not sure I even want to ask this—"where *is* Plum Island?"

Brainbox says, "It's near the Hamptons."

"You're shitting me," I say.

"No," he says. "It's off the North Fork of Long Island."

"Aw, crap."

That's only a hundred miles from here. Two hours' drive in the old days. Now? Who knows.

Brainbox smiles at me. "So, Generalissimo, what are you going to do?"

DONNA

JEFFERSON AND BRAINBOX COME IN, and everybody springs into defensive postures, like, grabbing butter knives from the bar and taking cover and all. It looks a bit ridiculous because we don't get the drop on them in the least.

They just sit down on the couch and look around in an important sort of way, a "your mother and I have something to tell you" sort of way.

Only instead of a divorce, it's a suicide mission.

Jefferson holds up that goddamn medical journal, which is all covered in blood and goo. He does this whole spiel about bioweapons, whatever those are, and some place called the Sugarplum Fairy Disease Emporium or something, and how he and Brainbox are going to find a cure.

Why not. The Sugarbaked Ham Infection Center is "only" a hundred miles from here, so, you know, fun!

Then he does a totally Jeffersonian thing, which is to give this whole big speech about how he can't ask any of us to volunteer; in fact he *insists* that the rest of us go home to the Square.

But SeeThrough refuses to go home. She's all up for the trip, in keeping with her new action-hero image.

Peter: (Raises his hand like he's in class or something.) "Hello, my name is Peter."

It takes a second for people to shake off the gloom and respond with a bored-sounding "Hello, Peter."

Peter: "Um, I would just like to say that I signed on for a good time? And so far, I barfed, I got shot at, and somebody tried to feed me human flesh."

Jefferson: "Your point being?"

Peter: "My point being, I'm not gonna go home with my tail between my legs. I'm gonna stay out, party hearty, and turn that frown upside down. Sign me up."

So now everybody is looking at me.

Me: "I vote *nobody* goes east. We all go home. Screw the hero routine. You want to bushwhack a hundred miles into unknown territory? After what's happened to us going *forty blocks*? And what happens if we get there? Brainbox, like, tweaks some margarita mix and then nobody dies anymore?"

Brainbox: "There's no way margarita mix—"

Me: "Shut up, Brainbox. You know what I mean."

Jefferson: "If we don't do something, it's only going to get worse."

Me: "What's that supposed to mean? How can it get *worse*?"

Jefferson: "It can get a lot worse. Tell me something, Peter. How are the scavenging expeditions going lately?"

Peter: "It's getting harder and harder to find food. On the plus side, you can still find shitloads of themed iPhone covers."

Jefferson: "Okay. Donna, how are your medicine reserves holding up?"

Me (frowning): "Frank and I are talking about growing poppies to manufacture our own morphine."

Jefferson: "Terrific. How many acres? Can we support everybody on the food we're growing right now, Brainbox?"

Brainbox: (Shakes his head.) "No. Not without foraging for canned foods and stuff."

Peter: "Or eating other people. Don't forget that."

Jefferson: "That's my point. The whole thing is going down the tubes. Those…monsters back at the library are the exception now. But they won't be when the city's food supplies are used up. And that's sooner rather than later."

Me: "So why is curing the Sickness going to help anything? At least now people are dying off, right? If everybody gets cured, there're more mouths to feed."

Jefferson: "You're not looking at the big picture. See, nobody's thinking about the long term, because there *is* no long term. If you know you're going to die within the next few years, you've got no reason to make a stable society. If people knew they were going to live…they'd have a reason to grow things, a reason to put stuff back together, maybe even build…I don't know…something *new*."

Again, typical Jefferson. While everybody else is figuring out new ways to cook rat, he's working on restoring civilization.

Don't go thinking that I find this admirable. To me, it's just denial. He's no different from the glue sniffers or the sex junkies or the suicides. Some people just do not want to deal with the world the way it is.

Okay, so maybe it's a little admirable. But still pointless.

Me: "Dude. I was down for a trip to the library and back for dinner. Now you want to save the world?"

Jefferson shrugs. Like, no big deal. Uch.

Brainbox: "Put it this way. What have you got to lose?"

SeeThrough: "Yeah. You're going to die anyway. Why not try to do something useful?"

Me: "Look, Black Widow, I don't want to act ungrateful for what you did back at the library, but just because you kicked a little ass doesn't mean you have a right to tell *me* where to get off."

Peter: "She kicked a *lot* of ass, actually. C'mon, bitch. You got some homework to do or something?"

Me: "Shut your cake-hole. I know why *you're* going. You just want to be famous."

Peter looks pissed off at this, but it's true. He always figured he'd end up a celebrity, back before It Happened. It's surprising the number of kids who thought they'd be famous. Like it was a viable end in itself. Like, they got so used to broadcasting their opinions that they figured they were as important as the people everyone actually *listened* to, and they were only waiting for the world to bow down and kiss their ass. Peter, however, had thought about it more extensively than maybe anybody I knew. And, weirdly, I actually agreed with him. He should have been famous.

Peter drops the scandalized look and laughs. Nobody but me joins him. It's more of a snort than an end-of-the-episode kind of laugh.

End of the episode. I find myself thinking in terms of dead clichés all the time now. All the juice was gone, but we were still sucking on the orange. Things were getting kind of old even before It Happened. Music, clothes, movies. Everything felt like a remake or retro or a mash-up or a callback or a sample. Everything was, like, been-there-done-that. Everything was biting on something else's style. Even when It was Happening, all I could think of was *This is just like* Contagion, and later, *This is just like* Lord of the Flies *meets* The Hunger Games.

This is my way of making an excuse for saying—*I've got a bad feeling about this.* I'm feeling... if we keep going, we won't be coming back.

Me (to Jefferson): "You're going no matter what?"

Jefferson: "No matter what."

Me: "Fine. I'm in."

Inappropriately cheerful applause. Jefferson seems pleased. Not just pleased that I'm going, but pleased that I'm going *with him.*

Screw Wash and his stupid letter.

It's not like I know what the use would be in going back to the Square anyway. If the whole world has caught the Sickness, ain't nobody coming to save our bacon.

But it can't be more dangerous than what Jefferson has in mind.

JEFFERSON

THE WAY I FIGURE IT, the only way out is through.

It's too dangerous to head back to the Square to reequip. The Uptown band may still be south, waiting for us. So we're going to head north, then east over the Triborough Bridge to the island.

But first, we'll reequip at the Bazaar. We're low on supplies. I never saw where the Ghosts put our packs, and we only had a little food anyway. Our night-vision stuff is gone, and I lost my rifle in the fight at the library. Peter's got his Glock, and Donna has her Ruger carbine back. But ammunition is a problem.

In the early days, everybody just emptied their mags at anything that moved, like they were in an action movie. It was a while before we realized that people weren't making any more bullets.

If only we had your average Walmart to pillage, we'd have piles of ammo. No such luck.

Wash wanted to manufacture his own, but he couldn't find the right tools. You need a special press, a caliber, all sorts of stuff.

Some kids got into archery, but to be honest, at about fifty yards, you can dodge an arrow, even from one of the new compound bows. And if you're working in close quarters, they're pretty near useless; try firing an arrow down a New York stairwell. Forget it. That's the reason I carry Dad's *wakizashi* instead of the longer *katana*. It's more useful at close quarters. Watch *The Twilight Samurai* if you want to know what I'm talking about.

So the Bazaar is our first stop. I went there lots, back when it was a train station, but I haven't seen it since it became the Mos Eisley cantina or something.

Once we got things organized in the Square, we didn't really need to trade with anybody from outside. The foraging grounds of lower Broadway were ripe, and Brainbox managed to MacGyver the stuff we didn't have. Besides that, Wash was against going too far uptown. We didn't get much news from abroad, but based on the few accounts from randoms and stragglers that we did get, things were hairy. The word on the Bazaar was that it was the Wild West.

But the word was also that you could get anything—absolutely anything.

I didn't put much stock in that. I have a theory, which I call the Bullshit Radius Theory. That is, that the accuracy of somebody's account of the truth is in inverse proportion to its distance in space and time. So if somebody tells you about something that happened yesterday, it'll be more accurate than if they tell you about something that happened a week ago. And if they tell you about something that happened two miles away, it is bound to be less accurate than if it happened next door.

It's nobody's fault. It's just human nature. People bullshit. They can't help it. They twist memories to serve the story they're telling about themselves, the one in which they're always in the center of the screen, and the world is propagating in a horizon around them, like in a video game. It's hard enough to know what happened inside your head a second ago. Knowing the truth about something after it's been drip-filtered through distance and rumor and fabrication and misunderstanding? No way.

The only constant is change.

Donna would put this attitude down to my Buddhist side. Maybe she thinks...maybe she thinks I can't even believe I'm in love with her, because I believe everything changes. I guess non-attachment is not much of an argument for a relationship.

For instance, the Buddha abandoned his wife and kid. Just took off in the middle of the night without saying good-bye. Treated his family like it was collateral damage. Another thing you'll lose anyway, so why even bother.

I've always kind of worried about his kid. The poor guy was called Rahula, which by some accounts means "fetter" or "hindrance." I wonder if he was one of those damaged celebrity children. *My dad? Yeah, he's the Buddha. Yeah, it's cool, I guess. I never really knew him growing up.*

I asked Dad about it once, and he looked at me like I was completely nuts.

"Well, you're a Buddhist," I said. "So would you just up and leave me and Wash and Mom?"

"Don't be ridiculous."

"But that's because you love us, right? And, I mean, isn't that a problem? I mean, isn't that an *attachment*?"

"Don't be ridiculous."

See, he couldn't even say, *Of course I love you.* That was kind of an issue with Dad. If he had really been pressed, I think he would have said it was silly even to ask, because it should have been obvious that he loved us. But deep down, I think that he wouldn't say it, because it made him weak. It made him *attached*.

Basically, a lot of people just don't have the ability to explain what they believe most deeply. What they hold most dear. And that's kind of a tragedy, isn't it?

But when he passed, I realized what he couldn't explain. See, no matter what, we up and abandon people in the middle of the night. It's called dying.

Still, the Buddha could have made it up to his kid. No matter what your philosophy, that was a Grade-A dick move.

We emerge from the hotel to find ourselves on Forty-Fourth Street, which is where our panic left us last night, I guess. The sun is out, and the smells aren't so bad.

We walk eastward to Fifth, our eyes sniffing for trouble.

I feel strange without my rifle. As if my arms have become very, very short, and I don't know what to do with my hands. As if I've lost my voice. That's the way we talk to one another nowadays. Through gun barrels.

On Fifth, there's a smoked-out Duane Reade, a Staples, a Best Buy. Somebody has marked up the awning:

YOU BEST BUY AT MY SHOP, FOOLS
TODDLY'S IN THE GRAND CONCOURSE

There's a big arrow spray-painted on the ground: DON'T DIE NOW! ONLY TWO BLOCKS MORE!

This makes me antsy. It seems too much like the traps Wile E. Coyote used to set for the Road Runner. I bring us to a halt and then zigzag my way across the street while the others watch me, bemused. When I make it across the street, they zigzag across, too, making fun of me.

Past Fifth along Forty-Fourth, there's a Brooks Brothers on the left and the Cornell Club on the right.

"I guess that's, like, the university?" says SeeThrough.

"Yeah," I say.

"Didn't you want to go to college there?" says Donna.

"My mom did. But it's too cold and depressing."

Everybody starts laughing.

At the next corner, Peter suggests that we approach from Forty-Second "for aesthetic reasons."

"For once, I don't want to enter from the back," he says, and then, pleased with his innuendo—"Boom! There it is."

We take a right and head down Madison. All the while, I'm imagining Cheekbones and his pals waiting for us to get close enough for a head shot. There's plenty of places to mount an ambush. Scaffolding, subway entrances, a low rooftop on Forty-Second...

Donna and SeeThrough, meanwhile, are completely oblivious to the danger, smiling and whispering about something.

Halfway to the vanishing point down the canyon of buildings, you can see the Chrysler Building—my favorite. I was always annoyed when they blew it up in movies. The spire shines like nothing has happened.

And then we encounter a trickle of randoms, like ants heading back to the hill. We automatically clump closer, but they don't take much notice of us. Most of them seem intent on the Bazaar. They're pulling handcarts, pushing shopping carts, hefting stuffed Day-Glo backpacks smutted over with grime. Everyone is armed; a few even have guns. I see Glocks, some shotguns, but most of all the ever-popular AR-15 in its various incarnations.

I miss my gun. How messed up is that?

There's a crustiness, stench, and disorder in appearance that in the old days I would have associated with homeless people. I suppose we are all homeless now, depending on how you interpret the term. The crowd gets thicker as we get closer to the Bazaar. I notice some kids look more dressed up. Some sport looks you might have called "fashionable" back in the day; some are wearing costumes or even uniforms. There's face paint, tattoos, body armor, scarification.

Sitting on the fringes of the last approach to the Bazaar are beggars.

The only time I can remember seeing beggars this young was around Tompkins Square Park before It Happened. Those were young runaways, I think—kids walking on the razor's edge of society.

These ones have already fallen off the edge. We all have. *We're all beggars now*, I think, hefting the hotel pillowcase that's replaced my rucksack. We're all bag men and hoboes and scavengers. There's no society to be on the margins of.

Or is there? Why haven't I seen beggars anyplace before? It's because nothing out there supports them. They starve or they get killed or they kill themselves or, God help us, they even get eaten. The fact that people are begging here, at the edge of the Bazaar, means that they have some hope, however slight, of being helped. It means that there may be some kind of surplus for people to give away. Maybe it means there *is* a society, of sorts. What a thought.

Donna thinks I'm a dreamer or something. But I can't help feeling we could rebuild. We could make something better than we had Before. She's all tied up in the past. Still mourning the crappy world we left behind. She even carries her iPhone with her. Like one day she'll turn it on and somebody will call. *It's Apple here. We have decided to reward your loyalty. You have shown great faith, and all will be restored to you.*

A statue of an eagle perched on a sphere looks down on us from the corner of an ornate colonnaded sandstone building. The eagle has been painted in red, white, and blue, and the sphere has been turned into a globe. Atop the main entrance, there's a big clock with hands of gold, and above that, three gods look down on us impassively. We took a school trip to study them once. There's Hermes, with the winged shoes, for speed; Hercules for strength; and Minerva for commerce. She's holding her hand to her head as if she has a migraine.

The abandoned streets around Grand Central Terminal, now known as the Bazaar, have become a sort of outdoor market. There are more people milling around than I have seen since It Happened. Hundreds, maybe thousands. Smoke rises from a hundred little cook fires and melts against the hulking silhouettes of abandoned office buildings. Under a blue-green wrought-iron overpass, people haggle over scraps laid out on folding tables. Kids are leaning over the upper roadway's edge, sunning themselves and chatting like they're perched on the balcony at a party.

Some shop windows from Before, when the civic building was colonized by commerce, have been miraculously preserved. Inside, the mannequins have been stripped. Each is headless, a fact that has been emphasized by red paint pouring down their chests. Signs over them read:

NO FIGHTING—TAKE IT OUTSIDE
NO PUBLIC DEFECATION—USE THE PLATFORMS
DON'T MESS WITH THE GENERATORS
NO BARTER

Red awnings over the windows read BANANA REPUBLIC.

"I don't get it," I say. "No barter. How are we supposed to buy anything?"

Donna shrugs.

We had counted on trading a gun for some supplies. I wasn't happy about it, but I couldn't see any other way to get what we needed.

You see, after What Happened, money became useless. It only worked if you thought it meant something. Otherwise it was just scraps of green paper. When the government collapsed, nobody believed in money anymore. I suppose you could say nobody bought it. What could you actually *do* with a dollar bill? Wipe your nose, if you didn't mind the dirt.

Money was a good *idea*. A way of keeping track of how much you owed somebody. If you owed somebody some money, they kind of had a rooting interest in your being around to pay them back. So in a way, capitalism was a method for people to keep connected. That kind of glued people together, gave them a better way of getting one another to do things than just using flat-out force.

The problem was that things got out of hand. Some people piled up too much, and other people had too little. Which was a way of saying that some people owed other people more than they could ever, ever pay.

But when the grid went down, and the banks closed, and the ATMs stopped giving out cash, the only numbers that mattered were calories and calibers.

So we started trading stuff we actually needed.

And barter sounds great, at first. But this got complicated, too. How many pairs of boots was a mattress worth? What if the person who had the mattress you wanted already *had* boots, and what she really wanted was toothpaste, but you didn't have any?

At first the answer was IOUs. If you gave me a mattress and I didn't have something you wanted, I would give you a signed IOU—"I owe you for one mattress." It was just a way of remembering that, sometime, you'd have to pay up that debt. But soon people realized they could sign them over—so that somebody would come to me, eventually, with an IOU I'd given, say, to Peter. They'd given something to Peter for the IOU—and now I was expected to pay *them*. Of course, I wouldn't pay them by giving them a mattress. That would be pointless, since the whole thing started when I bought the mattress in the first place. I'd pay them the equivalent of the idea of how much the mattress was worth. Maybe it was a pair of boots. Maybe something else.

This got kind of sticky, because maybe nobody could agree on the value of a mattress. So for a while, people wrote IOUs in credits or even dollars—and we were back to money again. Except the problem was, you could make up whatever amount you wanted when you paid for something. Like, what if you give me an IOU for a thousand credits in exchange for a can of soup? The next guy can outbid you by offering ten thousand credits—but what does that really mean? It's all made up. We were back to square one.

So eventually, the tribe settled on just remembering who needed what. There were few enough people that you could just remind someone that you did them a solid, or you could tell them that you owed them one, or whatever. It made trading with anybody from outside harder, but we didn't want anything to do with the outside.

Plus, after all the dying was done, things weren't that scarce. By things, I mean real *things*. I'd never realized how much people had spent on stuff that you couldn't put your hands on. Phone calls, the Internet, entertainment. *Entertainment*—what a word! Paying to kill time. That was all gone for good. But if you wanted it, there was enough *stuff* to go around. Like, actual things that actually existed in physical space.

For a while, there was even enough food. But that was changing. Like Wash had said, the shit was about to hit the fan.

In the Square, we tried to distribute the things that were in short supply fairly and evenly. We shared the food we scavenged. If you didn't want to do that, if you were only out for yourself, well then, you were welcome to leave.

I guess that made us communists. I don't know. It wasn't like we were trying to take anybody's freedom away or anything. We were just looking out for one another.

So now I'm looking at a bunch of spatchcocked rats grilling over a garbage can, under a sign that reads, URBAN MINI RABBITS—FRESH—CAUGHT THIS MORNING!—FOUR DOLLARS.

Dollars.

The food smells delicious. I haven't eaten anything but a candy bar since yesterday, and my stomach is writhing and twisting. I can see the others are feeling the same way.

"Um, does anybody have any *money*?" I ask. Everybody kind of shrugs, since we haven't used it in over a year. We dig in our pockets. Finally SeeThrough comes up with a crumpled twenty-dollar bill.

"Five rats, please," she says, smiling.

The vendor, a crazed-looking blond kid, looks at the bill. "That's not stamped," he says. Then, when it's obvious that none of us understands, he says, "Oh. You're virgins. Look, go to the ticket booths. I'm busy." Somebody hands him an identical-looking twenty-dollar bill, and he starts to make change.

We head into the terminal.

Past the brass doors, there's a long marble ramp, maybe fifty feet wide. The first thing you notice is the fumes pouring toward you, propelled by their own heat. I hear the rumbling of motors up ahead.

"Diesel," says Brainbox. "It doesn't explode."

The next thing you notice is the crowd—milling back and

forth, strangely relaxed. None of the habitual alertness to danger. Nobody even pays us much mind, like they're used to seeing strangers. It's almost like walking on the streets Before. I dodge the foot traffic, unaccustomed to making space for people, my hand on the hilt of my sword.

The girl is on me before I know it. "Ten dollars for a hand job," she says.

I'm struck dumb. The girl's face is round and sweet. Her eyes are circled in dark blue, her hair is bright pink. She stinks of perfume.

"Or my boyfriend can do it for you," she says. I shake my head, prying her hands off me.

"Or both. Or he isn't my boyfriend. Or he can watch. We can do whatever," she says.

I shake her off, and we keep going. I actually say, "No, thank you," like I was being offered a doughnut or something. Judging by their looks, the others are as stunned as I am. I guess we forgot that money could buy *that*, too. Sometimes money was like a big invisible clawed hand gripping the back of your neck, forcing you to do things you didn't want to. Sometimes you got control of the invisible hand and made people do things they didn't want to.

Now I see this kind of deal being arranged all along the ramp. Girls and boys, rubbing up against customers, taking cash.

We keep descending.

At the bottom of the ramp is a wide marble-walled room with soaring ceilings. Big chandeliers hang down, and the exposed bulbs are *actually working*. There are about ten big diesel generators, each around the size of a car, chugging away on either side—"Twenty-five K's," Brainbox says, meaning each one puts out twenty-five thousand watts. Each one is more powerful than anything we have back in the Square. And each one has an armed guard. In camouflage and uniformly shaven-headed, they're the closest thing to authority that I've seen in a long while. The camo reminds me unpleasantly of the Uptowners.

We enter the Grand Concourse. And it's almost like stepping outside again. That's partly because the vast ceiling, a hundred feet high, is painted blue like a late afternoon sky, complete with constellations marked out in gold. Partly because the inside is bigger than a football field. Hanging at one end, there's a gigantic American flag, strangely intact except for a few bullet holes.

Dad used to take me and Wash to Mets games, and we'd change here from the Lexington Avenue six line to the Queens-bound seven line, or from green to purple, the way we saw it. He would always make us get out at Grand Central in the middle of the trip, even though it meant spending twice as much. He'd walk us around the Grand Concourse, and we'd pretend not to gawk at the crowd. We were city kids, and we didn't want to seem like tourists. And we'd synchronize our watches to the big clock on top of the information booth in the center of the hall. The faces were made of opal, Dad said. He'd buy us the "funny papers," which is what he called comic books, at Hudson News. If we had time, he'd take us downstairs into the vaulted belly of the station for lunch at the Oyster Bar. Wash and I would whisper to each other in the corners of the parabolic arch in front of the restaurant and be amazed to hear each other every time. Dad would eat Kumamoto oysters under the vaulted brick ceilings, and we'd crunch on the salt crackers, saving space for hot dogs at the ballpark.

"Isn't this something else?" Dad would say, before getting back onto the subway. And he'd go a little misty-eyed. Which was weird, because he didn't do that much, not even when we sang the national anthem before the game.

Where there used to be waves of commuters heading for the trains and clumps of tourists gazing openmouthed at the ceiling, it's now nothing but feral teenagers of every description. Ragged, costumed, dreadlocked, wigged, made-up, armed, unarmed, talking, gesturing, clamoring, singing, dancing, buying, selling. It sounds like a thousand YouTube videos open on your laptop, all playing at once. You can feel it on your skin.

What looks at first like chaos resolves itself once you notice that hundreds of marquees, tables, and cubicles, everything from reproduction Moroccan tents to salvaged trade-show booths, are arranged in a rough horseshoe shape around the central clock. There's a sort of esplanade in the middle, and the shops are stacked several rows deep. Signs advertise all kinds of goods. Ammunition, medicine, tools, water, canned food, clothes, fuel, cosmetics, jewelry, maps. Everything swirls around this hub, but there are substorms of activity going on. Animated conversations, kids making out, kids getting high, kids eating. Up one of the grand stairways to the side of the hall, there's a bunch of kids in drag. Above that, on a platform overlooking it all, a band, an actual live band, is playing. Opposite that platform, on the other side of the hall, there's the old Apple Store, airy and bright, like Space Church or something. The logo is still there, only it's graffitied to say WELCOME TO THE BIG (APPLE). EAT IT.

"You're new, aren't you?"

The voice belongs to a short, smelly kid dressed in black. He's got a scraggly beard, and beneath that, a pair of goggles hanging around his neck and a black dust mask with a skull and crossbones design on it.

"What? No," I say.

"Really? Because you look like you have no idea what's going on," says the guy.

"Who asked you?" I say.

The guy shrugs. "Just offering to help is all."

"You know what?" says Donna. "We *don't* have any idea what's going on." She smiles at the guy like she's known him all her life. "I'm Donna. What's your name?"

"People call me Ratso," he says. He shrugs again. "It's from a movie."

"What's your real name?" asks SeeThrough.

"My name...is for my friends," he says in a fake British accent. Then, "Never seen that? No? Whatever." The guy's behavior is off-putting.

"What do you want?" says Peter.

"Like I said," says Ratso, "I just want to help."

"Why?" I say.

"Why not?" says Ratso.

"You want to help?" I say. "Can you tell us why our money doesn't work here?"

"Lemme see," he says. SeeThrough shows him the twenty. He snatches it out of her hands and, before any of us can take it back, has inspected both sides and returned it. "Thanks, pretty lady. It's not stamped. Ain't worth shit."

I'm kind of embarrassed, because we're living up to Ratso's first impression. But it's too late to pretend we know what we're doing.

"Okay, so where do we get our money stamped or whatever?"

"You don't," says Ratso. "Here, give me that again, will you?" SeeThrough hands him back the bill, and he unceremoniously tears it in half. "Worthless, see?"

I grab him by the lapels of his black coat. "Easy! Easy!" says Ratso.

Yesterday you could have burned a pile of hundred-dollar bills in front of us and we wouldn't have minded. Now that things suddenly have a price, we care, a lot.

"I can get you money," says Ratso, and I let go of him. "Have you got any stuff? Any stuff to trade?"

"I saw a sign that said no barter," I say.

"It's not barter. I'll show you. Let's go to the bank."

Ratso straightens his lapels and heads off to the ticket booths. We look around at one another like a bunch of morons, then follow him.

DONNA

SO, THIS BAZAAR place is a big family-size bucket of crazy with extra cray sauce.

I can tell right off the bat that Jefferson is loving it. Like, *Here, in the center of our great metropolis, we can rebuild! A new society rises like a phoenix from the ashes of the old!*

Which is a lot to say for a flea market in an abandoned train station.

I've got to admit that it looks like there's *fun* to be had, which is not to be sniffed at in these crappy times. Peter's eyes are zapping out on stalks like in a cartoon. Okay, some of the clothes people are wearing are cute. There's even, like, these girls? These model-y girls walking around in full-on evening wear like they're on the red carpet. Each of them has a boyfriend or a bodyguard or whatever trailing around with them. Weird. There's also these douchey guys—they're all guys—in camouflage gear with shaved heads stalking around, glowering like cops.

There's a bunch of them by the ticket booths that line one wall under a dead electric billboard labeled NEW HAVEN LINE DEPARTURES. That kid Ratso takes us to a window with no line in front of it. A grille of tarnished brass separates us from the teller, a plump boy with a jeweler's loupe tilted back on his forehead.

I'm wondering how on earth he managed to stay overweight post-apocalypse and daydreaming about eating when his voice wakes me.

Plumpy: "What've you got?"

Ratso: "What've you got? To sell, he means." (Then, to the teller.) "Take it easy on him; he's new."

I kind of like Ratso; at least, I'm willing to give him the benefit of the doubt. But I can tell he makes Jefferson uptight. I mean, it doesn't take much.

Jefferson: "Somebody give me their gun."

And I'm like, *Uh, sorry you lost your gun, pal. I'm hanging on to mine. Nobody else wants to give up their gat, either.*

Me: "Why don't you sell him your samurai sword?"

Jefferson: "Please don't call it that. It's a *wakizashi*, and it's been in my family for centuries."

Me: "Well, my gun is a *carbine*, and it's been in my family for more than a year."

Jefferson: "Why don't you sell that teddy bear you stole from the library?"

Me: "Are you *high*? This is a *relic*. Pooh stays with me."

Plumpy: "Look, you don't have anything to sell, move on."

Jefferson (remembering something): "Oh!"

He takes a pharmacy bottle out of his pocket and shakes it.

Plumpy: "What is it?"

Jefferson: (Steps to the window, opens up the bottle, and drops an orange pill onto the counter.) "It's—"

Plumpy (smiling): "Adderall. Haven't seen that in a while."

He leans back and calls to someone in the back of the booth. A wiry-looking kid in a beret pokes his body around the window, lights up when he sees the tablet, reaches his hand out, and snatches it before anybody can react.

Jefferson: "Hey!"

Wiry Guy: "Gotta test it."

He uses the butt of a revolver like a hammer to smash the pill into powder, then leans his head down to the counter and snorts it. He looks up. Smiles. Nods to the plump kid.

Plumpy: "Ten bucks a pill. Take it or leave it."

Jefferson: "Okay, that's two hundred dollars for twenty tablets, including the one you just hoovered."

Wiry Guy: (Shakes his head.) "Bank fee."

So we hand over the Adderall for a hundred and ninety bucks.

There's an ornate stamp in the space over the face of the president. The two towers of the World Trade Center with NEVER FORGET in, like, medieval script.

Jefferson: "Oh."

Ratso: "Only bills with the stamp are valid. All other bills get seized."

Jefferson: "Seized by who?"

Ratso nods toward the thugs with the camouflage.

Brainbox: "If everything has to be stamped, then presumably there's no coinage."

Ratso: "Correctamundo."

Jefferson: "Why don't people just fake the stamp and issue their own money? All you would need is some ink and a bunch of bills you can get anyplace."

Ratso: "Oh, I wouldn't do that."

Me: "Why not?"

Ratso: (Makes a face.) "Trust me, you don't wanna know."

Brainbox (to Jefferson): "Fiat currency."

Jefferson: "Backed up by a state monopoly on violence. Amazing."

Me: "If you guys are quite done with AP Economics, can we get cracking?"

Jefferson: "Well, you want to go shopping?"

Uh, yes?

We scan the tables and booths around the big clock. Not buying anything yet, just sizing up what's available and how much for. We don't meet the eyes of people hawking their wares. We must look like a bunch of tourists on a budget.

Jefferson eyes some boxes of ammo at a stand called Aw, Shoot. He's moving on to one of the competitors, International House of Killing People, when he stops in his tracks, alert.

I think it must be the Uptowners.

I slip a finger over the trigger guard of the carbine.

But it's not trouble. It's coffee.

Jefferson is staring at a shiny chrome espresso machine with a grinder sitting next to it. There's a dude with a red Mohawk standing behind the folding picnic table that supports it, nodding and smiling at Jeff, like, *Hell, yeah, this is what it looks like.*

Mohawk Guy: "Just about to open a new can."

Jefferson: "No way."

Yes way. The guy opens a silvery tin of coffee beans, and it lets out a hiss of air that was trapped before It Happened. He holds it up for Jefferson to sniff. Jeff sucks in every last molecule of coffee smell.

Mohawk Guy: "Espresso or cappuccino?"

"*Milk?*" says Jefferson. We all gather around to look as the guy opens a cooler that has ice—*real ice*—in it. A bunch of little plastic cartons are neatly arranged inside.

Me (astonished): "How did you get the ice?"

Mohawk Guy: "They make it at Camp Arctica, downstairs. Got some machines. The milk is my secret."

Jefferson, who has been squeezing our roll of cash tightly in his fists, looks back at us with begging kitten eyes.

Me: "Go for it. Live a little."

Jefferson: "How much for a double cappuccino?"

Mohawk Guy: "All I *make* is doubles. Two bucks."

Jefferson looks back again. We nod. Jefferson hands over a ten and gets back eight dollar bills, each with the red stamp.

The guy, who tells us his name is Q, pours the beans into the grinder. "A Mazzer," he tells us proudly, which seems to mean something to Jefferson. Then he goes through the ritual of preparation—

grind, charge, tamp. Finally he loads the little handle thing into the machine.

Jefferson: "Can I—can I do it?"

Q pauses, then says, "Why not?" Jefferson reaches out and reverentially presses down the arm that starts the water flowing. We watch as the thick black liquid drips into a chipped ceramic cup.

Jefferson (to himself): "Civilization."

Q: "You guys must be—"

Me: "New in town, yeah. We get that a lot. So how does it work? You pay off the goons so you can operate?"

Q: "I pay the *bank*. They control the real estate. The 'goons,' as you call our fine constabulary, are in their employ."

Me: "And you—you must have to buy everything you need here, right? You can't eat dollar bills."

Q: "Well, you'll find that a lot of people in the area accept bank dollars because they know they work here. But I don't have much reason to wander. I live up in the old MetLife Building."

Me (to Jefferson): "You believe this?"

But he holds up his hand to silence me. His eyes are closed as he savors the coffee.

Peter: "So what's the catch?"

Ratso: "The catch is that you can only buy things with bank dollars, and the bank buys wholesale and sells retail. And the bank controls the electricity business."

With my eyes I follow the cord leading from the espresso machine. It joins up with a standard surge protector, which plugs into some kind of rectangular thing that Brainbox knows the name of, which has a thicker cord stretching toward a hexagonal box by the entrance to the hall, and an even thicker cable snakes around the entryway toward, no doubt, one of the big generators with the armed guards.

Q (annoyed): "This guy with you?"

Me: "Kinda."

Q: "Take my advice. Stay away from Mole People."

Ratso (with an innocent look): "No such thing as Mole People."

Jefferson takes a deep breath and puts down his cup, which has nothing but a fleck of foam and a smear of coffee round the edges. "Thank you," he says to Q. "Thank you all," he says to the rest of us, smiling.

Q reaches for the cup, but Ratso snaps it up first. He quickly licks the inside of the cup clean.

Ratso: "Waste not, want not."

Q: "Watch him." He snatches the cup back and sprays it with soapy water from a plastic bottle.

Ratso shrugs and moves on, and we follow.

You heard about Mole People even before the Pocky. The rumor was that there were homeless people who lived in the subway tunnels. I always found this pretty easy to believe, because anything horrible was possible in New York, and generally people didn't do anything about it. Don't get me wrong—there was amazing stuff, too. But just to get on with life, you had to ignore all kinds of stuff that would make you hurl if you thought about it. For instance, I once saw this guy fall off a skateboard, and everybody rushed up to help him, and they called an ambulance and everything. But if you saw some guy just lying on the ground, and he looked, you know, *poor*? Well, people would just walk on by. Like there was some rule that everybody knew: *Only render aid to people like you.*

So, yeah, people living their whole lives underground? Why not?

Didn't make much sense *now*, though. It wasn't like rents were high or anything. I figured the Mole People were a Pocky myth. You always heard about some guy who knew a guy who never came back after he went on a scout in the subway.

But I never saw signs of them. No two pinpoints of light flashing from the deep or anything.

Ratso: "You guys want food and ammo, right? This way. I know a guy's got MREs, Tasty Bites, whatever you need."

Me: "Hey, Ratso?"

Ratso: "What is it, pretty lady?"

Me: "Why did that guy say you were a Mole Person?"

Ratso: "Like I said, there's no such thing as Mole People. Everybody knows that. He just doesn't like fixers. So he calls me names."

Jefferson: "Fixers."

Ratso: "I help people. I fix situations. I'm a matchmaker. I introduce supply to demand."

Jefferson: "You're a middleman."

Ratso: "That's a very pedestrian way to put it, but sure." He stops in the flow of people, like he really wants us to understand.

"Now, your average doofus, he doesn't understand that I lubricate the wheels of commerce."

Peter: "You're grease."

Ratso: "Yes. Johnny Starbucks over there, he doesn't understand the world. He thinks your ground-level economy is frictionless. What he doesn't know is that it takes people like me, working hard to help people like you. Like the way I got you a good price for those pills."

Jefferson: "You did?"

Ratso: "'Course I did. See, you don't know that the bank usually buys Adderall at eight bucks a pop. But when I'm around, they know they can't get away with it."

Jefferson: (Doesn't look convinced.) "Yeah, thanks."

Me: "Thanks."

Ratso: "My pleasure, Donna."

Jefferson: "So where do *you* fit in? What do you charge for all the lubrication?"

Ratso: "Who, me?" He looks like he hasn't given any thought to it. "I do it because I'm a people person. I love humanity. I never *charge* for my services."

Nobody seems to buy this, so Ratso adds, "Of course, any consideration you might offer, I would see it as a generous donation toward other travelers in need whom I may be able to help in the future."

Jefferson: "Got it." He frowns, and I can see he's thinking about telling the guy to shove off. He looks at me. I make an "oh, come on" face, batting my eyelashes. He sighs.

Jefferson: "Fine. We're looking for a week's food for five people. A bunch of equipment. Maybe a gun for me, if we can afford it. And ammo."

Ratso: "How much ammo?"

Jefferson: "Too much."

Ratso: "I like the way you think. Going on a trip?"

Jefferson: "None of your business. Just help us find what we need."

But we don't have nearly enough money for all the food we need, let alone guns and ammo. Ratso haggles for all he's worth, and he beats the prices down a lot, but we're still looking at a good thousand dollars.

Ratso looks sad—guilty, even. Like he's let us down. Then—and you can practically make out the lightbulb above his head—"I've got an idea."

Jefferson: "We're open."

Ratso: (Turns to the girl who sells MREs.) "You'll stay at that price for a couple of hours?"

Salesgirl: "Things change."

Ratso: "An hour? Pretty please?" He holds out his hand to shake.

The food seller nods. Shakes his hand. Ratso is off like a shot.

I see her wipe her hand on a cloth as we turn and follow him.

Ratso leads us out of the crowded stalls to a corner of the hall, then past an old subway entrance that's gone dark and down some big ramps.

A floor below the Concourse, there's a whole other level. It's all flat arches and dark brick, really claustro to the phobia. There's no sunlight at all, and it's lit up by a hodgepodge of work lights, desk lamps with the shades gone, old halogen torch lamps, hanging bulbs, crash-landed upside-down chandeliers. The light and the shadows are coming from every direction, so everybody looks like they're in a club in some kind of crappy rap video. There are even some strobe lights flickering away.

What makes it seem more like a club are all the bars and restaurants—if you can call them that—lining the walls.

It seems like there's a bunch of different businesses or whatever, because the theme changes every thirty feet or so. Like, there's a hookah bar, there's a place called the Ashram Galactica that is done up all fancily, there's a place that's all pink, there's a pub-themed place called the End of the World, complete with a hand-painted sign. There's even, judging by all the boys, a gay bar, the Regrette Rien, whatever that means. Peter really wants to stop for a drink, but Jefferson won't let him. They have some kind of movie-quote exchange.

Peter: "I'm starting my approach."

Jefferson: "Stay on target."

Peter: "They came from behind."

Me: "What the hell are you guys talking about?"

Peter: "Oh, never you mind, missy."

Then I hear a roar from deeper in the crowd. Above a bunch of shouts, I hear a whine that doesn't sound human.

Me: "What's that?"

Ratso: "That's my idea." He wades into a sea of backs, toward something glaring in the background.

Whatever is back there, I don't like the sound of it. People are screaming their voices ragged; I hear thumps and whines and angry music.

Me: "I've got a bad feeling about this."

Jefferson: "There you go." He dives into the crowd, following Ratso.

JEFFERSON

I **FOLLOW RATSO** into the crowd. There's a treacly mash of sound in the air, a soup of chatter and shouting and grunting that the curves of the Guastavino brickwork turn into tides and eddies.

Everyone's face is turned toward something lit up in the diesel haze at the center of the scrum of bodies. As I get closer, I can see a big, round podium with a bunch of powerful lamps cranked toward it.

I see a flurry of motion and then there's a *THUMP*, and my view is blocked. I push forward to get a clearer view.

There's a slender kid on the platform in a hockey mask and a cobbled-together outfit of leather and football pads. The white plastic is smeared with blood, the padding torn. He's leaning over, catching his breath, while he eyes his opponent.

It's a German shepherd, its maw rimmed with blood, drooling with exhaustion. Around it, in various attitudes of death, lies an assortment of other dogs. Many of them still have tattered old collars on, like the shepherd does.

"Five minutes!" announces someone at the side of the ring— a kid in a frayed prom tuxedo. Some in the crowd cheer, and others groan in exasperation.

"That's the over-under," says Ratso, smiling. Somebody just lost some money.

The kid in the hockey mask straightens and raises a sticky wooden baseball bat. He stares at the dog.

A girl next to me shouts, "Finish it! We haven't got all day!" And the crowd starts to chant, "Kill it! Kill it!"

The dog hesitates, cowering in the corner. It looks just like anybody's pet, eyebrows twitching in a mute question.

Then it seems to turn into a wolf. The curtain of its lips draws back, revealing black gums and yellow teeth, and it makes an angry lunge for the kid with the bat.

It moves fast, but the kid is ready and brings the bat down on the shepherd's back, knocking it to the ground. Then, as the crowd counts, he flails at the dog over and over, until it stops moving.

Finally the kid pulls the mask off, and I realize that it's a girl, about sixteen or so, freckle-faced, flushed with relief and triumph.

"Jesus," I say.

"Don't bring him into this," says Peter, at my elbow.

The crowd starts to disperse, money flashing between hands as bets are resolved. Some ring attendants in plastic aprons slosh water across the flooring and scrub it with rags, then spread sand over it.

"We got ten minutes before the next event," says Ratso.

"I'm not betting on anybody killing dogs," says Peter.

"Oh, the next one isn't a baiting match," Ratso says brightly. "It's man on man."

"Ow!" I'm gripping Ratso's shoulder so hard it even hurts my hand. "What's the matter?" We're over by what used to be some sort of food counter back in the day.

"We're not betting on *people* killing each other."

"Take it easy! Nobody's killing anybody." Ratso flexes his shoulder while he explains. "It's to a knockout or a submission. Geez, do you think the whole world's gone psycho?"

"I could show you a few things," I say.

"Well, they might go full-on gladiator someplace else, but here it's strictly Marquis of Queensberry. Sort of."

"So it's, like, MMA or something?" asks SeeThrough. She's got a predatory gleam in her eye. "How much can we make?"

Ratso looks at a dry-erase board nearby. "It depends on the odds."

"Can you get me in?" asks SeeThrough.

"In what?"

"In a fight. How much does *that* pay?"

"Depends. The fighters take a piece of the action. A lot more than just betting."

"Find out," says SeeThrough. "I want to fight."

"You?" says Ratso. "Listen, no offense, but—"

"Just do it," I say. Ratso hurries off.

"What are you doing?" Donna asks SeeThrough.

"I'm trying to get us some money."

"You're trying to get yourself killed," says Donna.

"I'll be fine."

"You'll be fine because you're not gonna fight," Donna says. "This is sick."

"It's okay. You heard Ratso. Marcus Queens whatever. We need money, right? Do you have a better idea?"

Ratso comes back. "I can get us a tag-team slot."

"Excuse me?" I say.

"You know, like in wrestling. Two guys per team. When one of them is tired, he can tap out, and the other guy comes in. First team that taps out loses. The winners get ten percent of the take," says Ratso. "Five hundred bucks guaranteed. Plus you can bet on yourself. Best thing is, the odds are against you."

Makes sense. SeeThrough looks tiny and hapless, still singed from her escape in front of the library.

"I'll go with you," says Peter.

"Forget it," I say. "You're missing half an ear. I'll go." I turn to Ratso. "Sign us up."

Ten minutes later, I'm trying to ignore the beating some kid is taking in the one-on-one match. My heart is going double time, and my shoulders are bunching up with stress.

"Have you ever done this?" asks Peter. "Fought somebody hand to hand? Like you meant it?"

"Uhh...not without a sword."

"All right. You're gonna be fine." SeeThrough looks me in the eye, her face serious. I think for a second about how odd it is that this little girl is coaching me. But only for a second. I remember how she took me down at the start of this trip.

"I'll try to win it quick," she says. "That way you don't even have to go in."

"Uh-huh."

"Take your shirt off," says Peter. "You don't want somebody pulling it over your head, like that dude."

In the ring, one kid has pulled the other kid's shirt over his head, tying up his arms. Unable to see or move his hands, he's getting pummeled.

"Jeff, you don't have to do this," Donna says.

"Please don't give me a way out," I say. "I might take it."

Ratso hands me a plastic jar of Vaseline. I don't know what to make of it.

"Put it on your cheekbones and your chin," says SeeThrough. "It'll keep the gloves from cutting you."

I do as she says. And I try to calm down. It's one thing killing somebody in anger, when your back is against the wall. It's another thing entirely to agree to batter a guy into submission with your fists. I've sparred before. Wash wanted to show me how to "take care of myself." But I always knew he would stop if things got out of hand. He'd pull his punches; he'd keep it friendly.

Wash would do this in a heartbeat. And he'd win, too.

Wash is dead.

I take my shirt off. Weirdly, in all of this, I still have time to worry about whether Donna thinks I look good. I spread Vaseline on my cheekbones and my eyebrows and my chin, copying SeeThrough.

Ratso brings over some gloves. They've got a little padding around the knuckles, but the fingertips are open. SeeThrough tries on both pairs, but they're too big for her. She hands me a pair. "Wear these. Otherwise, you might break your fingers." I nod.

"Don't let them get your legs," she continues. "If they know jujitsu, they'll want to get you down on the ground. So, like, punch them and kick them and stay standing."

"Stay standing. Good idea," I say.

I'm hoping that the one-on-one fight will last a little longer, so that I can still my mind a little, but they're down on the floor now, the stronger kid punching the weaker kid in the face over and over again until he stops defending himself. The crowd cheers as the referee stops the fight. Again, a flurry of money. They drag the loser off as the winner does a whole post-fight celebration thing that looks like he's reenacting something he saw on TV. He waves to nonexistent cameras, kisses his fist, and points a finger up at the sky. But all there is up there is brick ceiling.

He's still high-fiving his buddies when the referee makes his way over to us.

"Where you from?" he says.

"Washington Square Park," I say, without thinking.

The ref nods and heads back to the ring.

SeeThrough grabs me by the shoulder. "If you go in, keep your hands up and your head down. You ready?" she asks.

I nod. "You?"

"You know me," she says.

"C'mon," says Ratso, taking us by the elbows and leading us to the edge of the ring. SeeThrough and I follow Ratso in, slipping through the chains that serve for ropes. Ratso says, "I'm gonna go place the bet. Give me the money." It crosses my mind that he might just take off with our bankroll, but I put it into his hands anyway.

"The odds could still get adjusted," says Ratso. "Try not to look too confident."

"Okay," I say, thinking that should be pretty easy.

Our opponents slip into the ring. There's a wiry red-haired guy, about sixteen, and a kid with a shaved head and a long scar running along his jawline. They look at SeeThrough like she must be joking.

If she's as scared as I am, she's not showing it. She's mad-dogging them, staring back at their smiles.

The referee raises a bullhorn to his mouth.

"Ladies and gentlemen!" he barks. "Children of all ages! Grand Central Entertainment is proud to present an elimination tag-team matchup between the Clinton Claws and the Washington Square Wizards!" The crowd cheers.

SeeThrough looks at me. *Wizards?* I shrug. The "Clinton Claws" are working the crowd, holding their arms up like gladiators. I look at the menagerie of hostile faces and raise my hand and wave. It comes off a little toddler-like.

The referee continues. "There will be no stoppages, except for tagging in. Restart at neutral corners."

The ref gestures for us to come to the center of the ring. SeeThrough slaps me on the back, and we approach the Claws. One of them is zoning out, listening to an old iPod nano. I can hear metal leaking out of his head. The other is looking laser beams through my eyes into the back of my skull. I shoot them a wink and smile.

The ref, a floppy clip-on bow tie hanging from one side of his collar, leans in and gives us our instructions.

"All right, I want a fair fight, but not *too* fair. Everything's cool except for eye gouging. That, I don't want to clean up. Any questions?"

"Yeah. What kind of pussy name is Wizards?" asks the red-haired kid.

"You'll see," I say.

SeeThrough and I return to our corner, where Ratso has reappeared.

"Nice comeback," says SeeThrough. She holds out her hand, and I slap it.

"Kick some ass," I say. "Please." I step out.

"So far so good," says Donna as I join them around the ring post.

SeeThrough shakes her head back and forth to loosen her neck as the red-haired guy gets out of the ring. The bald kid takes his headphones out and howls, flexing. His ropy muscles stand out under thin skin, and I can see all the cords straining in his neck.

A bell rings. Cueball runs like a rocket for SeeThrough. She shifts sideways and flips her foot out and down. It looks as light as a dance move, but it catches him right on the knee. Suddenly, Cueball's kneecap is sickeningly out of place, sliding around the left side of the leg while the skin sucks into the new arrangement of bones, and underneath, like a shrink-wrapped joint of meat, you can make out the knobs of the tibia and the femur kissing.

A big "Ohhhhhhhhh!!!" from the crowd—appreciative, joyous. Cueball is in agony, curled around his knee, teeth bared.

SeeThrough doesn't hesitate. She steps up to him and stamps on his knee, then his face. With every kick, the crowd roars.

Blood pouring from his nose, Cueball finally grabs SeeThrough's leg. The desperate grab stops her for a moment, and he uses his weight to bring her down to the canvas.

He pays for every moment, as she elbows him in the face again and again, but finally he's able to make a stab for his partner's hand.

The referee jumps in and ushers SeeThrough back as the red-haired kid enters the ring.

He's seen what happened to his buddy, so he's cautious, even though SeeThrough is sucking air now, exhausted.

"Let me go in," I say. SeeThrough shakes her head. She steps into the middle of the ring.

Red circles around, flicking little jabs at her face, which she tries to catch. Finally she grabs a left hand that Red leaves out too long. She turns the wrist, putting all her weight into it, but Red swings around and manages to fall on her, bringing her down to the floor, and SeeThrough loses her grip.

Then he slowly forces her arm back, hyperextending the elbow. SeeThrough has lost the advantage of her speed and her skill—now it's a contest of strength that she can't win.

When the arm goes straight, SeeThrough casts a look over to me. I reach through the chains for the tag. If she reaches over to me with her free arm, she'll lose the only leverage she has.

The wolves, riding the change of momentum, are howling for blood; they chant Red's name and tell him to break SeeThrough's arm off. Reddy keeps heaving on SeeThrough's arm.

She growls and reaches out, slapping my hand just as something audibly pops in the arm Reddy is holding. The referee dives in to untangle their limbs. SeeThrough curls her body over her limp arm, and I get into the ring as Reddy, a smile smeared over his face, backs up to wait for me.

As Ratso jumps in and helps SeeThrough out of the ring, I try to block out the shouting of my blood. My arms are hot with adrenaline; they feel heavy. My breath is running out of me as fast as I can take it in.

Red creeps toward me. I'm expecting him to rush for my legs, but he doesn't. Maybe he thinks I know more than I do.

I try to cast my mind back to those sparring sessions with Wash, and my kung fu lessons with Sifu, SeeThrough's father. Keep your hands up. Fight at your distance.

I can't let him close with me. So when he starts toward me, I go into the motion of a roundhouse kick.

Red takes the bait and lowers his hands to stop the kick, but it continues, then hooks around, and I catch him on the face with the sole of my foot—a perfect hook kick.

He's dazed for a second, and I think of rushing him, but I don't want to get tangled up. Reddy sets himself again, and when I leave my next kick out there too long, he grabs it, rushes ahead, and drives me back into the chains.

As the chains go taut, they rattle like snakes. Out of breath, I reach my arms under Red's, keeping him from reaching down for my legs. This feels, and probably looks, weirdly like a hug, and I'm suddenly staring into Reddy's freckled face and blue eyes.

He head-butts me, and I turn my face just in time to avoid getting my nose broken, with the result that he hits me on my left eyebrow. I feel the skin split open, and blood starts to trickle down into my eyes.

I push him off, and he stands back and watches as I start to go blind.

DONNA

THE KID'S GOT HEART; you've got to hand it to him. Jefferson looks like some kind of really elaborate Halloween costume, say "sweaty boxer zombie." Blood's running down his face and into his left eye, and he keeps on smearing it across his cheek as he tries to clear his vision.

Problem with your cuts from blunt trauma, like punches, is that they go down to the bone. Now, if I had some Avitene flour or some thrombin, I could do something about it. As it is, I'm trying to figure out what the hell's wrong with SeeThrough's arm. The bicep is spasming, which means she can't get the arm straight again. So I won't be able to tell for a while.

Meanwhile, Jeff is getting his ass whipped. The redheaded kid realizes that he can't see much, so he's in no particular hurry. He's playing to the crowd, smacking Jeff around with sharp jabs and kicks.

Maybe this is the part where I'm supposed to go all gooey and boo-hoo. But what I'm figuring is, *For Christ's sake, Jeff, take a dive and let's go home. Let's just go home and die in peace.*

"I'm going back in," says SeeThrough.

"Like hell you are," I say. "Peter, will you keep this idiot from reinjuring herself?"

"Okay," says Peter. I jump up to the edge of the ring where Ratso has positioned himself. Meanwhile, Jeff takes a kick to the stomach.

"Ratso, throw in the towel," I say.

"What towel?" says Ratso.

"Let's end this before Jeff gets really hurt." Red nails him with a jab-straight-hook combination, then steps back as the crowd urges him on.

"I can't," says Ratso. "Only your boy can call it. That, or get knocked out." Jeff barrels toward Reddy and has his left hook blocked.

"Jeff!" I shout. "Jefferson!"

They've circled around, and he can see me. He shoots a glance over.

"It's okay, Jeff. You can stop! Stop this! Just quit! Just—"

And in that little bitty snippet of a moment, before Jeff turns back to face the guy who's beating him into a pulp, I see a look of such deep hurt and disappointment that my heart actually skips a beat. I stop in midsentence as his eye asks me, *How could you say that?*

He lowers his head. He looks beaten.

Then he looks angry.

Red is enjoying himself, clowning around for the animals. He goes into an exaggerated windup, and Jefferson rushes at him, cocks his arm back across his body, and elbows him in the face.

Like that, Red is on the ground. He's conscious, but the fight is gone out of him. A couple of teeth on the canvas. Blood and spit pouring from his mouth. He flops onto his front and starts crawling for his partner, Baldy, who reaches his hand out for a tag.

The crowd is silent.

Before Red can get anywhere, Jeff grabs him by an ankle and pulls him into the center of the ring.

Red tries to cover himself as Jefferson, sitting on Red's back, hammers his head again and again, leaning over and tucking his fists to reach his face.

After a few blows, Red stops moving. He doesn't even have the strength to tap out.

Jefferson keeps going at him.

The crowd loves it.

The referee rushes in and grabs hold of Jeff. Peter jumps in, and I follow. We hold him back as he lunges toward the kid on the floor.

"Stop it!" I say to Jefferson. He's crying now, spitting blood.

"Jeff, stop. Stop it, honey. You won. Stop it. We won." I hold his head, and he quiets down, bends over, and starts sucking air.

As Red gets pulled from the ring, we help Jeff down. People reach out to touch him. *Yeah, bro. Good fight. Way to go.*

Ratso goes to collect our money, and the crowd starts talking about the next fight.

Turns out Baldy and Red were certified badasses, and we weren't supposed to stand a chance, so the odds were hella long. SeeThrough and Jefferson's appearance on WWE Raw got us two thousand bucks. Our money back, times ten.

That's a whole heap of cash, so we're able to load up on tasty vittles and bullets a-go-go. The shopkeepers of the horseshoe bazaar treat us like long-lost cousins. And nobody says boo to Ratso, the chaperone of all this newfound cheddar.

By some unspoken agreement, each of us is morally allowed to get one silly piece of crap just for the hell of it. Which is great, because there's actually a whole row of stalls devoted to things that don't do anything worthwhile. That's the new high-ticket item: uselessness. There's fancy earphones that people wear hanging from their ears like jewelry. Ironic T-shirts. Makeup. Toys. Gold rings, dead watches. Video game controllers.

I get myself an I HOPE I DON'T BLACK OUT, 'CAUSE THIS IS AWESOME! shirt. Peter buys one that says, I TAUGHT CHRISTIAN GREY ALL THAT SHIT. SeeThrough gets a cute little notepad of stationery with WE ARE HAVING A TERRIFIC PICNIC TIME! on it and a fancy gold ribbon for a sling.

Brainbox, meanwhile, checks out a pile of LEGOs. He picks up a shiny, nubby piece and gives it the good old Brainbox once-over, which involves holding something really close to your face and staring at it like there's a secret message written somewhere in tiny script.

"Find something you like, BB?" I ask.

Brainbox looks at me but doesn't say anything. He turns to the shopkeeper and asks, "Why is it so expensive?"

Shopkeeper: "Google it. Couple of weeks ago some kid passes through and says he'll buy all the LEGO he can. He paid some serious bank. I'm saving this for him. If you want to get it, you'll have to beat his price."

I look at the rest of her stuff, a jumble of crappy plastic toys and supereducational wooden things made in, like, Vermont or something, aka the Kind of Toys That No Kid Wants to Play With.

Brainbox pays way too much for ten little bricks of LEGO.

Me: "What's that for?"

Brainbox: "I don't know yet."

When the shopping spree is done, we still have a few hundred bucks left, and Ratso suggests we celebrate.

Peter: "I could use a drink."

Jefferson nods. I would have expected him to be pretty cocky after he put a beat-down on that guy; I mean, most dudes are all boasty after a fight, forcing everybody to talk about it and everything. Jeff just seems sad and a little irritable, like he used to be when the Knicks lost. Maybe it's because a new gun for him is out of our price range.

Ratso says he's going to take us someplace special. He leads us up the stairs from the Grand Concourse, into a side passage, up some more stairs. We pay off a couple of bouncers with sweet Heckler & Koch submachines slung under their armpits, who let us past a ratty velvet rope into this place that Ratso says used to be some rich guy's office a hundred years ago.

"Ladies and gents," says Ratso, "the Campbell Apartment."

Homeboy lived large. Wood-paneled walls, high ceilings with painted beams, cozy leather couches. Somebody has kept the place up—like, except for the teenyboppers all over the place, it probably looks the same as it used to. There's music playing over speakers jacked into a little red generator with an exhaust duct leading through an empty pane in a big gridded window. Loads of people are drinking and dancing and smoking up.

Waiters and *waitresses* roam around. It could almost be pre-apocalypse.

"Now we're talking," says Peter. He goes to order us a round of drinks.

Ratso stares at the ceiling, his mouth hanging open.

Me: "Nice place."

Ratso: "Oh, yeah. I bring all my high-profile clients here."

Me: "High-profile clients?"

He smiles and shrugs. "Actually, they never let me in before."

Me: "Well, you're with the Washington Square Wizards now."

Ratso (defensive): "The name wasn't my idea."

We get a nice corner booth, because some kids who saw the fight make way for us. They hold their hands up for high fives, and Jefferson reluctantly complies.

Peter comes back with a cute, clean-cut boy in a white shirt and black tie carrying a tray of martinis.

Me: "*Martinis*? For real, Peter?"

Peter: "Girl, stop bitching. When's the next time you're going to get a decent cocktail?" He turns to the kid carrying the tray. "This is *Dominic*," he says meaningfully. "Dominic, this is everybody. Dominic is renowned as the best cocktail waiter in all of Manhattan. Maybe the world."

Peter says stuff like this all the time, just to stir things up. He's always like, "This is Donna. Donna is a performance artist."

Dominic: (Nods.) "You folks let me know if you need anything else." Then he shoots a look to Peter before heading back to the bar.

Folks!

I raise my glass. "Here's to SeeThrough and Jefferson. The Harold and Kumar of violence."

Everybody raises their glass except for Jeff.

Jefferson: "Bad luck to toast yourself."

Me: "Ugh, Jeff, okay. Here's just to...violence. Judiciously applied."

Clink-clink-clink. Jefferson also won't toast without meeting your eyes, which slows things down a bit. Everybody laughs as they goggle at each other. When Jeff looks at me, his eyes are all sad and dewy.

I've never actually had a martini. It tastes like decay.

Me: "Gross. Is this what it's supposed to be like?"

Peter (savoring his): "Oh, yes."

SeeThrough coughs and spits a mouthful onto the floor. People look over at us like, *Who are these barbarians?* It's kind of weird, after everything, to suddenly be someplace with standards. Just sitting here is kind of blowing my mind. I'm still getting used to the idea of a space where strangers congregate and buy stuff. Thought that was all done with.

SeeThrough is still coughing, so I slap her on the back a few times and sit her down.

Me: "So, slugger...what's the deal with you and Brainbox?"

SeeThrough: "The deal?"

Me: "Yeah, like...are you guys *together* or something?"

SeeThrough isn't playing along with the whole gossip idea. "He's over there," she says, pointing at the huge marble fireplace, which has an old metal safe in it. Brainbox is twiddling the knob experimentally.

Me: "Never mind."

SeeThrough: "Ohhhh. You mean 'together' that way." She thinks. "He talked to me."

Me: "What?"

SeeThrough: "He talked to me. Even when I was FOB."

Me: "What's FOB?"

SeeThrough (smiling): "Fresh off the boat. When my parents and I came from China, nobody would talk to me."

Me: "Brainbox doesn't talk to anybody except Jefferson and W— except Jefferson."

SeeThrough: "He talks to me."

Me: "Oh. Well, do you...like...*like* him?"

SeeThrough laughs, and it's like the sun breaking through clouds. I don't think I ever saw her laugh before. Maybe I wasn't paying attention. She shakes her head, but she can't shake off the big smile.

Me: "*You like him!*"

She keeps shaking her head.

SeeThrough: "You think he likes *me*?"

Me: "Who knows what Brainbox thinks? He *should* like you."

SeeThrough: (Holds up her drink.) "*Gambei.*" Which I guess means "cheers." She squinches up her nose and swallows it. I do the same.

Peter does indeed find something to ask Dominic for, which is another round of martinis. Dominic also brings over some pigeon fried rice and a box of Entenmann's chewy chocolate-chip cookies, which are not chewy so much anymore. Still, this feels like the high life.

I'm on, like, my tenth cookie when Jefferson sits down opposite me. He's been leaning against the wall, looking gloomy.

Me: "Looking good out there, champ. I think we can get you a title shot."

He touches the strip of duct tape over his eyebrow.

Jefferson: "I got lucky." He scowls as he sucks down some martini.

Me: "Don't like your drink?"

Jefferson: "I don't like this *place*."

Me: "*Dude.* Live a little."

Jefferson: (Snorts.) "That's a slogan for our times. *Live a little.*"

Me: "You know what I mean. You won. We're, like, rich. We're all stocked up. And nobody carded us. This is a good time. Savor it."

Jefferson: "I won by beating a total stranger's face in. And this place?" He looks around. "The moment there's a tiny bit of stability, people just start copying the way things were. Velvet ropes. Bouncers. Waiters. It's pathetic. Like there wasn't any other way to do things. It's all the same. The strong eat the weak."

I have a flash of dinner at the library.

Me: "You think people are doing it better anyplace else? Like, they're living it up in Europe or something? Well, *let's go.*"

Jefferson: "It's probably the same everyplace. Because everyplace had become the same."

Me: "So, what did you have in mind? Utopia?"

Jefferson: (Shrugs.) "Why not? What is there to lose?"

I take another sip of my martini. It burns like acid. It's doing something to my brain, letting thoughts drift loose and float to my mouth. I don't usually talk about Before.

"You mean if you could have things back the way they were, you wouldn't do it?"

His face wrinkles. "Obviously, I wish people hadn't died. I wish my mom and…and Wash were back. But what was so great about things Before?"

Me: "Real food? The Internet? Running water? *Coffee?*"

Jefferson: "Didn't you feel like anything was wrong then?"

Me: "Sure. Lots. But not as much as what was right."

Jefferson: "You always complained about everything."

Me: "Yeah, well, I didn't know what I was missing."

Jefferson: "War. Racism. Commercialism. Fundamentalism."

Me: "I can't believe you're making an argument for the end of the world."

Jefferson: "It's only the end of the world if you don't think there's a future."

Me: "I don't. *We don't have a future.*"

It comes out a little more aggressively than I had meant, and it hits hard enough, I think, to slop over into another meaning. Like, *There's no future for you and me, either.* At least that's how Jefferson seems to take it.

I don't know, maybe that's how I mean it. I don't know.

Jefferson: "Okay. I see."

I'm tempted to explain, to, like, extract what I meant from what I didn't mean, but then I'm not sure if I can.

Ratso: "Is this great? Is this great, or what?" He slips into the booth next to us. He's kind of tanked.

Jeff shakes off the hurt look, laughs, and pats Ratso on the shoulder. "Sure, buddy. It's great." He looks around for our people. Peter is helping Dominic deliver drinks. SeeThrough has walked over to Brainbox, and he's showing her how the generator works.

Maybe *they* have a future.

Ratso continues, "When I saw you people, I knew you were class. I said to myself, 'Ratso, these people are not a bunch of Johnny-Come-Latelies. They are Top Shelf.'"

Me (laughing): "How come you talk like that?"

Ratso: "Like what?"

Me: "Like an old movie."

Ratso: "Oh, that. Well, this may seem funny, but English isn't my first language. My parents moved here from Russia when I was six. I learned English from TV and Netflix."

Jefferson: "So what's your real name?"

"Vitaly," he says. Vitaly. Emphasis on the middle syllable.

Jefferson: "I like that better than Ratso."

Me: "Netflix was so awesome." I take another gulp of martini. "That scientist dude oughtta pay for all the good shit he screwed up."

Ratso: "What scientist?"

Me: "Oh. I was just saying, if, like, some scientist was responsible for the Sickness."

Ratso: "I thought It Happened because somebody had sex with a monkey or something."

Me: "Well, that slutty monkey has gotta pay, then."

Jefferson: "The world was a bubble. A bubble inside a bubble. It was just waiting to go off the rails."

Me: "You're mixing metaphors, Debbie Downer. Here's to bubbles."

"Here's to bubbles." Ratso clinks his glass with mine. "So..." he says, "what brings you to Grand Central? What are you kids up to, anyway?"

Jeff and I share a look. He shrugs.

Jefferson: "We're going to save mankind."

Me: "Wouldn't we be saving *teenkind*?"

Ratso: "*That's* why you won the fight. You're following your destiny. I *knew* it. I saw you taking that beating, and I thought to myself, *Only one thing's gonna save that kid now.*"

Jefferson: "Which is what?"

Ratso: "What?"

Me: "What's gonna save him now? I mean, then?"

Ratso: "Oh. The power of Destiny. Like, with a capital *D*. Did you hear the capital *D* when I said *Destiny*?"

Jeff and I crack up. But Ratso is, like, really intent on being taken seriously.

Ratso: "Seriously. No foolin'. Take it from a guy who does not have a Destiny. Some have it; some don't. Me, I'll probably be stuck running from the Uptown Confederacy for the rest of my brief life."

We stop laughing.

Me: "What do you know about the Uptown Confederacy?"

Ratso: "Uh, just that they run this place."

Jefferson: "They run this bar?"

I reach down and take the safety off my carbine.

Ratso: "This bar and the whole building. Grand Central. They own the bank. They provide security. They're pretty much in charge."

I sober up quick.

Ratso: "What? What's the problem?"

Jeff looks wide awake himself.

Jefferson: "We've gotta go."

Ratso: "But—"

Jefferson: "Get out of my way, Ratso."

Somebody has his hand on Jeff's shoulder.

He sits down opposite us. A blond kid with high cheekbones.

Cheekbones: "Take it easy. What's the hurry?"

JEFFERSON

CHEEKBONES SMILES and takes the olive out of my martini.

"Having fun?" he says. He pops the olive into his mouth.

I look around for the others. The only one of ours I can see is Peter, who meets my eyes and then notices who's sitting with me.

"Look at me when I'm talking," Cheekbones says, his voice rising just a little. Then he sits back. "You know, when you were about to shoot me, I told myself that if I made it through, I'd track you down sooner or later. I never expected you'd just *show up* like this. How lucky can a guy get?"

"I don't suppose you'll accept an apology," I say.

He grins. "Nah." He reaches out and takes a chocolate-chip cookie from the center of the table. "How's whatshisface? The kid who shot my pig?" he asks as he cracks the cookie with his teeth.

"We were just going, dude," says Donna.

"You let bitches talk for you?" says Cheekbones, ignoring her.

"Don't call her that," I say.

"Or what?"

"Or I'll have to wash your mouth out with soap."

Cheekbones acts like he didn't hear that. "So what brings you to our neck of the woods?"

"They're going to save mankind," Ratso volunteers.

"Shut up." Now he takes my drink and downs it.

"What do you want?" I say.

He smooths his hair back, exaggerating his ease. "Restitution," he says.

"Tell you what," he continues. "I'll wipe the slate clean if you leave me the bitches. This one and the skinny little Asian one."

"Not gonna happen," I say.

"What the fuck is your deal, dude?" says Donna.

"Oh, did I offend you? Guess what—*I don't care.* Up here we're done pretending everybody's equal. If God wanted bitches to call the shots, he would have made them strong enough to defend themselves."

"Why don't you try me?" she says.

"Get your finger off that trigger, bitch." Now he looks at Donna. "This is my house. One shot, and the rest of my tribe comes up here loaded for bear. *We will torture you to death.*"

"Donna—take it easy," I say.

"*You* take it easy," she says.

"Come on," says Cheekbones. "It's no big deal. Just lie there.

You'll pay off your indenture in, like, a year. After that, you'll be all nice and broken in. Find a sponsor, and you're cool."

So that explains the girls with the armed guards. And the ones selling themselves on the way in.

"You know what?" says Cheekbones, smiling. "I'll even jump you in myself."

"Watch your language, cowboy. Do you go down on your mother with that mouth?" It's Peter. He's standing behind Cheekbones's seat. Dominic is at his shoulder, looking scared.

Cheekbones slowly lowers his smile and the drink.

The point of Peter's knife rests lightly on the pulse of Cheekbones's neck.

"Put the knife down," says Cheekbones.

"What's the magic word?"

"Put the knife down, please."

"No. But thanks for asking nicely."

"Is there an exit to the street?" I ask Ratso.

"There's some back stairs, but the exit's blocked off," he says.

"Let's go."

Peter puts his hand on Cheekbones's shoulder and guides him up to his feet. He lowers the knife to the middle of his back.

"You're not getting out of here," he says. "I've already alerted everybody."

I take the walkie from his belt. It's switched off. "I don't think so," I say. "I think you were already here when you lucked onto us."

We walk to the back of the bar. The crowd and the music work in our favor. Nobody sees the blade at Cheekbones's back.

Dominic the waiter unlocks a door leading to a staircase heading down, and we all slip in. The landing is pitch-dark, and we take out our flashlights.

"Are you going to kill me?" asks Cheekbones. I taste a drop of fear.

"That would be the easiest thing to do," I say. "Donna, you got any duct tape left?"

We tie Cheekbones's hands behind his back and bind his ankles together. I rip off a piece of my shirt and stuff it into his mouth, sealing it off with tape. He doesn't do the old-fashioned moaning and whimpering thing. He doesn't struggle or make noise. Instead, he looks an unambiguous message into my eyes. The message is, *I will be the death of you.*

Well, maybe.

I sit him down at the edge of the stairs that lead into blackness and debris.

Donna looks him right in the eye and kicks him down the stairs. We hear muffled barks of pain as he tries to stop rolling and right himself.

"All right," I say. "We're walking out of here. Everybody just stay cool. I'm betting that loser didn't tell his people he'd found us before he sat down to gloat. Any objections?"

"Just a question," says Ratso, raising his hand. "So—you know that guy?"

"Yeah. Long story. I'm sorry we got you involved. You want to come with us? I don't think things are safe here."

He nods. "Oh, I agree." He thinks. "Well, like I said. Destiny."

"Sure," I say, and head back into the bar.

People are none the wiser, and we make our way out easily. Peter blows a kiss to Dominic as we go.

We don't say a word as we head past the bouncers fingering their guns. "You guys have a good night," they say.

When we emerge from the stairs to the corner of the Grand Concourse, the buying and selling is still going on. But it's hard to look at it the same way. It's as though a spirit hovers over the place—all its actions and transactions in service of the Uptowners. All of it seems like whoring now.

There's some sort of ceremony or ritual happening on the balcony at the other end of the hall. Some camouflaged guards stand around a boy, his head hanging. Another kid is reading off some sort of proclamation. Everyone in the Concourse has turned to watch. The high arched windows are blocks of blackness above them.

"What's that?" I ask Ratso.

"Looks like a counterfeiter."

"What are they doing with him?" asks Peter.

But Ratso doesn't have to answer, because the guards put a stained hood made from a sewn-up *Angry Birds* T-shirt over his head and start strangling him with a rope. He struggles, kicking wildly, and the guards hold his limbs.

We're frozen in place as the life shudders out of him.

"Shit," says Donna.

"Let's go," I say. "Take it slow. Nobody runs."

We head for the big marble stairs, but just as we do, the walkie I stole from Cheekbones crackles to life. "Lock the doors down," I hear Cheekbones say.

Above us, the guards at the exit doors pull them shut and prevent anyone from leaving, leveling their guns at anyone who gets near.

"We've got intruders," Cheekbones says. "Four male, two female. Mongrels. There's a tall black kid and a couple of Asian kids. And that Mole Person who always hangs around the Bazaar."

"There's no such thing as Mole People," Ratso says, to nobody in particular.

As the guards scan the crowd, we try to look casual rounding the stairs. We walk toward the center of the Concourse. I can see guards all over the place getting the message:

"Kill the fuckers."

There's no order to stop, no warning shots. I hear the *TACK-TACK* report of an assault rifle, and a stranger to the right of me falls to the ground.

The crowd scatters like ants from a hill getting hosed down as the guards take potshots from above.

"This way!" shouts Ratso, running toward the passage to the old subway station.

As we reach the garbage-strewn, sepulchral mouth of the

subway, a lone guard raises his gun. Peter shoots him in the leg, and he goes down.

"Sorry!" shouts Peter as we head farther into the darkness.

I don my headlight and turn it on, the light playing over a heap of debris and rows of wire fencing that block our way out.

"They're at the subway entrance!" I hear an unfamiliar voice say. Then, the stomp of boots heading our way.

We search the fence. There's no way through, and Ratso is nowhere to be seen. Then I hear him call from a corner.

"Over here! Quick!" he says. We rush over to find a corner in the chain-link fence that's been torn from its mooring and bent backward.

We follow Ratso as he shimmies through. My leg catches on the edge of the fence, and I tear it free as the guards finally appear, silhouetted against the lights of the Concourse.

Brainbox slips up to the hole in the fence and rolls something along the ground toward the guards.

"Grenade," he says calmly.

I hunker down and cover my ears as the stun grenade goes off, and I watch as the silhouettes contort and stumble.

"Where'd you get that?" asks Ratso, amazed.

"The library," says Brainbox.

Ratso's face registers confusion. "Come on, they're gonna follow."

"How do you know?" says Donna.

"Because," says Ratso, "they *hate* Mole People."

DONNA

SO HALF AN HOUR AGO, I was sipping cocktails, hobnobbing with SeeThrough and Peter in an episode of, like, *Post-Apocalyptic Gossip Girl*. Now, for about the fourth time in two days, I'm being hunted by murderous psychopaths.

This is a great cardio workout. But, generally speaking, evading capture by cannibals, enraged hippies, and machine-gun-toting jocks? Not my thing.

Ratso seems to know the terrain, which levels the playing field a little against the numbers and outright bloodlust of the Uptowners. He leads us through the dark as light from our headlamps splashes over bricked MetroCard-dispensing machines, empty ticket booths, redundant turnstiles. We jump from the platform and haul ass down the tracks. Every once in a while, a rifle-mounted lamp from the Uptowners' guns catches us, and we dance between bullets that ring the steel support beams like giant chimes.

I blame Jefferson, of course.

This is what happens when you try to change the world. See, things may have been kind of shitty back in the Square, but they were at least *dependably* shitty. We had settled into a sort of groove. Then came this whole stupid adventure. When you go around acting all heroic and effing around with the status quo, the status quo responds by kicking you in the nuts.

So now it's first-person-shooter time. Sopping concrete with gray snowdrifts of God knows what. Rusting metal rails and crunching gravel. Slimy, spray-painted walls and scattered plastic cones. Any minute now, a mutant is gonna jump out of the shadows.

Ratso, who seems basically to see in the dark, takes us through a side passage from the Lexington Avenue subway line onto a football-field-sized patchwork of tracks leading farther into the dark. I notice a sign that used to say LOOK OUT FOR TRAINS, which has been modified to say LOOK OUT FOR RATS. Indeed, we encounter a chorus of squeaking and skittering rodents as we run across the metal lines. I glance at a fleeing rat, and our eyes meet for a moment; I could swear she gives me a sympathetic look—like, *I been there, honey.*

Ratso leads us on a long, looping sidetrack—dipping back downtown and then up again—hoping to shake the Uptowners. We huddle in a dank black alcove under some graffiti by somebody called Revs, and I listen for the sounds of boots over my roaring pulse and my ragged breaths.

After a while Ratso says, "C'mon. We've gotta go farther down."

The flashlights of the Uptowners reappear and grope over the tracks toward us as we follow Ratso to a blank wall. He kicks it, and a camouflaged door opens, revealing a narrow set of stairs covered in grime and soot, like everything else under the station. We clatter down these stairs and emerge into another dirty plateau of rails; then sprint along them, uptown this time, the sounds of the hunters growing more and more dim.

I keep running, quiet, tired, and scared, the alcohol pounding in my temples and sapping my strength. Ratso guides us through channels of bare rock, down long flights of stairs, along switchbacks, and down graffiti-painted hallways, until I have no idea where we are, what's up, down, east, west. He never hesitates, navigating by some kind of mental GPS.

Eventually he stops, and we listen some more. I can only hear the dripping water and the scrape of bits of paper being shushed along by underground breezes. I smell oil and tar and rot.

Ratso's listening with everything he's got. His eyes are raised, sipping the air.

Finally, he's satisfied. He disappears through a hole in the wall I never saw. His head pops out moments later.

"This way," he says. "No talking until I say."

We slog up a narrow track, past a broken-down subway train. From the green 6 in the window, I can tell we're back on the Lexington Avenue subway line. Then we duck into another tunnel, where the air is filled with dust. A big 61 is painted on the wall.

I see shapes moving in the darkness, but Ratso grabs my carbine and lowers it when I take aim. "Don't worry about it," he says.

And then I notice more shapes, behind our group, on either side...
and the shapes resolve themselves into people.

Mole People.

They're skinny and dirty, wearing ragged clothing and armed
with machetes and baseball bats and homemade spears. They're
quiet as shadows. Before I know it, one of them materializes at my
side—a wiry girl with matted blond hair and staring blue eyes.

I half expect her to start fingering my possessions, like we're in
some movie about Amazon tribesmen or something. But instead,
she says, "'Sup."

"'Sup, girlfriend," I say.

She looks about thirteen—really young for this world, though her
size could be due to malnourishment.

The rest of our pilot fish are youngsters, too—I'd say nobody
over fifteen. That's odd because youngsters don't make it very far
in New York. Not strong enough, not independent enough, not mean
enough. You see a few randoms scraping by, and there's some kids
as young as SeeThrough in our group, but generally they don't live
long in the Rough and Tumble.

Ratso is on a first-name basis with everybody; or maybe
I should say a nickname basis. The Moles have names like Gaga,
Bieber, and Honey Boo Boo, which I'm guessing their parents didn't
give them. There appear to be at least three Bellas. My little friend is
called Taylor.

Our fixer paves our way with a big fat smile, like in that *Peter and* the Wolf cartoon where the kid is high-stepping it at the end with a snapping wolf hanging from a pole.

The tunnel widens into a platform. Past that, illuminated by a bunch of campfires, there's a work site dotted with abandoned construction equipment. Tents are staked into the dirt all over—everything from cute little kids' pup tents with grimy cartoon animals all over them to big canvas deals. I see shadow people through the nylon, faces peeping up from plates of food, lit by the flames.

The cavern has decorations hanging all over the place. There's a bunch of paintings with dudes in red jackets riding horses after packs of dogs, Asian tapestries, mirrors with fancy curlicued gold frames, shiny golden drapes. Puffy couches and ornate chairs line the walls, and there's a gigantic grandfather clock with four faces sitting in the middle of the jumbled tents.

Ratso: "*My* house. Not bad, huh?"

Me: "Groovy."

Kids are pouring out of the tents to gawk at us. I figure maybe seventy or eighty in all.

I'd call their look "Insane Tween Posse." There's some black-clad emo happening, especially among the outnumbered boys. But most of them are decked out in crappy mall fashion, accessorized like they're wearing everything they have in case they need to move at a moment's notice.

Ratso: "Visitors! Be cool, everybody! Nothing to be afraid of!"

I wonder who he's trying to convince—them or us. We're surrounded, seriously outnumbered, and generally pulverized.

The Moles kind of circle around us for looky-loos, and nobody knows what to say. Peter tries to break the ice with, "We come in peace," but nobody laughs.

Silence.

Ratso: "Well, come on, make them welcome and stuff." Still nothing.

I rack my brain for something to break the ice. Turn to Taylor.

Me: "Ummm...that skirt's really cute?"

Her robin's-egg-blue thousand-yard stare, set off against the filth of her face, suddenly twinkles away as she smiles. "Really? I got it at Urban Outfitters. Before, you know."

Me: "Totally suits you."

Taylor: "Your skin's really beautiful. I would kill to have skin like that."

Some more girls step forward.

Mole Girl: "You're so pretty. Isn't she pretty?"

Another: "And she's so skinny. Uccch. I wish I was that skinny." (She is.)

Another: "Your hair looks awesome."

As the International Language of Girl builds cultural bridges, the boys look lost.

Jefferson (to some kid): "Um, your shirt is cool?"

There's a clanging sound, and everybody looks up at an old railway car that looms over the platform.

Talk stops. Ratso goes tense.

Two girls appear in the car's doorway. One looks like a kind of

Victorian Morticia Addams; the other one's a psychedelic cowgirl—Day-Glo colors, pink raccoon eye shadow, glittery hat. They look, stylistic gulfs aside, related. *The Harajuku Twins*, I think.

The Twins seem to have the only guns in camp. Morticia packs an old British Sten gun, practically an antique. Cowgirl has, if my tutelage under Washington serves me, a Kriss Super V, this boxy, snub-nosed little submachine gun that fires big .45 bullets at about twenty rounds a second.

The Harajuku Twins are not to be taken lightly. In my brief Pocky experience, I've found that the nastiest weapons tend to gravitate toward the nastiest people. Like, we're in a situation where shots get fired in anger pretty often? If you're packing something like a Super V and don't use it, chances are, somebody else is going to come into its possession.

Morticia scans us like she's the Terminator or something. There's a period of nervous hush, which she ends with a pithy:

"W." Pause.

"T." Pause.

"F?"

This is directed at Ratso, who all of a sudden looks like a Pomeranian who just got caught taking a dump on the carpet.

Ratso: "Baby! I brought home guests!"

Morticia gives him a look that, I confess, I am guilty of having served up myself on occasion. The gist of it is, *Oh hell, no.*

Me: "I like your gun."

Morticia: "Shut up, bitch."

Normally if a girl said that to me, we would, like, have words. But at the moment, I am just too tired and too hungover and too exhausted and generally too chewed up and crapped out to bother.

Ratso: "Okay, first off, it wasn't my fault."

Jefferson: "That's true. This is my fault. Ratso was helping us, and we got in trouble with the Uptowners—do you know about the Uptowners?"

Cowgirl does a little *snort* that removes any doubt.

Jefferson: "Well—they were going to kill us. So Ratso helped us to escape. And here we are. We pose you no harm."

Morticia: (Looks at Ratso.) "Oh, Vitaly."

Cowgirl strides through the crowd and confronts him. "Why don't you just give them an effing *invitation*? Draw them a *map*? You led a bunch of a-holes who the Uptowners were after *here*? Are you *smoking crack*?"

Ratso: "...No?"

Morticia suddenly notices Taylor standing next to me. "What the hell are you doing here? Back to your post!"

Taylor: "Sorry!" I think I see her blush through the soot. She runs off toward where I first saw her, and some of the others follow.

Ratso: "We lost the Uptowners. No way will they find us."

Morticia: "Oh, STFU. You are SFS."

Cowgirl: "Get in here before you make everybody totally space out."

I'm not going to say Ratso is *whipped*, but he isn't exactly the Man in Charge, either, if you know what I mean. He seems to be *involved* with Morticia, though whether he is pet or boyfriend is another matter.

Morticia and Cowgirl, whose real names, after much hemming and hawing, are divulged as Tricia and Sophie, are indeed twin sisters. It would seem they are either the most charismatic or most bossy figures in this teen underground scene, so they run the show.

As the full Polaroid develops, it's not as easy to make them out as the bad guys. They have a lot on their plates, what with being responsible for all the Lost Girls and Boys who've banded together here for security in numbers.

This kind of answers the question that we are too polite to ask—"Who the hell would want to live underground?" It should have been obvious.

Prey.

The predators are all around. Anybody bigger, faster, and meaner, same as in the jungle. But the Uptowners are the worst of them all. They are numerous, organized, and particularly douchey.

Morticia and Cowgirl lay it out for us. How, as the plague hit, loads of families from Uptown headed to the Hamptons to wait it out, leaving their nannies and their maids and their doormen to die in the crowded city. How they came back toting guns when the police force collapsed. How the adults fought pointless battles to preserve their real estate and then died of the Sickness, how their children picked up their guns and picked up the fight against anybody from "outside." It was easy enough for them to tell who didn't belong. They started clearing out anybody who wasn't white. Mistakes were made, of course; that's the deal with ethnic cleansing. But as a rule of thumb, it worked, for the ones who survived.

The boys, thanks to years of life wasted on *Call of Duty*, had a knack for violence and a jump start on ignoring the suffering of others. So, unsurprisingly, they were the first ones to grab the guns and go hunting. But for a few notable exceptions, like Tricia and Sophie, the girls were unprepared and underarmed. While Wash and Jeff and the rest of us were trying to establish some kind of, I don't know— fair?—society down in the Village, Uptown turned into a rapeocracy. Rule by the strong and especially the male. The weak, or the meek or whatever, were there to serve.

There were plenty of girls who resisted, and plenty of boys at that. Suffice it to say, they weren't sufficiently brutal. They were driven out, put down, just plain slaughtered.

After a whole pisspot of blood got spilled, Uptown ended up in the grip of the "Confederacy." An alliance of what was left of all the private schools in the area, with a thousand "warriors" in uniform imposing order on thousands of others.

Now they control the territory from Grand Central all the way north to the edge of Harlem. They have a Tom and Jerry thing going on with the Moles; to date, their Good Guy Base hasn't been discovered, but the Moles need to pop up aboveground to get food. Thanks to their knowledge of the subway system and other bits of dead infrastructure, they've managed to survive.

Mole HQ is in a station underneath the Waldorf-Astoria hotel on Park and Forty-Ninth. Which is either Really Ironic or Really Stupid. Basically, they're right underneath Uptown territory. They've burned out the entry floor of the hotel to make it look uninhabited, and the Uptowners are too spoiled for choice to bother investigating. As for the station itself, nobody knows about it. It's a "dead stop" once used by, like, superrich visitors to the hotel who had their own railway cars. Cowgirl tells me that Franklin Roosevelt would be driven right onto a private car so that he could leave New York without anyone noticing that he was disabled. The station was bypassed and disused, and now the Moles are the only ones who know how to get here.

We offer to be on our way, but the Twins decide that it'd be safer to stick around overnight, in case the Uptowners are still searching the tracks near Grand Central.

After a while, some platters of food are brought in—rat stew and a bowl of stale rice with rainbow-colored spores.

Peter crosses himself and says a little grace while Morticia scoops off the mold and reverently places it on a bronze platter under a picture of Edward from *Twilight*. She closes her eyes and whispers something.

Peter: "You know that vampires aren't real, right?"

Morticia: "Of *course* I do. Do you know that *God* isn't real?"

Peter: "Says who?"

Morticia: "Says *me*. Either he isn't real, or he's a total douche."

Peter: "No need for that."

Morticia: "Oh, *sorry*, did I hurt your *feelings*? Well, ask yourself this. If God is all-powerful and all-knowing, then he *knows* we're here, and he could make it *suck less*."

Peter: "We can't blame God for things *people* do."

Morticia: "Why *not*? What's his game? Why would he make us if he didn't make us right?"

Peter: "He wanted us to have free will."

Morticia: "Hah! How can you have free will if he knows everything that happens and he has power over it all?"

Ratso: "Babe, c'mon. These are our guests."

Morticia, sullen, pokes a spoon into her rat stew.

Morticia: "I'll stick with Edward, thank you very much. God's just a myth. Like the Tooth Fairy or the Old Man."

Jefferson: "What do you know about the Old Man?"

Morticia: (Shrugs.) "Same as everybody. He's just a story for people who want their mommies and daddies back."

Cowgirl: "I heard that he was immune to the Sickness, and he's trying to cure it by injecting his blood into kids."

Morticia: "That's *shit for brains*. Excuse my sister. She's an idiot."

Cowgirl: "It could happen! There's always somebody, like, resistant to diseases, right?"

Morticia: "You're dreaming. All the adults were screwed. And nobody's going around *injecting* people with his own blood."

Ratso: "He exists."

Then, when he has our attention: "I *saw* him."

Morticia: "*Bullshit* you saw him."

Ratso goes quiet. But then, after a little chewing, he says, "I was over by the East River. There was this pigeon that couldn't fly? Anyway, as far as I was concerned, it was dinner. So I'm following it, and I get close to the FDR Drive. Across the road, I see this guy get out of a boat? And he's dressed in a big plastic astronaut suit? For hazardous materials and stuff, like in the movies?"

Morticia: "How do you know it was a *he* if he was all covered by the suit?" Like she's said it a million times before.

Cowgirl: "Maybe it was just some kid."

Ratso: "Why would a *kid* wear a suit like that?"

Cowgirl: "Kids wear a lot of stupid stuff." She ought to know.

Jefferson: "Did you see his face?"

Ratso: (Shakes his head.) "Hell, no. I saw him look up at me? I know that because the sun was behind me and the faceplate caught the light? And I ran the hell away. Left the pigeon there and everything."

Brainbox: "What color was the suit?" He's barely said a thing all day.

Ratso: "Blue. I think. Why?"

Brainbox: "Nothing."

Morticia: "Does it really matter what color suit it was? The whole point is, nobody's left. We're it. Nobody's coming to save us."

I look over at Jefferson. "You want to tell them?" I ask.

He tells them. About everything we've done since the Uptowners showed up with that damn, delicious pig. The library and the cannibals. Plum Island.

The Harajuku Twins are not impressed.

Morticia: "I'll believe it when I see it."

Ratso: "Well, I think it's groovy. Tomorrow I'll take you up to 110th Street on the number six line. That'll get you past Uptown territory."

Morticia: "And out of our Kool-Aid."

Jefferson: "What's on 110th Street? Why can't we keep going?"

Ratso looks embarrassed. He glances at Peter.

Peter: "He wants to say 'black folks,' but he's worried I'll take it the wrong way."

Ratso: "That's right. Sorry. Anyway, I can't help you through the tunnels there."

So, bonus newsflash? There's some kind of race war going on between the Uptowners and Hispanic people and African Americans. Things haven't worked out in a very touchy-feely way up north. I guess people didn't really get why the white boys should keep all the phat apartments, especially now that 90 percent of the residents were dead. And the Uptowners weren't feeling very much like sharing their toys. Lots of kids got killed; now things seem to have simmered down for the moment. But the long and the short of it is that we're on our own once we get to the top of Central Park.

The park is a no-go because all the animals escaped from the zoo and have been generally living it up, at the expense of picnickers.

So, great.

Taylor, my little friend, pops her head in after knocking. She tells us our "rooms are ready." Some other kids come and take away our bowls. We thank the Harajuku Twins and leave the car. Ratso stays behind, and as the door slams shut, I can hear Morticia start to lay into him.

Taylor, whose turn at watch is done, takes us to the "rooms" that have been set up on one end of the construction site. They're basically just areas that have been cordoned off from each other with white plastic sheeting. But the beds are super fancy and soft, and there are plush chairs and lacquered wooden tables and bedside reading desks. There are candles everywhere, and they make the plastic look like milky glass, and you could almost forget you were underground.

"This is super cute, Taylor. Thank you."

Taylor looks totally stoked that I like the rooms. The others mutter with gratitude, and she's just, like, fit to burst. As the others put their stuff down, Taylor kind of hovers up to me, looking embarrassed.

Taylor: "We're, um, doing something?"

Me: "Uh-huh?"

Taylor: "Would you, like, like to come?"

Me: "Oh—sure!" I'm so goddamn tired I can't imagine anything better than falling asleep, but I figure I have to appease the natives or whatever.

Her face explodes into a smile.

Me: "Can my peeps come?"

Taylor (even more stoked): "If they want!"

I'm surprised when Peter and SeeThrough both decide to tag along. "Something is my favorite thing to do," says Peter.

SeeThrough: "Yeah. I *love* something."

Jefferson: "I'll be there in a second. Brainbox wanted to talk."

We follow Taylor through the cavern and into a little lobby sort of space, where a bunch of other girls are waiting. There's a buzz of anticipation when they see us. Smiles and whispering.

They scrape together some chairs, upturned paint buckets, and milk crates for us to sit on. Then, with a nod from Taylor, one of the girls fetches a little box with satiny red embroidery on it. It looks like a case for a saint's finger bone. And she handles the box like whatever's inside is precious.

I'm thinking we have been invited to a church service or something when she opens the box and I see that there are four chubby little copper and black batteries inside, lying against cushioned silk.

She gently fishes the batteries from the box and leans over to mess with something I can't see. Some plasticky clipping and clacking noises.

Taylor hands me a binder encrusted with glitter and stickers and plastic jewels and crap. She looks me in the eyes significantly like she's giving me something very precious. I nod a churchy, appreciative sort of nod, and open the book.

It's a list of pop songs with numbers by them.

The girl with the batteries stands up again, and now she's holding a microphone. She gives it to Taylor, who smiles sheepishly and clears her throat.

Peter looks at me, like, *Aw, yeah.*

Then music starts up. Bouncy, cool twanging with a looped, chimey bass line. It's that song from 2012 or something, the big hit where the guy complains that his ex had her friends pick up all her records and stuff, and then she says that he was a loser.

Taylor starts singing in a sweet, fragile voice, pacing through the words like she was walking carefully on stepping-stones in a stream.

And that song—ugh, I heard it so many damn times that it made me sick. Like, it was as if I ate fifty cupcakes in a row. I was, like, eff these losers and their relationship issues. *Move on dot org.*

But the way she sings it, it's so freakin' beautiful? Like, it isn't about some hipster and his stupid ex. It's about everything. It's children singing to their missing parents, it's a lamb singing to a lion, it's Life singing to Death.

So I start crying. Tears escape from my eyes; I can feel them trying to find their way down my face, getting stuck on these ice floes of soot and grime. And I think, *Thank God, thank God, I can still do it, I can still feel.* A lever inside me has been pulled, and a subroutine is running, and my body is dumping toxins overboard.

I look over at Peter and SeeThrough, secretly so they don't see that I'm crying. But they're too busy listening to pay attention to my tears. Both of them look like they're floating in a bubble of their own, running their own little brain apps in their Brain OS's. Or maybe we're all in the same place, just it's dark there, and we can't find one another.

Taylor finishes in time for me to keep from full-on losing it. She seems unaffected by the emotion of the song as it winds down and fades out, like she's in the eye of the storm. She looks to me, her face open and vulnerable. I smile a big smile and applaud. She laughs and bows.

Then another girl gets up, and "Call Me Maybe" starts playing, which, again, I didn't have any time for. But as she sings, my mind is flooded with all the precious stupid things we had and lost— flirting and wondering if a guy liked you and giving out your phone number, and clothes and texts and accessories and looks and laughing, and stupid TV and stupid music and stupid pizza and stupid games and stupid magazines and stupid makeup and stupid books and stupid everything.

And the girls sing some Justin Bieber, and then Peter and I do the Black Eyed Peas, and for all the world it's like we're back in time. The music has made a little wormhole, and we're Before, and everything is fun and goofy and cool. And everything is almost perfect, but I find myself wishing Jefferson were here, too. I want to see him smile. And then, boom, it's like a dam breaks in my heart, and I am just drowning in feelings for him, and I think, *What am I, insane?* Not to have kissed him and held him. And I know it's probably just the music and singing all these songs about love; I must be hypnotizing myself—but it feels very real, and my heart is just bursting for him, and I decide that I HAVE to go, I have to find him and tell him what I've discovered, that if you can just hollow out a space together with someone, you can hold the entire world at bay.

I make, like, my excuses and hug Taylor and thank her, and I start back toward our "rooms," and I hear the next track come on behind me, another silly tune, a teenage girl singing Jay Z, all boasty and blustery, but my heart is in another place—it's out of my chest, it's with Jefferson, and I have to go and get it back.

I pull aside the plastic sheeting and find his bed—

And he's lying there. His feet are on the floor, his chest gently rising and falling. Asleep, he looks like a little boy, his hair mussed and his mouth open.

I feel like I am on a ledge looking over a great height.

He's away somewhere peaceful, better than this world. His spirit is wandering someplace safe, his body is trying to put itself back together. It feels selfish to wake him.

I decide it can wait till tomorrow. This feeling isn't going away.

But first I lean over him and gently touch my lips to his face.

I've never done this. Like, touched him. I mean, I've *touched* him touched him, but not, like, lovey-dovey or anything. The closest we ever came was a dare in first grade. And he didn't even follow through. So.

My breath on his poor wounded cheek. A kiss on his eye. A kiss on his forehead full of worries.

And his mouth.

I'm surprised when it smells of mint.

The music is still going on, but I don't want to go back.

Instead I go to my bed and I take out my iPhone. I power it up and find my favorite movie of Charlie.

He steps forward onto the rug in front of the mantel, and Mom and I applaud. He grips one hand in the other in front of his little belly and starts to sing in his whistly, lispy, out-of-tune voice:

> *We sing … with pride …*
> *We sing with pride, our hearts open wide …*

We sing…we sing…with pride…
We sing with pride…we sing with pride…

His face so serious, his eyes wandering up to the ceiling, his body swaying this way and that. He loses the thread of the lyrics and brings the song to an end, bowing. Then he is seized by embarrassment and makes a run for the phone, and the movie ends as he grabs it.

I watch it again. I have watched it a hundred thousand times. Sometimes I just look at movies of Charlie over and over again until the phone's batteries run down, and I find Brainbox and beg him for more juice.

As long as he is here to sing to me, some whisper of me is alive.

But who knows when I will get back to the Jennies. I power the iPhone down and lie back, caressing the screen with my thumb, and in time, I fall asleep.

JEFFERSON

DONNA AND the others leave with that Taylor kid and the other feral nymphets, and I find Brainbox. He's looking at a piece of plastic.

"What's with the LEGO?" I say.

His eyes flick my way.

"Nothing. I want to talk about that pig."

"Which pig do you have in mind?"

"*The* pig," says Brainbox. "The one that Cheekbones and the rest of them wanted to sell us."

"*Sell* is an interesting word to use."

"Okay—they wanted to *trade* us the pig for two girls. Remind you of anything?"

I shrug.

"It made me think of that stuff they taught us in grade school," says Brainbox. "The triangular trade and everything. Like, molasses for slaves for cloth."

"What's the third part of the triangle? Pigs for girls for what?"

"Doesn't matter," says Brainbox. "What matters is, why did they even bother to come trading? And where did the pig come from?"

"They wanted to trade because they wanted girls for—you know…"

Brainbox frowns. "I don't buy that. I mean, yeah, they treat girls like objects or whatever—I get it. But I don't think that was the *real* reason they wanted to trade with us. I mean, why us, particularly?"

"High-quality women?" I say.

"No. I mean, yes, but not for *their* purposes. Why not capture people instead? They had no idea what kind of…*society* we were."

"They didn't really care," I say. "When we didn't want to trade, they tried to force us to."

"Right, which is not what you do with an equal trading partner."

"But why not just take our stuff?"

"Dangerous," Brainbox says. "Unnecessary, if you can extract what you need another way. An unequal exchange. With…a colony. When you colonize, you don't have to kill somebody to take *their* stuff. You force them into your system, and they *give* you their stuff, for things they don't need."

We're on to AP Economics again. I can practically hear Donna sighing in annoyance.

"Mercantilism," I say. "But *girls*?"

"Weren't you listening to those twins? Girls are trying to *escape* the Uptowners. What if they do escape? Or what if they fight back?"

"So they want to enslave us. And they want our...stuff," I say. "Everybody wants something. What else is new?"

"It's more complicated than that. Who raised the pig? And what about the milk?"

"For my cappuccino."

"Yes. How did they get milk? It's been two years since It Happened."

"It could've been, like...canned, or that kind that comes in boxes, right?"

Brainbox shakes his head. "UHT milk lasts a year at most."

"Okay," I say. "So they've got some cows, too. So?"

"They've got enough pigs that they have a *surplus*."

"Right. You don't trade away what you *need*." I'm starting to see what Brainbox means.

Frank has worked like hell to squeeze a few crops out of our little plot in the Square, but we still resort to scavenging, and even that's running out.

The Ghosts are growing vegetables in Bryant Park, but they don't have enough to survive without cannibalism.

And the Moles are starving underground.

"They have farms," I say, amazed. "Not, like, patches here and there. Not some vegetable garden. Something big. Upstate, or Long Island."

"Exactly," says Brainbox.

"But what if they don't own the farms?" I say. "What if they're trading partners, or colonies, or whatever?"

"Doesn't matter," says Brainbox. "The point is—"

"The point is, where there's a surplus, there's a *future*," I say. A surplus means you can store up food. It means you can sustain life.

It means you can start again.

If.

If Brainbox is right about the Sickness. If we can do anything about it. If we get to Plum Island. If.

"If we figure out the Sickness, Brainbox..." I say.

"Then?" he says.

"Then we do something about the Uptowners."

"Do what?"

I think about the Uptowners in their thousands, and our little tribe seems insignificant. And our expedition feels like a wood chip on the ocean.

I can hear music from the other side of the cavern; laughter, chatter.

I wish I could just go there.

But my head is full of hope and fear. Hope that despite everything we've lost, we might build something good. Maybe something better than it was Before.

Fear that it'll be too late; that if we somehow live through this, we'll just drown in the hatred of our enemies.

I'm too tired to go all that way toward the music. Too sad to look at Donna and still not touch her.

We don't belong, my heart says to me. I want a future, and all she wants is the past. So she doesn't love me. She loves that phone of hers more. Charges it up and keeps it close, like Before is going to call her.

But I'm here now.

I leave Brainbox twiddling with his radio and head to my bed. I lie back. Maybe I ought to get up. Maybe things would be different this time.

And then I'm asleep.

In my dream, I hear the endless static from Brainbox's crank radio. Then, suddenly, out of the ocean of noise, I hear a voice. I imagine that I open my eyes, and I see him look at me, and fiddle with the knobs, and the static comes back.

Impossibly big—obese—raindrops hit a metal roof.

A mouse is screaming.

And then I'm awake. Peter is shaking me.

"What?"

The raindrops are gunshots echoing through the tunnels.

"They found us," says Peter.

I'm up, and adrenaline is jetting hot through my veins. I see the others, gray silhouettes on the plastic sheeting, gathering their gear.

Fear is running through the hole like a fire, eating the air. A few of the Moles are heading toward the shooting, but most of them are running, leaving everything. Some cling to each other, frozen in place.

Ratso appears, his eyes wild. He's got a rifle in hand.

"Go!" he says. "Get out of here! The Uptowners have found us. We won't be able to hold them long."

I don't like the idea of running. Not if it means leaving the Moles to get hunted down.

"Ratso—is there a side tunnel? Can you get us around behind them? We can lead them away from here, can't we? Give the others a chance to escape."

Ratso focuses, nods. He gestures for us to follow him. We pass by the railway car, and I see the Twins heading toward the Uptowners, their guns at the ready. The Goth girl and Ratso share a look as they pass.

We follow him to another door that groans and yields to a stairway heading down. We slip down mucky stairs, then through a service corridor of some kind. I have my Petzl on and can just keep up with Ratso, who runs as though the way were fully lit.

Stairs leading up, and a blast of cold air as we empty onto a row of tracks. We've doubled back behind the Uptowners, I think. The gunfire is coming from a different direction now.

"Okay," says Ratso. "What's the plan?"

I hold my breath, trying to slow down my heart.

"We engage them," I say. "Try to draw them after us or at least split them up."

"Hurry up, damn it!" says Donna. "Before they kill them all!" And she rushes ahead toward the shooting.

We follow as best we can, until we make out the light of muzzle flashes splayed against tunnel walls in the distance.

They're too busy trying to shoot their way into the Moles' cavern to see us coming. We get to within fifty yards or so, picking our way among the girders holding up the ceilings. Rats are streaming past our ankles, away from the fight.

I can see a doorway leading to the Moles' encampment. There's a little figure crumpled on the ground, wedging the door open. Somebody else is doing a good job of holding the advance of the Uptowners, popping into the open to fire a shot and then hiding.

The Uptowners are trying to pick her off, inching closer and closer every time she ducks out of sight. Soon they'll work their way around to a position from which she can't hide. The popping of the guns is intermittent, a ragged backyard Fourth of July with an occasional burst of typewriter-era newsroom. Nobody has the ammunition to really open up.

Ratso, who I guess doesn't understand this, suddenly unloads his AR, hosing down the middle distance with a five-second spray of bullets. Then nothing. He looks at the empty gun as if it's broken.

It does the trick, though. The Uptowners stop firing and scurry to new positions, shouting to one another. In moments, shots are coming our way, clanging off beams and raining filth from the ceiling. I throw myself to the ground as Ratso falls backward onto his rump.

Meanwhile, Donna has made her way to the doorway, dangerously close to the Uptowners. The others are following her, which means that we'll lose our flanking position if I don't do something. I wish I had my old AR-15. I miss her worse than my parents right now. My brain has just enough time to process what a twisted thought this is as the Mole defending the doorway appears again.

It's Taylor, the skinny blond girl with the plastic earrings. She pops out to take another shot at the Uptowners, and her luck runs out. A bullet catches her in the chest, and she falls backward out of sight.

I hear Donna scream, and she gets up and runs, pumping rounds out of her carbine. As she reaches the doorway, Peter and Brainbox try to cover her.

The rest is fractured. I see four Uptowners get up from their positions and advance, shooting their way into a position between me and Donna. I scurry over to Ratso. As I reach him, he groans.

There's gore where his right eye used to be, and his mouth hangs open slack. I hear a sound like a wooden rattle coming out of his throat.

I grab his collar and start dragging him backward, slipping and struggling, as the Uptowners keep advancing. Behind a pillar, I put my fingers on his neck, which is useless, because my heart is beating so fast that my fingers are throbbing and I can't tell his pulse anyway.

His remaining eye is unfocused. He doesn't see me.

He's gone.

I close his eyelid with a sweep of my fingers. Something out of a movie, I realize. I grab his gun. His hands yield it, but remain tensed like claws.

The Uptowners are getting closer, and there's no way to reach the others now, not without running across their fire. I test Ratso's AR and confirm all the bullets are spent. I've got no choice but to run.

I scamper to the next pylon, away from the firefight. A couple of shots from the Uptowners tell me that at least I am drawing some heat away from the others. But I don't know who's in a worse spot, me or them. I haven't got anything to answer the Uptowners with, and bit by bit, I get pushed farther and farther away from Donna.

When the four Uptowners on my tail try to flank me, I'm forced to run, torn between hoping they'll follow me and an animal urge to survive, even if it means the others are taken.

I push down these thoughts, leaving them on the garbage heap of impulses to deal with later, the landfill of recrimination I'll sort through someday to see if there's anything useful.

Madly, I scan the darkness. At length, a great hole opens up in front of me, blackness inside the blackness, and I dive down it, the lights of my pursuers painting spots of dirty gray all around me, bullets kicking up ash and dirt spatter.

They stop shooting, conserving their bullets for the kill, and I hear nothing but the sawing of my breath and their boots behind me, cursing, spitting, and shouting as they follow. I crack my shins on an electrical box, pick myself up, and head along a current of cold air. In the darkness, my eyes conjure blotches of color that float and blend and jump, like the light show that I used to perceive on the inside of my eyelids when I tried to go to sleep in my bedroom at home Before, when I was little and it was new, before I dismissed it and it became nothing but black to the voice in my head. I'm rediscovering the colors inside the dark.

The sounds of pursuit die out. I stop and listen as the voices dim and are suddenly muffled, as though they've taken a turn.

And finally I'm alone. My hands ache from gripping the gun so tightly; my lungs burn. There's no sound but the dripping of water as my eyes dilate and the rough tunnel slowly fades up.

Somewhere out there in the dark are my friends, alive or dead. Maybe twenty, maybe thirty feet above, maybe more, is the wreck of New York. But I don't know how to get there. I'm lost.

I start to cry. A child in the dark, crying. I think of Mom and Dad, her under the earth, him scattered in the ocean. I think of Wash.

And that stops my tears. I think of what he would have done. He certainly wouldn't have sat around snuffling.

I take a deep breath and stand up. I'm in a tunnel, tracks

leading either way. I grab the Petzl from where it hangs by the elastic around my neck and slide it onto my forehead. Switch it on and pray I don't run out of juice and that the Uptowners aren't close by.

I keep heading the way I was running, lining myself up between the rails, equidistant from the walls. I make a great target this way, but the feeling of being centered somehow holds back my fear to the point where I can manage.

I walk for maybe ten minutes, trying to make sense of the cryptic numbering on the track pillars, wondering where the trains are. I guess somebody had time to hole them up in their yards, hoping someday the world would be right again.

The thought that we ever lived our life in public, brushing up against each other, breathing each other's air, trusting one another's judgment, seems like an obscene miracle.

The black gunite walls give way suddenly to white tiles, oily and cracked, and I realize that I'm approaching a station. I slip to the wall and crouch, inching my way up, the empty gun aimlessly pointed in front of me.

A blue mosaic tells me that I'm at the Rockefeller Center stop. I've made a loop—south, west, and then back north. As I crawl along the depressed tracks, the lip of the platform runs level with my eyes.

Then I make out movement in the gloom of the platform, up by a set of stairs leading to the surface. It's hardly more than a change in the density of the darkness, but my eyes are sensitive now after hours of creeping around.

I grab my headlamp, snuffing out the light, and jump under the overhang of the platform's edge.

I hear slow steps, one after the other, distinct. One person. They seem to be searching the platform for something or someone. They don't know I'm here.

I press myself into the wall so there's no way to see me without leaning over the edge.

I can hear the stranger breathing. Slowly, I reach for the pommel of the *wakizashi* and thumb the blade out of the scabbard. There's a wooden scraping, thunderous to my ears.

The breathing stops.

Second after hour-long second pass by with nothing but the *thump-thump* of my heart and drips falling from the ceiling.

He's heard me. Why else would he stop in his tracks? And now there's nowhere to go. If I try to make a run for it, I'll be exposed the moment I leave the overhang of the platform.

Then the footsteps start again. Close, practically above my head, then farther and farther away. I guess at where the stranger can be...I guess at whether he's looking this way or turned away....

And I slowly, quietly lift myself onto the platform, the sword in my teeth like something from a pirate movie. It would be embarrassing to be killed looking this way. The thought flashes through my mind as I make it to a prone position on the platform.

The stranger is a shortish black shape in the gloom. I make out skinny legs, a wiry frame, the rectangular barrel of a handgun.

If I'm quick and quiet, I can take him. I hold my breath, push myself up, and grab the sword in my right hand.

And then she turns and points her gun at me.

I'm surprised that it's a girl. In the darkness I had been imagining a soldier from Uptown, and the change in perception is a shock.

She's blond, slender, and, my annoyingly beside-the-point brain tells me, beautiful. Big blue eyes and a Cupid's-bow mouth. Full, round breasts and a smooth stomach beneath a ripped T-shirt. It stretches against her body as she tries to catch her breath. She seems as scared as I am.

But so much for that. She has me dead to rights, down to the little red laser point on my chest.

"Put down the sword and the gun," she says in a clear, confident voice.

I hesitate. "But—"

"But what?" she snaps.

"But then I'd be defenseless," I say.

She smiles a crooked smile. Something about her looks familiar. "You're bright. Put them down."

I lean down and put the gun and the sword on the ground. Of course I have a fantasy about somehow throwing the *wakizashi* and skewering her in an uncanny burst of dexterity, but it seems pretty unlikely.

Plus, weirdly, the idea of just *wasting* this beautiful girl seems wrong.

This mental scruple puts me at a hell of a disadvantage. I should just see her as a threat, same as everyone else, but it's hard to shake this kind of prejudice.

I can practically see Donna facepalming.

"Take two steps forward and stop," she says. So I do.

Now the weapons are behind me, and she's still a good ten feet away. I try to calculate how many shots she could get off before I get to her. Enough.

We stand there as she eyes me up and down.

"Well," I say, "do what you're going to do."

"Where are the others?" she says.

"What others?"

"Don't bullshit me," she says. "I know you're running with four others. Two bitch—" She catches herself. "Two girls and two boys. And the Mole. Are they hiding back there?" She looks into the shadows. "I'm going to kill your boy if you try anything!"

"We were separated," I say.

She blinks. "Bad news for them."

"They're doing better than I am," I say.

"Naw. You're lucky." She blows a stray lock away from her eyes. "Okay," she says. "Let's make a deal."

"Huh?"

"I save your ass from my—from the Uptowners. In return, you let me join your tribe."

"What tribe would that be?" I ask.

"Washington Square, of course."

"How do you know that?" The question sits there. Then I add, "I can't make a deal like that."

"Why not?" she says. "I thought you were the boss."

I recognize her. It's the girl who was with the Uptowners when they tried to trade us the pig. The girl they wanted to use to convince people everything was cool.

And I can see the bruise that was covered up before, just above her mouth on the left side.

"What're you doing?" she says.

"What do you mean?" I say.

"Are you eyeballing me? Are you *checking me out*?"

"No!" I say, even though the question is kind of ridiculous under the circumstances, and even though I had been checking her out only a moment before.

"Jesus," she says. "Boys."

The red dot skips off my body for just a moment, and I move. I'm on her before she can get a shot, my left hand around her wrist. I figure if I can get the gun from her, I can get away, go back, and find the others.

She wraps a leg around mine, jams an elbow into my windpipe, and brings her head down on my nose with a thud. My eyes sting; my ears crackle. I won't let go of her wrist, though, and she pulls the trigger, firing into the darkness. Still, I don't let go.

She's stronger than she looks, and it's a stalemate for a while. The only sounds are our raspy breathing and the growls in the back of our throats as we struggle for position.

Then, suddenly, her mouth is on mine.

Which is unexpected.

I don't know if she's biting me or kissing me for a second, and then I realize, the latter.

Our bodies are still fighting, but our mouths are kissing. I don't know how this happened.

Her leg is still wrapped around mine, but in a different way, somehow. Meanwhile our hands are still at war, but as they start to get reports from other parts, they slack off. With a clatter the gun falls to the platform, and now our hands grip each other like fighting octopi.

Her other hand wanders down my back, coming to rest on my tailbone. And mine is on hers. And we mash into each other.

I remember once I was despairing of ever getting any action and Washington said that you never knew when things like this were going to happen, and that it went down exactly when you thought it was the last thing possible. But this is kind of ridiculous.

So I'm making out with the girl who was about to shoot me. And, okay, I don't have much to *compare* it to, but it's amazing. Like eating when you're incredibly hungry, like cold soda on a hot day. I feel her little stomach heaving against mine, her tongue, the arc of her back, her feet pressing against my legs.

A little voice asks, *What about Donna?* But after a while, it shuts up.

She didn't care anyway.

DONNA

HAS THIS EVER HAPPENED TO YOU? You wander for years with a great guy right under your nose, and then when you realize you're nuts about him, there's a gun battle and you're driven apart by bloodthirsty enemies?

Are you with me, ladies?

Yeah.

After what seems like forever, which was probably an hour or so, we stop for a rest.

I make a *compartment* for what happened—the screaming and running and crying—and put it all in *there*. Now for what matters. Jefferson.

Useless thoughts infiltrate and set up shop. If I had woken him up last night and told him what I was feeling, maybe he would have been with me when the attack came, maybe he would have stuck closer, and we wouldn't have been separated, and I wouldn't have lost him.

I push the thought away, but you can't, really, can you? I mean, that's just a metaphor, just another *like*. Thoughts aren't really like people coming to bother you, and minds don't have doors that you can close on them. Thoughts are more like water, or wind, or the smell of something burning; they find a crack to get through.

Jefferson, I was right. It was a bad idea to try to fix the world. And now you're somewhere out there in the dark, alone.

But I'll come find you and protect you.

We're huddling in the middle of the tracks, which would be, like, dangerous if there were trains. Now it's as safe as it gets. Miraculously, I have the rest of my peeps with me. As for the Moles, the ones who weren't caught or killed have disappeared into the dark, which probably says a lot about our chances.

We've prodded our way forward a couple of times only to find the way blocked by the Uptowners, like they were waiting for us, driving us toward something. Like we're surrounded.

Me: "Anybody know where we are?"

Everybody shakes their head except for Brainbox, who says, "We're on the E line below Fifty-Third, two hundred yards west of Fifth Avenue."

Me: "Is that a rough approximation?"

Brainbox: "No."

Peter: "Not to sound, like, *concerned* or anything, but what the hell are we going to do?"

SeeThrough: "Uptowners everywhere."

Me: "I noticed."

Peter: "Aren't there manholes we can get out of? Maintenance stuff?"

Brainbox: "Different system. You're thinking of electricity and steam."

Me: "Okay, so how do we get out, exactly?"

Brainbox: "There's a disused line from Fifty-Seventh and Seventh to the Sixty-Third and Lexington stop."

Me: "Everything's *disused*. The whole world is *disused*."

Disused, diseased.

Brainbox: "What I mean is that they didn't use it for passenger trains. Maybe the Uptowners don't know about it. It connects with the line they were building up Second Avenue."

Me: "How do *you* know about it?"

Brainbox: "While *you* were doing karaoke, I was learning about tunnels from the Moles."

Me: "Okay, so we find Jefferson and get out via the secret tunnel, right?"

The others sort of avoid my eyes, like, *Let's not tell her that the goldfish died.* Except they can't just go to the pet store and buy a new Jefferson while I'm away at school.

Me: "What?"

Peter: "I'm willing to do that, honey. You know I am. Just…how do we know he made it?"

Brainbox: "He's probably dead."

Me: "Jesus, Brainbox! What's wrong with you? Jefferson wouldn't count *you* out like that!"

Brainbox: "I didn't say I was *happy* about it. Just that he was probably dead."

Brainbox is right, of course. In principle. He continues, "Besides which, even if he's alive, don't you think he'd be in a better position to know what to do for himself? He might be up and out of the tunnels by now."

SeeThrough: "I'll go with you." She looks at the others. She pushes Brainbox. "Idiot! Donna *likes* Jeff. If you were out here alone, you'd want me to come get you."

Brainbox: "I do want to get him. I was just pointing out that he's probably—"

Me: "Okay, okay. I get it."

Brainbox: "Which makes it not the best decision."

Me: "Yeah, but I'm the boss now. So what I say goes."

Peter: "Uh, Donna? I'm down with this, but who made you boss?"

Me: "I did. Unless somebody else wants to take responsibility."

Nobody else does.

We eat a quick meal, some packets of tuna, some canned beans, which, fortunately enough, have lids you can open just with your hands. Beats cutting your way in with a knife, though the sound of the aluminum top tearing free still seems to ring through the tunnels like a violin note.

We creep back the way we came, figuring maybe the Uptowners have given up and Jefferson might be hiding back there.

We come to a fork in the tunnel that we hadn't seen when we were hauling ass away from the Moles' place. We take one and stumble farther through the darkness.

This isn't "the dark" of your room at night. That was in a world of windows and streetlamps and office buildings lit up at night, and the LEDs of clocks and the standby lights of speakers and TVs. Little voices of electromagnetic radiation speaking to your eyes even when they were closed. And it's not vacation darkness, in the twittering of the stars and the pale glossy moon. This is earth darkness. Thousands of tons of dirt between you and the sun, lightbulbs dead, the air swallowing up life. If it weren't for the others being here, I would be full-on *Paranormal Activity* freaking out up in this bitch.

I think of Jefferson alone out there, and my heart hurts.

And that's why I fire on the shapes in the distance.

Because I think Jefferson's alone. After about a half hour of stumbling around, we hear the sneezy sound of a handgun going off. We track the sound around some bends and up onto a platform.

When we make something out, we hit the dirt, or the metal, as I do, bruising my hip. Alerted, two shapes kind of straighten up like prairie dogs, and I line one of them up in my sights as best I can.

I figure the Moles would be smart enough to stick to the walls. I figure it can't be Jefferson.

So it's good that I miss, because after some pointless shots back and forth, which serve to scare the crap out of all of us, I hear a familiar voice.

Jefferson: "Donna?"

Me: "Jefferson! Are you okay?"

Jefferson: "I'll be fine if you stop shooting at me."

Me: "Who's that with you?"

Jefferson: "Long story. I'm getting up, okay? Don't kill me."

And it is Jefferson. Of course, I mean, maybe in some story it would be, like, a shape-shifter who copied his body or whatever, but obviously it's him, and the relief floods over me.

I get up. Cross the distance between us and hug him to me hard, and I notice just a teensy little bit of reserve, just a few pounds per square inch less pressure than I'm giving him, and then I tell myself not to be so insecure and persnickety.

Over his shoulder, I see some blond chick.

I don't say *Who the hell is this?* but I sure *think* it pretty loud.

Jefferson: "This is Kath. Kath, this is my friend Donna."

Blond Chick: "Hey."

Me: "Hey."

I put just the right degree of coolness into "hey" so that she's on notice.

Pause.

Me: "So, Kath, what brings you to the subway tunnels?"

Jefferson: "She says the Uptowners are after us."

Peter: "We know *that*."

Blond Chick: "They're waiting for you. All the tunnels across the East River, all the ways downtown."

Shit.

Brainbox: "What about the line at Sixty-Third?"

Me: "Shut up, will you?"

Jefferson: "We can trust her."

Me: "Okay, uh, why?"

Jefferson gives her, like, a significant look.

Jefferson: "Tell them."

Blond Chick: "I'll lead you out of here. If you take me with you."

Peter: "Oh? Where do you think we're going?"

Blond Chick: "I don't care. Away from here."

Me: "And what if we say no?"

She shrugs. "Then we're *all* dead."

Jefferson: "We've already said yes. *I've* already said yes. We need help to get out of here."

Me: "So what's your angle? You some kind of, like, political refugee or something?" I look Kath up and down. Golden hair, bee-stung lips, nice boobs.

Big trouble for little Donna.

Tits McGee: "I have good reasons to leave Uptown."

Me: "Like what?"

She loses her poise for a nanosecond. Then: "Do you know anything about what happens up here?"

Yeah. The Twins told us plenty.

Me: "Fine. Fine, Generalissimo." I try to look through Jefferson's eyes into his brainpan.

I can't tell what's going on. Is he being smart, or is he rescuing princesses?

Me: "But I'll take her gun." I walk right up to her and hold my hand out. She doesn't go for it, which leaves us in a bit of a macho standoff.

Tits McGee: "You're smoking crack."

Me: "*You're* smoking crack." Not, like, dazzling repartee or whatever, but the chick has spoiled my composure.

SeeThrough: "Stop smoking crack!"

Jefferson: "Give it to her, Kath."

She shoots him a look. Then shrugs and hands me her gun.

I slip it into my waistband against the small of my back. Which is kind of a cool-looking move, except that the cold metal on my butt gives me the shivers, and I'm worried about shooting myself in the ass accidentally. I try to carry it off as best I can.

McGee: "Fine. Let's get out of here."

Brainbox: "The Sixty-Third Street—"

She straight-up shuts Brainbox down. "Forget it. We—*they* found the spare tunnel ages ago. Our only chance is Fifty-Ninth and Fifth."

Me: "Our only chance? What's so special about Fifty-Ninth and Fifth?"

McGee: "What's so special is that I'm supposed to be guarding it."

So, perfect. We're trapped like rats, and our only hope is Little Miss Benedict Arnold.

Her bright idea is to pop up at Fifty-Ninth and Fifth and make our way into Central Park. *The* park. Which the Uptowners don't control. Which makes sense, because it's full of wild animals.

I guess it beats being massacred in the subway. But not by much.

There isn't time to hold out for the perfect plan. We're running out of darkness above, according to the Hello Kitty Limited Edition Military Chronometer. Without the cover of the nighttime, they could have us dead to rights aboveground, and we can't afford to wait the day out down here. Too many people on our tails, too much risk.

So, Tits McGee leads us uptown, explaining on the way that she was some kind of high-ranking ho-bag or something, which is why she was trusted with a gun. She and some dude were assigned to a subway exit. She's going to lull this guard into a false sense of security or whatever. At which point, we knock him out. Then we leg it into the park.

Which sounds awesome, except for one thing? It's really hard to just *knock somebody out*. I know in movies and stuff, you just bop somebody on the head and they collapse into a heap, and then later they wake up with a mild headache.

In fact, the line between knocking someone out and smashing their head open like a melon, scattering their brains everywhere, is pretty thin. Even if you *do* pull it off and conk somebody on the head just so, odds are that the conkee is going to suffer from intracranial bleeding and concussion, and maybe slip into a coma. Which, I know they're after us and everything, but still. It's hard to stop being Dr. Donna, Medicine Woman.

I argue that we should take the guy hostage and do the old tie-'em-up-and-gag-'em routine, only this time we make sure they can't get out as easily as Cheekbones did. There's some controversy about this, but I say I'll handle the prisoner taking.

We head east for a few hundred yards, then turn north. Up a couple of narrow stairways—Brainbox says we're skipping from the E to the F lines even though the tracks didn't used to connect. At one point we hear voices from above, and we hunker down and try not to soil ourselves. Then the voices fade.

I make sure I'm behind McGee, so I can put a bullet in her brain if she screws us over. Just sayin'.

Before long, we approach a platform. It's not as crapped-on as your usual subway stop. The white tiles are still shiny, and the Roman mosaic thing saying TO 59TH STREET in little stone pixels is clean. McGee says the guard is up on street level.

There are three exits farther up, on Sixtieth, but they're across the street from the park. The closest way out, a big stairway that forks into two smaller ones, is up against the park border; if we get up to the street, it's just a quick jump over the wall and we're in the cover of the trees.

Kath says she'll go up one branch of the stairway and distract the guard. I'm supposed to sneak up the other side, rock up behind him, and take him prisoner. *Very* eighties TV.

This is all established in hissed whispers as we skulk underneath the platform. McGee nods at me, and I give Peter a silent high five, and SeeThrough and I totally mangle another high five, and Jefferson looks into my eyes.

Jefferson: "We'll be ready if anything goes wrong." He's loading the mag of his AR with ammo we got at the Bazaar.

Me: "Nothing's gonna go wrong. Right?"

Jefferson: "Right. Be careful."

Then he looks at Kath and says, "You, too."

Humph.

We all make our way onto the platform and shuffle over to the exit.

It's still dark outside, but even so, you can feel a difference in the pressure of the blackness. A breeze is blowing down the stairs, bringing a fresh smell. The green of the park.

Without warning, she starts up the stairs.

I hear, "Where have you been, yo?" A dude's voice.

McGee: "I went down in the tunnels and got lost."

Dude: "Who told you to go down there?"

McGee: "Evan."

Dude: "Oh." Like, no argument.

"So..." the dude goes, "are you available later?"

And I think, *That's a weird thing to say. Not Are you around?* but *Are you available?*

McGee: "What about now?"

Dude: "Dude, don't tempt me."

Over the edge of the balustrade I can see a husky guy in camo with an AK slung over his shoulder, his hand on the trigger.

The other hand, I'm guessing, is on McGee's ass, because she's kind of rubbing up against him, and I can see her face over his shoulder.

I could swear she's rolling her eyes for me, like I'm in on some sort of joke.

I raise the carbine to my shoulder and say—just in kind of a regular *Hey, there!* voice, not a shouty *Freeze, scumbag!* kind of voice—

"Get your finger off the trigger."

Said dude stops groping McGee and turns around. He's actually blushing. His hand flutters away from the gun, and he squinches his eyebrows together as he tries to figure out what's up.

"Get behind me," he says to McGee. She giggles; he doesn't get it.

Me: "Okay. You're coming with us. Down the stairs."

Dude: "What?" He still doesn't get that he's been played.

This is taking too long. So I decide to get all street, or, as Peter likes to call it, *Git all rue.*

Me: "Did I stutter, bitch? Get down the fucking stairs."

He's still processing. But his tone changes to pissed off.

Dude: "Who do you belong to?"

I don't know where it comes from, but McGee has a knife in her hand, and suddenly she's stabbing him over and over, his camo shirt is getting dark and bloody, and he's falling to his knees, and still she stabs him again and again. Finally she leaves him.

McGee: "Let's go! He's dead! Let's go!"

But he isn't dead; he's whining, "Wait! Wait!" But it's already too late for him, I think. I run up; he's not thinking of anything now but living and dying, and he actually slips the gun off his shoulder like he's trying to help me help him—

And Kath takes it from him and kicks him to the ground and out of my hands. His blood is on me and on the street, shining like rubies.

The others, confused and blinking, emerge from the station.

Jefferson: "What happened?"

McGee: "Let's *go*!" She sprints to the dirty gray wall of the park. She throws one leg over and then another, and she's in.

People in the building across the way—it's a hotel called the Pierre, according to the awning—are starting to take notice of what's going on. I see gloomy faces in the windows; someone opens up the glass and swears.

Me: "No problem! Sorry! I'll get him home!" Figuring that they might think that the guy bleeding out on the ground is wasted or something. It seems to work, and Peter, SeeThrough, Brainbox, and I jump the wall into the park—what's the word?—unmolested.

Jefferson is standing over the dying boy.

Me: "Jefferson—*now*!" He turns away from the boy and runs up to the wall. He throws me his AR and lifts himself over. He looks at me for an explanation.

Me: "Later." I hand the gun back to him, and we take off after the others.

JEFFERSON

WE TRAMPLE THROUGH rows of dead plantings under the trees and come upon a chain-link fence. We seem to be in a disused farming plot. Everybody is strung along the fence looking for a way out, and eventually Brainbox finds a meshed-in door of tubular steel unlocked.

There are tall trees all around us, their branches interweaving overhead and obscuring the towers that loom over our backs. Expensive real estate, and good vantage points for firing on us.

When I was a kid, I used to relish the moment when the natural eclipsed the man-made; just a little ways in, and you could tell yourself there wasn't a city around you at all. And if you angled your head just so, squinted so that the buildings might be mountains, it worked. In the predawn, with the cars all dead, the effect is complete; nothing but birdsong and the thudding of our feet as we race among the trunks. Wash and I used to burst into the park; the linear constraints of the trafficked streets broken, the peril of crossing the road slipped, we loosed ourselves from

Mom's and Dad's hands and ran jubilant and shouting into the fake wild.

We burst into a footpath and, beyond that, a road through the park running north. There we pause at the verge and look for any sign of the Uptowners. But Kath walks out of cover and stands there totally exposed.

"Nobody's here, I'm telling you," she says, and walks into cover across the street. There's a bounce in her stride, like she owns the place.

So we start across the road. It winds away lazily to the north and south. A mourning dove coos. All seems well.

My foot sends something skittering. I look down and see, in the purple light, a little bone with some ragged flesh still on it.

We come to a pond with a blocky stone bridge across it. I'm trying to piece together a map in my head, but this part of the park doesn't register. Somewhere near here was a skating rink, I know that much, and east of that, close to the park walls on Fifth Avenue, the zoo and the planetarium.

A splash on the opposite bank makes us raise our guns. Something has slipped into the water; ripples roll lazily toward us.

There's another splash, then another, and we see a row of dapper little birds conferring and diving.

The penguins seem untroubled by our presence, and utterly at home.

In the zoo there was a miniature rain forest, kept artificially humid, circled by a spiraling helix-shaped walkway. You could see parrots, snakes, and caimans, with cartoonish teeth and narrow snouts, as your skin wept, shocked by the change in temperature. Then you'd reemerge into the cool of the real world.

Nearby there were polar bears making endless cycles of their enclosure, banging up against the chunky glass with their massive paws, which is why we're alert as we follow the curve of the pond northward. It's hard to figure how they would have survived, but the post-apocalyptic urban myth holds that they're thriving, poaching the occasional human from beyond the walls. A softhearted keeper released them during What Happened, people say. Maybe he was worried that they would starve to death, or maybe it was just a symbolic gesture in tune with the catastrophe—*let nature out to do what she will.*

People say they killed the keeper and ate his soft heart.

We can make out to our right the low shapes of the zoo under the burly, boxy apartment buildings in the distance. I have a sudden desire to walk under the Delacorte Clock and watch the bronze animal statues as they circle. An elephant with a concertina, a hippo with a violin, a kangaroo and joey playing curving horns. Chimes clanging a jaunty tune in cold, skeletal rhythm.

Animals on their hind legs playing instruments. Where did the desire to make them act like us come from? We weren't satisfied with having shoved them aside, enslaved them, exterminated them, so we had to make them, in our minds, imitate us, like an empire forcing its ways on conquered nations?

Past the zoo, the tension eases a little. I catch up with Donna.

"She killed the dude," she says, her voice low. "Straight up shanked him to death."

"Why?" I ask.

"Why? Ask her. You guys are, like, tight, right?"

I can feel my face flushing, and I hope she can't see it in the dim light. A waning moon is finishing its circuit, about to make way for the sun.

"What do you mean?" I ask.

"Whatever, dude," she says. And she looks away, composing her face. "I—whatever."

Is she jealous? Why should she be jealous? She doesn't want me anyway.

"Just watch yourself, Jeff," she says. "She's a live one."

We pass by the skating rink, a square about the length of a football field on each side. We used to come here. The rink was wider than the one in Rockefeller Center, and Dad, who was kind of Japanese about these things, preferred the setting of the trees to art deco architecture and golden statues. Wash would glide—first gracefully, when he was picking up skating with his customary ease, then fast as lightning during his brief and expensive hockey phase. I would stutter around like a badly worked puppet as people steered clear of me.

Now the melted ice is a black, stinking pool crusted with green algae.

There's something malevolent about a lake with squared-off banks. The water pointed and resentful. We hear the splash of more penguins, but I can't see them.

"This was a fish farm?" says SeeThrough, who has fallen in step with me.

She isn't joking.

"Of course not," I say. "You never came here? Your parents didn't bring you?"

She laughs, like it's ridiculous. "No! My parents were too busy."

"Too busy? Like, they worked every day?"

"Yes, every day," she says, as if I'm stupid. "They had to pay for food, school, everything."

"I thought school was free for you. Because of your dad."

She laughs again. "Nothing is free!" she says, smiling. "You rich kids never understand that."

I never thought of myself as rich. I guess everything's relative. I have a flash of SeeThrough, learning to live in a new language, working hard every day, ignored.

"I'm sorry," I say.

"Sorry about what?"

"Sorry I haven't gotten to know you better."

"No worries," she says. She holds out her uninjured arm. I shake her hand.

Past the water, the land gently rises. I feel an ache in my calves as we climb toward an octagonal building at the top of the slope.

It turns out to be the old *Catcher in the Rye* carousel, obscured under a housing of red-and-white-striped brick and a green cast-iron roof. The barred iron gates are shut and secured with chunky padlocks. We fan around the building, looking at the horses frozen in tense, lacquered agony.

Across the way, through a tangle of wood, past smutted silver mirrors, I see Kath staring through the bars. She winks at me, her mouth twisting into an odd smile.

I turn away and look to see if anyone's following us. In the distance, I can make out a cloudy form hazing the undergrowth. Time to go.

Past Sheep Meadow, a grassy green hangout now rioting with long weeds, we come to Bethesda Terrace, grand stone steps leading to a swampy fountain with a stone angel in the middle. We hurry down a path to the east side and slip between the boat house and lake on the left and a pond on our right.

I flash to a day in preschool: I am climbing the *Alice in Wonderland* statue, my palms practically sizzling on the summertime bronze giant mushroom. Miraculously, someone starts giving away ice-cream sandwich samples. This windfall blows right through Mom's treat embargo. Wash and I even get seconds. After working the soily chocolate from our fingers with our teeth, we hop down to the pond. There's an informal regatta of model sailboats. Some are blocky and inert, some elegant and complex. A big man with a beard lets us steer one with his radio control box, and we wildly gyrate the toggles, sending the magnificent craft crashing into the side. He laughs and says no harm done. When we get home, Mom finds a book called *Stuart Little* and reads out loud about a clever little mouse who sails on that very pond and cuts his way out of a paper bag with his pocketknife.

I ask for a pocketknife for my birthday, and Mom says no. I start wailing, and Washington says I'm too small for a pocket-knife, and I say if Stuart Little isn't too small and he's a mouse, then I'm not too small.

Past the pond, the ground shifts up again. We are heading into a narrow channel of rock when I see something crouching at the edge, a sleek assembly of tensed muscle.

"Stop!" I hiss.

"What is it?" says Peter.

"It's a fricking panther or something! On the rock right there!"

Donna squints and then sees it. "Jesus," she says, and looks angrily at Kath, like this is all her fault.

Dawn is seeping into the sky. "We've got to move," I say.

Donna raises her carbine to her shoulder, stills her breathing, and fires at the big cat.

There's a resounding *clang*. The cat doesn't so much as move.

I laugh and start walking toward it.

"Wait!" says Donna, but I'm not afraid.

I walk into the channel in the rock and, reaching up, tap the bronze panther sculpture with the butt of my gun. It rings a low note.

"Let's go," I call to the others.

I lead them under a bridge and around the side of a hill to where a massive sandstone building juts into the park. A sloping wall of sectioned dark blue glass faces us.

"This way," I say.

DONNA

WE'RE AT THE PARK SIDE of Jefferson's happy place, the Metropolitan Museum.

We kick our way through the window. It would be much cooler to shoot it out, but it just doesn't work that way with fancy glass. I've tried. You end up wasting a bullet, putting a tiny hole in it.

So Jefferson and I kick and club the window, and it shatters into little fragments like crystals clinging onto a sheer film, like a curving skin of scales, and we peel it away.

The room is cavernous under the slanted windows. Thin wooden totem-pole things tower into the air. There are masks and figures, roughly carved and forbidding, in glass cases dotting the floor. In the middle of the room, under a sort of roof of wooden panels strung from the ceiling, there's a long, narrow dugout canoe. Hanging from the walls are these massive wooden sculptures—distorted, angry bodies, twisted animal forms.

Jefferson: "Come on. We can rest here until night comes again. I know a place."

Jefferson leads us through the galleries without pausing. These are his stomping grounds, all right. It looks like he knows exactly where he's going. It's weird to see him so sure of himself when usually he's, like, convulsed with self-doubt. Like, *Would the doorway to the right be insulted if I took the doorway to the left?*

We pass through a big-ass room full of Roman stuff, busts of chicks with totally random hairdos and dudes with no noses. Another room of ancient-y things. Creamy marbles, big black clay soup tureens decorated with people running in circles. Some of the smaller cases have been smashed open and looted. We slip through a darkened gallery and into the entrance hall of the museum, which is, like, two stories tall, with balconies running around it.

We hear a bellowing sound, like the groaning of a tree before it snaps. We freeze in place. Standing there, my body slips back a hundred thousand years—squirts of fear tell me that I'm being hunted.

The roaring gets louder. At the end of the gallery, I see a mass of filthy cream yellow, smeared with dirt and blood.

I stumble backward, terrified, and lift my carbine. As I fire, there's a clatter of reports from the guns of the others.

It lumbers toward us, nudging aside big statues like they're store mannequins. They smash and scatter on the floor. Bullets ping off the marble, chips flying into the air. Somehow, whether it's the wildness of our shots or the animal courage of the bear, we're not stopping him. As he crowds forward, we turn and run.

Jefferson takes the lead again, and we cut to the side of the stairs and find ourselves in a dark room full of medieval stuff. There's a big stone gazebo sort of thing in the center, jeweled chests, a statue of a lady holding a baby (Jesus, I guess—who else is it gonna be?). There are stained-glass windows set into the wall, but no light is coming through, so they're muddy and dark.

The next room is even bigger, with windows high up letting in sunlight. There are statues and plaques all over the place, but most importantly, a tall ornamental metal fence running across the back of the room with a hinged gate. We go through and shut the gate, and then we shift a stone statue off its stand and slide it in front to keep it shut.

The polar bear lopes into sight at the far end of the gallery. Jefferson and Kath open fire, and the echoes batter my ears. I pull the trigger on my carbine until the flat click of the receiver tells me it's empty.

The bear disappears under some arches to the side of the gallery, and we can't see it anymore. My head is buzzing, but I can still hear hoarse breathing, like something huge is dying. The shell casings dance along the ground, tinkling, and then nothing.

"I'm out," says Jefferson, pulling the mag from his gun.

"Same," says McGee.

Then—faster than I thought possible—the bear gallops into view and slams into the fence, twisting and snapping the metal bars. Its face leers down at us, yellow teeth as long as fingers running with spit and blood.

Peter fires his Glock, and the bullets ping and crack the bars and take the creature's ear off. It howls and reaches through the bars. Jefferson has his sword out and slashes at it, but the bear actually yanks it away, and it clatters to the ground on the other side of the fence.

Jefferson: "This way!" He pushes me out the doorway.

He leads us through rooms with fabric walls, elegant wooden furniture, portraits of lords and ladies in petticoats and waistcoats. We can hear roaring and the groaning of metal behind us.

And finally we come to a long hall, bright and airy, and there are gorgeous banners hanging from the ceiling. And in the middle of the hall there are armored knights on horseback, frozen in midstride, lances in hand.

Jefferson takes his gun, casting his eyes around, then walks up to a glass case and smashes it open. He takes a round metal shield out and fits it onto his arm. Next to it is a sword, which he yanks from its housing. SeeThrough follows him and grabs a long dagger with her free hand.

So we set to looting, arming up for the bear. Peter finds a sword that reaches up to his sternum. Brainbox takes a nasty-looking spear from the wall, and Kath gets an even nastier one with a sort of meat hook on the end. Me, I opt for a battle-ax.

Which is what my father used to call my mother. So, shout-out to Mom.

The bear lumbers around the corner, then rears up on its hind legs, massive square paws cocked toward its body. Its head is a good ten feet up, beady eyes gleaming down.

Brainbox charges with his big iron spear and nails the thing in the shoulder. The bear twists around and swipes at the spear, which splinters right in the middle. Brainbox totters and falls, and the bear lunges for him, black lips drawing back from the wicked teeth, but SeeThrough jumps on him first, sinking her dagger into its humped back.

Howling, the bear violently twists to the side and bites into SeeThrough's injured arm. He swings her this way and that, making her look as light as a doll, and then throws her through the air. She smashes through glass and into the back wall of a case of arms.

Peter raises his big-ass sword just as the bear's front paws land on the ground again, and before he can connect, it has turned and slammed into him, and he's down on the ground, yelling. McGee stabs at the bear as it tries to bite Peter, and I run up and bring my ax down on its shoulder. I feel the blade slice through flesh and bone.

Blood goes everywhere. The bear sort of hollers, and I back up as it lurches toward me. I slip on some blood before I can get away. Up goes its paw, I see the yellow claws flexing out—

And then Jefferson takes the swipe on his shield. He's thrown back into a glass case, crashing through it into the wall.

The bear pursues him and smashes again into the shield. Jefferson punches upward with his sword, and the point goes deep into the bear's neck.

But the damn thing won't die. It clamps its teeth onto the edge of the shield and actually bends it, and I hear Jeff screaming as his arm, stuck in the clasps of the shield, starts to come out of its socket.

Then Peter brings his sword down on the thing's neck.

And all I can say is somebody loved his job in the arms and armor department, because damn, the blade is sharp. The head comes clean off, still stuck on Jeff's shield, the massive body of the bear falling to the side with a *thump*.

Peter throws his sword to the floor and helps up Jeff from the case. They stand there leaning against each other, too tired to speak, as I fall to my knees, gasping.

Quiet. We all lie there for a moment just listening to the *hiss* of the bear's blood pooling on the floor.

Then we turn to SeeThrough.

Her breath is shallow. Her eyes are rolling up into her head. I take her wrist, and her pulse is high and irregular, like someone running panicked through a dark house.

I pull SeeThrough's shirt up to the sternum. There's a jagged, angry wound near the bottom of her rib cage. A puncture from a shard of plate glass. It hisses and blood bubbles around it every time she takes a breath.

Brainbox looks up at me. "Do something. Save her."

"I need a plastic bag."

Peter throws his pack to the ground and pulls a white plastic shopping bag out. He empties a pile of energy bars from it and hands me the bag. I cut a square of filmy plastic out of it.

I tear some strips of silver tape off a roll from my bag and carefully edge the square of plastic with them, leaving one side untaped.

With Brainbox's help, I roll SeeThrough onto her back and then flatten the plastic over the wound.

The plastic rises and falls with SeeThrough's ragged breath, first inflating and then stopping up the hole. The hissing sound goes away.

She's not going to make it. The sucking chest wound has been stopped up—the lung may even be inflated—but she's all broken inside, I can tell. Thank God she's not conscious. She moans and grabs at air, and her chest rises like she's trying to float out of here.

Me: "Take her hand, Brainbox. Try to calm her down." Then I look in his eyes. He sees that she's not going to live.

Suddenly she starts breathing fast, like she's running a race. Then, a kind of sigh.

Then, as lightly as a bird flying from a branch, she stops breathing.

We take SeeThrough's body through colored galleries, up wide stairways of shiny marble, along high balconies. Jefferson leads us to a corridor full of brush paintings and calligraphy, through a round doorway into a courtyard that looks like it's part of an oldy-worldy Chinese mansion. The paned glass has cracked above, so little birds have built nests in the tiled roof. You can make out little bright pieces of plastic in the nests, but it doesn't look like litter; it looks sweet and cheerful.

We wash her face and hands with some water from a stagnant pool, and set her down on a low step under a pointy green roof.

I kiss her on the forehead and tell her good-bye. Peter takes her hands and folds them over her stomach. He closes his eyes and prays to himself. Brainbox kneels down and leans his head against hers.

Jefferson kneels with his feet folded under him. It's a neat trick; like, no way could my legs take it. It looks like it's genetic or something. We all try to do it, too, but end up Indian-style.

He chants. It's Japanese, I think, kind of monotonous and in the back of his throat. I guess it's the equivalent of that part in movies where somebody says, "We should say something," and then some dude will come up with something that is all Simple Yet Beautiful. This doesn't sound simple, it sounds really complicated, and it makes me wonder if Jefferson went to Buddhist school the way some kids used to go to Hebrew school.

It's weird, because he's Jeff and he's not, like, somebody else is here, or part of him is somewhere else. Wherever it is, it looks less hectic than here. I feel like there's all sorts of things about him I didn't know—and then I realize that I don't remember him doing this for Wash or anybody else, and I start to figure that he's kind of still catching up on death. I don't know, maybe he's even throwing the Mole People in there, too. Sort of a mental mass grave.

Meanwhile, everybody tries to act appropriate, and we end up just sort of holding our hands in our laps and looking around. I expect McGee to be checking her nails or something, but instead she's staring at Jefferson like she's trying to count up his pores, and despite the fact that this is SeeThrough's funeral, I kind of want to punch her in the face.

After a while, Jefferson stops chanting, claps his hands three times, and gets up. "Come on," he says. We leave SeeThrough in peace. Everybody except for Brainbox. He holds her hand and stays for a long time after.

JEFFERSON

SO I GOT her killed after all.

I know there are all sorts of excuses, like she decided to come, we couldn't keep her from it. But the fact is that if I hadn't started this, SeeThrough would be safe at home in the Square.

It's not Brainbox's fault. When he sees something broken, he wants to fix it. He'd probably rewire a defused bomb if the challenge was interesting enough. Seeing him like this, pretty much unhinged by the loss of his what—his girlfriend?—I realize that he had no idea of the consequences.

And yeah, we're all going to die anyway, so why not? But that was always the case, even Before. Who could say they were going to live forever before It Happened? People just tried to keep their heads down and find something worthwhile to do, or tried, I don't know, to stay *entertained* or something, and not to think about the end.

So I decide to call a meeting to figure out what to do.

"What are we talking about?" says Kath. I haven't had time to explain everything to her.

"Whether we're going to save the world or not," says Peter.

"Oh," says Kath. "Okay, count me in."

Donna sort of snorts. "Who *asked* you? You're just some bitch from Uptown who got my friend killed."

"I saved your *life*," says Kath. "All of you."

"Was that the part," says Donna, "where you shanked some poor dude while his back was turned?"

"He was reaching for his gun."

Donna snorts. "With what, his *boner*?"

Then Brainbox says, "If she's willing to take the same risks as us, she should come with us." This puts an end to the argument since, somehow, Brainbox has become the custodian of SeeThrough's legacy.

"We can use all the help we can get," I say. "Anyway, that's not what I wanted to talk about. The question is, does everybody else want to keep going?"

I look at Brainbox first. He nods. Peter looks over at Donna.

"Jesus Christ," she says. "Why do you keep asking us all the time?"

"Because it's *your* life," I say.

Donna snorts again.

"Have you got a cold or something?" I ask. With maybe a little more animosity than I meant.

"Jefferson, I said I'd go" is all she says. "Stop...questioning my resolve or whatever."

Peter says, "Have you ever played poker?"

I'm confused. "No?"

"Well," he says, "there's a point? A few cards into a hand? Where you've bet so much that it feels like it'd be crazy to fold up your hand and lose it all. It's called being 'pot committed.'"

"So?" I ask.

"So...I figure we're pot committed. I mean, SeeThrough... Ratso...all the people who died...I can't just turn tail and go home."

Yeah. That's kind of it. "Only way out is through," I say.

Then Brainbox says, "Statistically, it shouldn't matter how much you've already bet." He looks up at us for the first time. "If you've got a bad hand and keep betting, you're just going to lose more."

There's an unspoken understanding that we're not going to move today. Our bodies and our minds are empty.

We parcel out SeeThrough's food and eat. I can't say that "she would want us to do it." What does that mean anyway? If she's up in heaven, she's got other things on her mind. But this is the way it has to be.

It's the notebook that gets me. We're going through her pack for anything useful, and some stationery with a cute little bug-eyed animal on the cover drops out. When I pick it up, the pages fall open, and I see, before I can stop myself seeing, the words *friends* and, surrounded by stars and hearts, *boyfriend*. In loop-ing girl script, hearts above the *i*'s and everything.

I pick the notebook up and hand it to Donna. She takes it and turns away, starting to cry.

I take the others to the furniture galleries, and we hunt down a place to sleep. Everybody flops down, exhausted, but I don't feel like resting.

Instead, I go find my *wakizashi*. Then I take a long walk through the museum, looking for old friends.

A lot of the smaller paintings are missing, along with pretty much anything made of gold. But the death of Socrates is still happening, Brueghel's peasants are still lying down in the fields. The sun still shines on Vermeer's girl with the water pitcher.

I think how easy it would be to steal. Just take a knife to the edges and roll it up. Tack it over my bed like a poster when I get home. If I get home.

Then I wonder what for. I know I'm supposed to think, *This is the precious legacy of mankind* or something. *Somebody* is supposed to think that. But right now nothing really seems to matter, least of all art. And I wonder why I am the way I am, what's wrong with me, why did I ever care about these things instead of Jay Z or getting high?

We're nothing but animals.

But I know I cared about SeeThrough. I care about what Brainbox is going through. I loved my brother.

I loved Donna, I thought. Maybe I still do. But I don't understand. How could what happened with Kath happen if I really do love Donna?

Uh, maybe because Kath gave it up.

All those things I'd spent so much time wanting and wondering about were just right *there*, like a bowl of candies on Halloween. Everything that was fraught and difficult and challenging with Donna. It was so easy.

Or maybe *Kath* was so easy.

As for me, well, I'm a boy. I was born easy.

Maybe it was a onetime thing.

Maybe Kath is really into me.

Maybe I should make sure we preserve this place, so people remember what humans could do.

Maybe I should burn it down and see if anybody cares.

I'm in a dark interior gallery, looking at a still life of a skull, when I hear footsteps nearby.

"Who is it?" I call out. Nothing.

Then, just where I thought the sound wasn't coming from, Kath emerges from the darkness.

"Thank you," she says. "For standing up for me."

"It's okay," I say.

"I was lonely," she says. Then, looking down, "No one back there likes me."

"That's just...they're just...not used to you," I say. She actually doesn't look very sad, or lonely.

"Do *you* like me?" she says, reaching up and tugging on her hair.

"Of course I do," I say.

"Prove it," she says.

"What do you want me to do?" I say, and she laughs. She lays her bag down on the floor.

She pulls her shirt over her head.

I clamp my hand over my headlamp. It doesn't seem right to leave her exposed in the glare.

I can't think of anything cool to say. Instead, I say, "Kath, I feel like I should think about stuff—"

"I feel like you shouldn't," she says, and kisses me. She's pressing up against me. My heart is exploding.

"Oh, *thank you* for standing up for me," she says, smiling.

I drop my things.

The floor is not so hard, really. Not exactly a bed, but, you know, everything's relative. Kath is soft and warm.

"This reminds me of *From the Mixed-up Files of Mrs. Basil E. Frankweiler*," I say, and immediately regret that I did.

"What?" says Kath.

Just say nothing, says my brain to me, but instead I say, "It's about this girl and her little brother who run away and live in the Metropolitan Museum."

"Oh," says Kath. We lie there for a while as I consider how much of an idiot I am.

"So what's the plan, boss?" she says, twirling a piece of my hair around her finger.

"The plan," I say, "is to head uptown and east to the Triborough Bridge."

"We've got to get past Uptown territory," she says. "Get out at the northeast corner of the park. Evan hates you. He and the others are gonna be after us."

"Who's Evan?" I ask.

"Evan led the expedition down to Washington Square," she says.

"The guy with the cheekbones? What's so special about him?"

"He's..." She looks away.

"He's your boyfriend?" I ask.

She laughs. Not a happy laugh.

"He's my brother."

"Your brother," I say, after a long while.

"I probably should have told you that earlier."

"Yeah, maybe." Now I can see it, of course.

"Don't feel *bad*," she says. "He won't be coming after me because he *cares* about me. He'll be after me because he thinks he *owns* me. Him and his friends."

Her body gets tight.

Him and his friends.

"Why didn't you run away?" I ask. Then I realize she *is* running away. "Sorry."

"Stop saying you're sorry. You're not, not really."

"I am."

"You're no different from anybody else."

"I am," I say.

"No, you're not," she says. "People are scum."

Now I feel my own body tensing up. I shift a little, and she rolls over onto her side, facing away from me.

"I don't know. Maybe you're not like them. Maybe you're different."

"I *am* different." *Lame.*

"Maybe," she says. Then: "That girl Donna wants to do you."

"No, she doesn't," I say.

She laughs. "Yes, she does. She's all possessive of you."

I try to work out the validity of this claim. "I haven't noticed."

"You're a boy," she says. "You're totally clueless. She wants to get rid of me, and she wants to have you."

"No. She doesn't. She could have. She didn't want to."

"Ugh, there's history?" She sits up. "All the good ones are taken. Oh, well."

And at that "oh, well," so dismissive, a stab of feeling. A shard of loss where I thought I couldn't feel any more.

She gets up, grabs her clothes in a bunch, and walks off, just like that.

"Where are you going?" I ask. But she doesn't answer.

After a while lying there, during which time I bang my head against the floor in self-judgment once or twice or three times, I get up and find my way back to the others.

I half expect that Kath will have taken off, but when I get to the Italian bedroom with the crazy plasterwork and pink bed, she's sitting on it, cleaning her feet with Handi Wipes she must have scavenged somewhere.

Donna and Peter are sort of regarding her with disdain. I figure it's because she's effectively claimed the bed for herself, so I make what seems like a reasonable suggestion: "The girls should share the bed."

Donna levels her eyes at me. "You wish."

"That's not what I meant," I say.

"I don't need the bed," Kath says, unwholeheartedly.

"Keep it, princess," says Donna. She makes a point of lying down with her head on her pack, pulling a tapestry over herself.

I lie down on the floor, too, despite the fact that I wouldn't mind a soft mattress. Something tells me it wouldn't be a good idea.

I remember lying next to Donna in the hotel and strike the thought from my mind.

In the end, it's Brainbox who sleeps next to Kath. He just walks up and lies down, and when she says, "Uh. Can I *help* you?" he says, "Yes, please face away from me."

It takes a long time to get to sleep.

DONNA

THIS IS JUST LIKE From the Mixed-up Files of Mrs. Basil E. Frankweiler, but with more killing.

And more jealousy. Really I should go looking for another place to sleep, except part of me thinks that if I leave the room, Peter will leave, too, and then Brainbox will leave, and then Jefferson will have sex with that Kath chick.

Probably he already has. Jefferson sort of wandered off acting all pensive a while ago, and then New Girl was like, "I'm going to the bathroom," and neither of them came back for a while. Then they, like, pulled the old "come back into the room at different times" gag that I've only seen about a million times at parties. Like, you try to act all casual but you can't help but check if the other person made a suitably ninja-like infiltration.

I'm super pissed off that Jefferson would sneak around like that. Then again, maybe I'm just a sore loser. Like, I had my chance. Then *again* again, I'm pretty sure this chick is a sociopath. Or, I don't know, some kind of escaped-sex-slave-nympho psycho. And I wouldn't want Jefferson to be mixed up with her even if I didn't have feelings for him.

Have feelings for him. That sounds like "have cancer."

Uuuuuugghh. Why?

See, this just proves that there is really no point getting involved with people. I mean, friends are fine. Friends don't have to be exclusive. So, like, it's not a zero-sum game.

I don't actually know what *zero-sum game* means. I just vaguely remember it from sociology as being sort of a bummer. I *do* remember what *negative bias* is, which is basically that you mind losing something more than you enjoy having it.

But can you lose something you never had?

I guess so. *That's* a bitch.

Why should I still care about him anyway? I mean, it's pretty obvious that he's got a thing for Sexy McSexerson.

Maybe I'm not sexy enough.

Maybe we should have had sex.

Maybe I'm scared.

It's less *scary* for boys. Like, if something goes wrong, it's usually the girl holding the bag. Or the baby or whatever.

Also, if you're a dude and you sleep around a lot, basically people think you're a stud. If you're a girl, you're a slut. Totally unfair.

It's weird. I always felt this mix of power and helplessness. Like, I could tell that I had some sort of hold over boys—even over men, like, much older men, because I had something they wanted. That was the power part. But then there was the bigger thing, the helplessness, which was that the whole game seemed rigged against you if you were a girl; like, people just made snap judgments about you based on how attractive you were, and the whole of society was basically urging you to be sexier, lose more weight, act like this, say that. Basically so that more people wanted to have sex with you. That was, like, the economic model of being a girl. Except the more sex you had, the *less* you were valued. How messed up is that?

Which was just the way it was Before, I guess. I suppose I should have been pretty stoked about the apocalypse. Like, for one thing, now you couldn't have babies. For another, there were no authority figures around to judge you. And there weren't any ads or magazines or movies with hot chicks in them making you feel inadequate.

Still, it was surprising how many old attitudes kind of stuck around. Even in my own head. Like—Kath? Part of me just thinks, *Total slut*. Those ideas were contagious. They made me hate myself and my own judgments.

Anyway I guess I kind of opted out of the whole game. Just—too much trouble.

Which is not to say Jefferson is your typical dude. I mean, he's almost *too* evolved. Like, maybe if he hadn't been Mr. Super-understanding Sensitive Guy, maybe he would have just grabbed me and kissed me at the library instead of making a PowerPoint presentation.

I don't know. I'm crazy.

Normally I could talk to Peter about this kind of thing, but we've been too busy being hunted down by various predators.

These are the thoughts I cycle through as I try to fall asleep. Jefferson is over there on the floor, like, ten feet away, but he might as well be in another country. What's-Her-Face is, I'm sure, sleeping it off up there in the fancy bed. Me? I'm trying to get comfortable under an ancient carpet.

I take Pooh out of the bag and hug him tight.

Around dawn, we break our way out of the park side of the museum and head north. We figure that now that the polar bear is dead, we're, like, the apex predators or whatever, so it's less tense than before. Except I keep searching my brain trying to remember if there were any other carnivores in the zoo. Pumas? Ocelots? Killer monkeys? What's next?

We come to a big-ass lake surrounded by fencing, which I guess was a reservoir. The water level is low, and the surface is carpeted with green algae. I think of filling my canteen despite the pond scum, but then I see that a bunch of bodies have collected on the edge. They're bloated and floating, and crows are hanging out on them taking occasional pecks.

The curve of the reservoir pushes us out toward Fifth Avenue. We decide it's better to risk going close to the border of Uptown than to circle around the other side and run up against who knows what. Still, it makes me think about what we're going to find once we get north of the park.

Confession? I've never been to Harlem.

Like, I know we were supposed to live in a post-racial society? What with Obama getting elected and everything. But even though I only lived about ten miles from a—I guess you would call it an *African American neighborhood*, it might as well have been an island. Like, *in theory*, everything was cool. I mean, I believe in equality, and you would *never* hear anything racist or whatever at my school. But that doesn't mean we *knew* a lot of black people. There were, like, five black kids at our school, and they tended just to hang out with each other, which I guess is what I would do under the circumstances. And kids don't really bother to reach out and Embrace Difference that much. Social life is gnarly enough without doing stuff that's actually challenging to your preconceptions.

So there's a sort of unstated unease as we get closer and closer to the north edge of the park. I find myself pulling up next to Peter. I mean, I know it's kind of lame, but he's African American, or African Apocalyptic American, or whatever, and I'm sort of hoping he'll reassure me that we won't get arrested and put on trial for slavery or something.

Me: "So…" But then I can't figure out what to say after that.

Peter looks at me and raises an eyebrow.

Peter: "Is this the part where we talk about Harlem?"

Me: "What? No. Actually, yes."

Peter: "Uh-huh. So let me guess. You want me to make you feel safer about being white?"

Me: "Yup." I mean, he's got me pegged; there's no point pretending.

Peter: "Look, girl, I don't have, like, Brother ESP or anything. The fuck am I supposed to know what people are gonna do to us?"

Me: (I'm drowning here.) "I just thought…maybe…your perspective or something…"

Peter: "Okay, here's some perspective. Probably? People are pissed off. Excuse me. *Brothers be* pissed off." He's kind of annoyed with me.

Me: "Okay, I totally get it." We keep walking for a bit. Then I ask, "Uh, why?"

Peter: "Because given the way things go, probably white kids have decided that the world ended because of something black folks did."

Me: "Oh. *I* don't think that."

Peter: "Gosh, thanks!"

Me: "The way the Moles talked about it? There's like some kind of race war going on. It's only…I'm kind of tired of getting shot at."

Peter smiles, his mood lightening a little.

Peter: "Don't worry. I'll just speak *jive* to them, and everything will be all right."

Me: "Look, I'm *sorry*. I'm just scared, that's all."

Peter: "Girl, ain't no brother want to grab your bony ass."

Me: "You know that's not what I mean. Jeez."

Peter: (Shakes his head.) "I don't know, okay? I can't speak for anybody else. You think I was, like, in the *mainstream*? A gay brother going to the homo school? For all I know, they're gonna burn me at the stake."

Me: "Yeah. Good point." I think for a while. "Well, why don't you just butch it up a little?"

Peter laughs. I think I'm back in his good graces.

And I remember that, while I'm feeling all sorry for myself because Jefferson seems more interested in Tits McGee, Peter maybe has it worse. Like, everything was cool back at the Square. There were plenty of gay kids, and nobody really cared how you acted, as long as you pulled your weight. But out here? It seemed like society or whatever was just as likely to backslide as move forward.

When all this is over and the world is saved, I've got to get him a boyfriend.

At the top of the reservoir, a channel cuts through the park where cars used to cross from east to west. As we let ourselves down, a pack of wild dogs scatter. They've been chewing on some bodies that, judging by the relative lack of smell, are pretty recently dead. There're shell casings all around them, but no guns. It looks like it was an ambush, so we're quick about getting out of the clear and into the trees on the other side again.

I can still make out the bright collars on some of the dogs, and I remember how hard we tried to redomesticate them down at the Square. The problem was, by this point the dogs were too busy living off corpses and getting hunted for meat. What bothered me most was the ones that were puppies when their masters died. I'd try to catch them so that I could cut the collars off, but they didn't trust me; they'd run just out of reach. And their breathing got more and more restricted as they got bigger, until they suffocated.

Maybe that's, like, a *metaphor* for the kids who were too accustomed to the way things were. I don't know.

We come to the northeast corner of the park. Here, in the elbow of the walls, there's row upon row of plantings that look like they've been abandoned. The stalks of the plants are yellow, and the dirt is dry.

We shimmy up to the exit. Still the same blocky limestone running all the way up Fifth. Over the edge of the walls, an abandoned public square, trashed cars, debris.

Jefferson starts across the street, trying to look casual but totally looking tense. The rest of us follow and get away from the open space as soon as we can and into the channel of street between the buildings. Street signs say we're leaving Duke Ellington Circle and heading down Tito Puente Way.

The plan is to strike east for the river. It's only a little more than a mile, the shortest path through unknown territory before we hit FDR Drive. There, if the way is clear, we can head straight up to the Triborough Bridge and over to Queens and Long Island.

After that, who knows?

It's nothing but dreary redbrick mid-rises for the first couple of blocks. Down the north-south streets, you can see rows of old-fashioned five-story walk-ups with shops on the ground floors. The little general stores they called *bodegas* in some parts of the city, all smashed up and burned out.

I think we're going to make it out easy by the time we see the first people on the street. A bunch of girls about my age just hanging out and talking on a stoop.

I almost said "a bunch of black girls," and maybe I should have said so to be clear or something, but they're just girls, really. To call them black just means that I'm thinking about them as different from me. Like, we're all going off what we imagine is "normal." To me, I'm just a girl. To them, I'd be a "white girl." Language trips you up. You can't ever say exactly what you mean, and every time you try, you actually end up saying something about yourself.

Anyhoo, it looks weirdly peaceful and natural, like something Before, and suddenly I wonder if *we're* the people to be afraid of, spattered in mud and blood and loaded up with guns and knives.

But then I notice the AK across the lap of one of the girls. There's something weird about the sheen of the metal parts, but the girl stares me down, and I have to stop looking.

We just keep walking, neither friendly nor hostile, and they don't stop us. And I figure maybe we can just make our way peacefully to FDR Drive. But when we pass them, they get up and follow. I see one of them say something into a walkie.

We walk another block, picking up company as we go along, and by the time we've gone five blocks, we're in a crowd of about a hundred kids. They seem more, like, curious than hostile. Like, *What are these fools doing here?*

Then I notice that *everybody* has a gun. Some of them AKs, some of them pistols, some of them these weird guns I've never seen before. A few of the guns look normal, but a lot of them have a glossy look, like they were made out of plastic or something.

It gets so crowded that we couldn't run even if we wanted to. I don't think we'd get ten feet. Still, nobody is making a move. They're just keeping pace.

And then I hear a sound that I haven't heard in two years. A fractured *WHOOP WHOOP*, offensive to the ears. For a moment, totally illogically, I think, *Oh! We're out of danger!*

That makes no sense, of course, and when the cop cars round the corner and pull up, it's not police who get out but some tough-looking kids, shaven-headed and cold-eyed. The crowd parts for them, and they walk up to us, machine guns at the ready.

Huge dude: "Well? What you waiting for? Assume the position, motherfuckers."

We're marched over to the cars and bent over, our legs kicked apart, and the kids from the cop cars take our bags away and start frisking us.

They take my clasp knife and my belt with all the clips and cara-biners. They handcuff all of us. Then they shove us into the patrol cars the way they used to do on TV—jamming us in with a hand on one arm, the other on the head to keep from banging it on the roof. The whole protecting your head thing is kind of a ritual, since from what I can tell, they aren't too concerned about our well-being. I fig-ure it's just a style thing, like, *We're the cops now, and we're gonna act like it*.

I'm stuck in the back with New Girl, who pushes as far away from me as possible. She has a weird look, her focus kind of floating off into space.

Me: "What's wrong with you?"

McGee: "Nothing. Getting ready."

Me: "For what?"

She refocuses on me. "Oh, it's never happened to you, has it? You're lucky, then."

Me: "What's never happened?"

McGee: "Oh my God. You're a virgin."

I think she means something really bad is about to happen to us. My heart starts floating up into my throat, choking me.

I'd been imagining a cold cell, maybe a bullet to the head or the more cost-effective knife across the throat. Not that.

I look at the back of our captors' shaved heads through the metal grille that divides the front seats from the back. We're rolling north, I think, but all of that is hazy. Instead, I'm fixated on the pink scar on the back of the driver's head where the shape of the skull juts out.

Beneath it, the skin folds a couple of times before his neck reaches his shoulders.

And I'm afraid.

And she looks at my face and laughs.

But they don't take us to a back alley or a prison or anything. They take us to a pretty red brownstone with flower beds in front.

A girl with one of those shiny guns and a gigantic dude with a suitably gigantic machine gun—a Maremont M60E3, part of my brain tells me—are smiling and talking on the stoop. They break off their conversation as the cars pull up.

We're handed out of the cars and led up the steps of the brownstone.

Birds sing. A sleek gray cat rises from its sunny spot and caresses its way past my ankles as we climb the stairs.

They deposit us in a little parlor to the left of the door, leaving us alone to find seats on the puffy old-fashioned chair and couches.

Kid with a scar: "Don't mess the place up, y'all, or there'll be hell to pay."

I can see what he means. The room is, like, immaculate. Clean rugs, old pictures on the wall—*new* pictures on the wall—somebody must have a printer and a supply of electricity. Polished wooden side tables. A grandfather clock lazily ticking off the seconds.

And a bowl full of apples.

I doubt they can be real, so I lean over to sniff them.

McGee: "What're you *doing*?"

Me: "They're *real!*"

McGee: "Who gives a crap?"

But I can see wheels turning in Jefferson's head.

Jefferson: "Let me do the talking."

Me: "Uh, how about no?"

After a couple of minutes, which I spend imagining nom-nomming those apples, a girl comes from upstairs and says, like we have an appointment or something, "He's ready for you."

The stairs are narrow and steep, and I stumble on the way because my hands are still cuffed behind my back. The guard with the scar actually hoists me back up, shrugs, and smiles.

We're led down a corridor into a back room that has a big window looking down on a garden with a tree in bloom.

Behind a desk, in front of a window, a handsome black kid sits. He's a little less than medium height—but he feels *compact*, not short. His hair is neatly buzzed, his clothes are clean and pressed—a soft black leather jacket over a crisp white shirt, khakis with sharp creases, shiny brown leather boots. I think, *He irons his clothes? He shaves with a razor?*

His eyes are beautiful, deep brown over long lashes.

He puts down a notebook with rows of numbers in it.

Him: "I can let your hands loose, right? If you try to escape, we're gonna have to kill you. I'm assuming that you are rational people, otherwise you'd probably already be dead. So…"

He nods to the guards and they undo our handcuffs. When we're settled back into some chairs, he says, "Okay, we good? I'll do you a favor and give you my name. It's Solon."

Jefferson: "The lawgiver."

Solon: (Smiles.) "That's right."

Jefferson shrugs when I look at him, and just says, "Ancient history."

Me: "You *know* him?"

Solon: (Laughs.) "No, he means real ancient history. Don't worry about it."

McGee: "Let's just get this over with."

Solon: "Get what over with?" He's confused.

McGee: "Come on."

"She thinks you're gonna *rape* her," says a plump girl I hadn't noticed before because she's been sitting in the shadows. Next to her is a skinny girl with a kind of brain-dead look.

Solon: (Frowns.) "You seem to have us mixed up with our benighted neighbors to the south."

Benighted?

McGee: "What?"

Plump Girl: "He means he'd shoot you in the head before that happened, Miss Thing."

McGee: "Whatever turns you on." I do sort of admire her attitude at that moment.

"We're not savages like you Uptowners," says Solon.

And at that moment, I don't know exactly why, I decide that I like him and trust him.

"We're not from Uptown," I say. "We're from Washington Square."

Solon looks at the plump girl, like he's asking her how possible this seems.

"I believe they ain't from Uptown. Ain't no brother in Uptown."

"Hell, no," adds the spacey-looking girl, who up to now hasn't looked like she was listening.

Solon (to Peter): "What do you say, brother? How did you end up with these folks?"

Peter looks Solon in the eye. "Brother? I don't know you. *These* people are my brothers and sisters. Well, not *that* crazy bitch." He nods toward New Girl.

Solon looks over at the plump girl again and laughs. She shrugs.

Solon: "How'd you get up here? And why?"

Jefferson: "The how part is easy. We fought our way through Union Square, escaped from cannibals in the library, won a cage match at Grand Central, went into the subway and managed not to get massacred by the Uptowners, then fought a polar bear in Central Park."

Solon: "Uh-huh. Okay, that *sounds* easy. Now tell me *why*."

Brainbox: "We're going to save mankind."

Solon: "Come again?"

Jefferson: "There's a lab on the eastern tip of Long Island. We think that's where the Sickness started. That's where we're going."

Solon: "And when you get there, you're gonna know what to do?"

Jefferson shakes his head.

Solon: "Then why are you trying to get there?"

Jefferson: "Beats waiting to die."

Solon thinks that one over.

Solon: "But you'll probably die on the way."

Jefferson: "We've made it this far."

Solon: "The night is young."

That stops conversation for a while.

Solon: "I'm going to explain my dilemma to you." He leans back in his chair. "I don't know if I can take you at face value. I mean, that is one messed-up cover story."

Plump Girl: "Sounds like bullshit." Except it sounds like *buuuuuuulll sheeeeeeeeiiit*.

Solon: "Then again, who the hell would come up with a cover story like that? And what bunch of idiots would just *walk into* our territory?"

Me: "Exactly! It's such a stupid idea it has to be true."

Jefferson (annoyed at me): "Look, we're not here to cause a—a dilemma. Just let us go on our way and you'll never have to think about us again."

Solon: "That's the problem. I don't think I can let you go."

Me: "Why? I mean—I get it. We're your prisoners, or whatever. But can't you just believe us?"

Solon: "Oh, I *do* believe you. I just can't afford to let you go."

Me: "But *why*?"

Then Brainbox speaks up. And it all makes sense. Well, at first it doesn't make any sense at all, but after, it does.

Brainbox: "Three-D printing."

Solon: (Looks surprised for a second, then smiles.) "There it is."

Me: "Three-D *what*? The thing with the glasses?"

Brainbox: "Three-D *printing*." He turns to us. "Have you noticed that everybody has a gun? Did you see how parts of them didn't look metallic at all?"

Yeah?

Brainbox: "Well—that's because they're not. They're made of plastic. Somebody here has managed to print gun parts out of plastic. They can make firearms. That's why people are buying up LEGOs. They've got agents trying to corner the market."

Solon: (Smiles.) "Go on."

Brainbox: "And they must have a metal shop, too—you can't make all the parts out of plastic. They won't handle the pressure of the explosions."

Solon: "Uh-huh."

Brainbox: "And you've got a supply of gunpowder. Or you're manufacturing it."

Solon opens his hands wide and looks at the plump kid. Like, *You see? I told you they were smart.*

I almost feel proud of us until the plump girl says, "And *that's* why we have to kill you."

Solon: "That's a little *harsh*. But, yeah, that more or less sums it up."

Me: "So you've got guns. Why does that mean you have to kill us?"

Solon: "We can't have everybody know about it."

Jefferson: "If the Uptowners find out, they'll attack."

Solon: "That's right. And we're not ready to move. Not yet."

Me: "Move where?"

Plump Girl: "Everywhere."

This takes a second to sink in.

Me: "So you're gonna just—take over?"

Solon: "I'm not happy about it. I've got enough headaches as it is. But the situation demands it. I've got the Uptowners to my south, I've got the Puerto Ricans, the Dominicans up here...and limited resources. If we get a technological advantage, I've got to use it. I've got to go to war so we can live in peace."

"Guns, germs, and steel, bitches," says the plump girl. "Don't hate the player. Hate the game."

"Let me get this straight," says Jefferson. "When you have enough guns, you can just roll all over everybody else. The Uptowners, the West Side, the Fishermen, everybody. But you're not ready *yet*. You're worried that we'll warn everybody."

"Well, I'm *not* worried, because you're my prisoners. But, yeah, I suppose you could put it that way." Solon smiles.

Jefferson levels his gaze at Solon. "But—why? What's the point? I mean—you're, what, seventeen? So you take over New York. You'll only be able to *enjoy* it, or whatever, for a year or so."

Solon shrugs. "I don't know. Maybe. Call it Manifest Destiny. Call it the course of history."

"She said 'guns, germs, and steel.' You're forgetting germs," says Brainbox.

"I'm *not* forgetting germs," says Solon. "Who the hell can forget germs? Without *germs*, we wouldn't be in this position. So, yeah, we've got germs covered."

Jefferson: "You could be in a *better* position."

Solon: "Explain."

Jefferson: "If you had the guns *and* a cure for the Sickness, well…" He makes an *it's obvious* gesture.

Solon: "And who's going to find a *cure* for the Sickness?"

Brainbox: "Me."

Solon: "You. After every scientist in the world dies of it, some nerd from the Village is gonna crack it?"

Brainbox: "Yeah." Not, like, bragging. Just, you know, saying.

Jefferson: "What if we don't make it? So we die trying. We're gonna die anyway, right?"

Solon: "And how do I know you won't just send a message to the Uptowners, telling them we're going to attack?"

Jefferson: "Two reasons. First, we hate the Uptowners as much as you do. They've been trying to kill us from the get-go. Second, you send somebody with us. Make sure we do what we say we're going to do."

Solon: "And how are you fools going to make it to the east end of Long Island without getting yourselves killed? Seems like you're pretty good at getting yourself in trouble."

Jefferson: "Oh, we'll use your contacts on Long Island. The farmers."

Solon smiles like Jefferson has just made a good chess move or something.

Solon: "What farmers?"

Jefferson: "The ones that grew those apples downstairs. The ones that make it possible for everybody here to look healthy and well-fed and allow them to work on projects other than hunting and gathering. Am I right?"

Solon: "It's possible that we have agreements with producers on the island."

Me: "But not all of them, right? I mean, that's why the Uptowners have milk and pigs." I want to get in on the acting-smart deal.

Solon: "That's right. That'll change soon enough, though."

Jefferson: "So what do you say? Can we do business?"

JEFFERSON

SOLON LEANS HIS CHIN ON HIS HAND, then looks over at the plump girl. She shrugs.

He holds his hand out to me. "You're alive," he says.

"Thank you," I say.

"What are you thanking me for? You're working for me now. *If* you find a cure, which I doubt you will, that cure belongs to *my* people. Understand?"

I think about how I could possibly deny a cure to anybody, how I could give life to some and not others. Then I think about the Uptowners. And my heart hardens.

"My people get the cure as well," I say. "Washington Square."

"Goes without saying," says Solon. "You need a little skin in the game, don't you?"

I reach out and take his hand. This will have to do, for now.

"Oh. There's another part of it. If you don't find a cure... well..."

If we don't find a cure, we're through.

"I'm sending some of mine with you," he says. "If you make it back here, you can go home. Until then, you belong to me."

Before we set off, they give us the tour.

They're proud of what they've accomplished, and it's hard to blame them. They've managed all kinds of things we couldn't or didn't down in the Square—generators, sanitation, medical facilities.

And a nondescript, heavily guarded building holding the gun factory.

In one room, piles of LEGOs are melted down over big propane burners, slowly and constantly stirred to get rid of air bubbles. In another, there's a lineup of small lathes where gun barrels are fashioned. Next to that one, a crew works on refurbishing spent bullet casings, casting lead bullets and tapping them carefully into place over gunpowder.

And then, at the center of it all, the fast-prototyping machines. Boxy, scrappy constructions that look like props from a sci-fi movie. They slowly extrude plastic parts, layer by layer, using instructions from a set of laptops running design software.

The strange girl with the eyes that never meet yours hands a newly minted piece to Brainbox, who turns it in his fingers, fascinated. According to the file open on the computer, it's an AR-15 lower receiver.

"This changes everything," says Brainbox.

Which is true. When there are enough plastic guns, the population of Manhattan is set to go down even faster than usual.

But I have a theory. Maybe if people actually thought they would live longer, they wouldn't be so ready to fight. It's easier to put your life on the line when you think you're going to die soon anyway.

Lastly they show us the hospital. In a long, tall-windowed room, they care for people giving in to the Sickness. It isn't any prettier than I'm used to seeing, but it's clean and comfortable and free from chaos. A nice, peaceful place to die.

There's a big crucifix hanging on the wall, suffering Jesus looking at the sufferers. Bibles by the beds, and people reading passages to the dying kids. There's something to this—this shared feeling of a story in which things make sense in the end— that seems to ease their pain.

I ask Solon why he thinks they've come through so well. He says, "We didn't identify with the way things were. So we had less to lose when America went down."

One of the kids who arrested us, the one with the scar on the back of his head, meets us as we're leaving the hospital. He's got a big pack on his back and a half-plastic AR-15 hanging from his shoulder. His name is Theo, he tells me in a barely audible rumble, quiet but powerful like the bass woofer of a party going on next door. I shake his hand, and his grip is like iron.

Theo is our minder, I guess. Him and our guide, who everybody calls Captain for some reason. If we stray from the path, they're supposed to do us in.

We clamber into the bed of a pickup truck and drive east toward the river. A police car keeps us company as we slide past a redbrick housing complex, lines of ten-story rectangles with overgrown bits of grass out front. Kids wave at us as we pass. It seems to me like they are waving good-bye.

We drive to the edge of the FDR.

"You got people chasing you?" asks Solon.

I hesitate. Then, "Yeah. Uptowners."

Solon nods. "Scouts on the south edge had a run-in. We turned 'em back."

I look over at Kath, who seems oblivious.

We come to the embankment above FDR Drive and stop.

"We aren't driving?" I ask Solon as we get out.

"Roads are blocked. Cars can't make it through."

"So—we walk?" says Donna.

"We're not gonna make you *walk*," says Solon, smiling. "Are we, Captain?"

"Hell, no," says Captain, but he doesn't explain.

"You ready, Theo?"

Theo nods. Solon hugs him. "Stay sharp."

Then Solon turns to us. "I hope you make it back. I do. And I hope you find what you're looking for. For all of us."

I don't know what to say. I don't know if we're his prisoners, his friends, his associates, his partners, his subjects. So I just nod.

Captain and Theo lead us down onto the roadway. Solon was right—it's littered with garbage, bodies, and cars abandoned at skewed angles. As we make our way to the East River, I try to reconstruct what happened. This car was driven by somebody who had a seizure and careered off that one. This car was abandoned when the way was blocked. Somebody fought over that one and got shot.

At the water's edge, tied to the stumps of two trees that once shaded the road, a tall, square construction pokes above the level of the roadway beside a big metal cylinder. As we get closer, it resolves into the wheelhouse and smokestack of a tugboat. A skinny kid makes his way up a precarious ladder from the deck below while I take in the brawny little ship, which looks like a giant bath toy.

Something about the homely, colorful boat seizes at my heart. Maybe it's the sheer unlikeliness—a childish, stout, romantic thing in the torn-up world.

"What's the matter?" says Captain, mistaking my look for skepticism. "You think brothers can't drive a boat?"

We board the *Annie*, which gives off a hum as my boots hit the deck. I've never been on a tugboat before, and I'm intrigued by the curious design. The sides of the hull dip close to the water, but the bow rises so high that you can't see what's in front of the boat unless you climb to the wheelhouse. Below, there's a sort of living room, decorated with old nautical prints in wood frames screwed into the wall and a few family photos of whoever owned it Before. Fourth of July fireworks from the water, the sheer side of a big container ship from the deck. There are bedrooms in back and in front, past a little kitchen that Captain calls the galley.

"You all are staying up top, in the wheelhouse," says Captain. "I'm gonna trust you not to fuck around with anything. Understand me? *Don't mess with my boat.*"

When he says *my boat*, I can't help looking at the picture of the former owners.

"What you looking at? Them? Trust me, the *Annie* isn't any use to *them.*"

We take our stuff up to the wheelhouse, where we find a clean, tightly rolled sleeping bag for each of us. I look down to the shore and see Spider, the kid who was manning the ship, working at the lines while Captain fires up the big diesel engines.

The next fifteen minutes or so are filled with the kind of boat stuff that makes you feel useless if you don't know how to do it. We shuffle around and try to stay out of the way. It's ridiculous, but I don't want to seem like a landlubber or whatever, so I spend a while acting like I'm used to this sort of thing. Donna curls up into a compact little ball by one of the saloon windows and takes a disco nap. When we get under way, the Rottweiler rasp of the engines taking on a higher note, I decide to go in and get her up, but she's already making her way on deck.

We stand side by side as the ship floats free of the land and glides up the East River, with the Triborough in the distance.

Our fingers are just a few inches apart on the rails. And I have an urge to take her hand. But it seems like nothing is going to bring them to touch.

"This is weird," says Donna. And I wonder how she's read my thoughts. But then she says, "After all the goddamn walking."

"And running," I add.

Donna pauses. "Do you think...do you think we're gonna make it there?"

"Yeah," I say.

"Really?" she says, her face brightening.

"Yeah." I want her to keep smiling. So I add, "Definitely."

Definitely maybe.

The *Annie* is surprisingly powerful and nimble. Captain swings the boat around to go by the south end of Randall's Island—"We could run aground up north. Fools might try to board us"—and we slip under the east leg of the Triborough Bridge, a cliff of metal gray and skeletal over our heads, with flocks of gulls colonizing the understructure. ("You ever had gull's eggs? Good eating," comments Captain.) Then under the old railroad bridge with the promising name of Hell Gate. This lets us into the wide, snaking throat of water sandwiched between the Bronx and Queens. He steers between two jutting green islands in the middle of the flow, then under the White-stone Bridge and the Throgs Neck, which reminds me of a D&D

character I had when I was in sixth grade. On the waterside, rubble, smoke, decay.

And then the way opens up, and we're in Long Island Sound. South of us is the island, sticking out into the ocean like a rotting fish. North of us, the coast of Connecticut appears and disappears in the mist.

At this distance, everything seems the way it was Before. Everything, except for the fact that I'm on a tugboat piloted by a kid from Harlem, heading for the Plum Island Animal Disease Center.

I let the drone of the engines and the buffeting and slapping of the water on the prow flow over me. It takes on the quality of a dream, the ship plowing its way endlessly through the sound, the water repairing the wound, the north coast of the island always in sight.

Captain has a dirty, marked-up map that, with his perverse insistence on changing the name of everything, he calls a "chart." The notes refer to the location of abandoned ships that have gotten stuck in the channel, marinas, diesel pumps, and "farmsteads."

After a few hours' slow but steady progress, we dart toward the land and stop at an abandoned old dockside with a domed blue-gray fuel tank looming over it. From the engine room, they fetch a device that looks like a giant metal hypodermic with a shovel-handle plunger and a big coil of rubber hose. They use it to siphon fuel from a pump on the quayside, and finally I can be useful, hauling canister after canister of stinking diesel back to the boat with the others while Donna and Theo stand guard. In an hour, we're off again.

We stop at little docks poking out of the undergrowth, where ragged kids stand, offering fish and vegetables. Looking at them I feel like we're explorers discovering tribes along the Amazon.

The vegetables are homegrown, fresh and muddy and idiosyncratic, each pepper or onion or carrot lopsided and twisted and different from the other.

Captain exchanges news and packets of letters with the locals. I trade some bullets for a bunch of carrots and onions. Holding the carrots by their green stems, I remember a school play.

First grade, Miss Emerson's class. *Rock Soup.* I am a suspicious villager; Donna is a starving Russian soldier. She makes a soup of water and stone, and offers to share it with me and the other peasants. But, she suggests, it would be ever so much better if only we added a few carrots. By the end of the play, she has hoodwinked us into making a rich beef stew with vegetables.

"Do you remember *Rock Soup*?" I ask Donna.

She just looks at me like I'm nuts.

Over my shoulder, I hear Captain exclaim, "The *Old Man*?" and laugh. I turn around and see that he's talking to a white kid with straggly dreadlocks, who gesticulates like he's insisting that Captain take him seriously. Captain waves him off, and we hop back onto the *Annie*, her engines still running.

We finally stop as the sun sets. I'm sure Captain has some

word for this time of day. Anyway, his chart indicates a safe harbor. We moor on a long rope (a "line," of course, not a rope). That way the current carries us into open water, and we can just cut ourselves loose if we have to.

In the dying light, we eat dinner together, our weapons laid down at our sides.

Spider, the first mate, serves up some thick, spicy brown stew. He's cooked the onions until they're sweet, and the carrots are soft and rich. The sauce tastes of curry. We ladle it over bowls of jasmine rice.

I pause for a second at a hunk of meat that bobs up to the top of the pot.

"What?" says Spider.

"Nothing," I say, and spoon it into my bowl.

"It's chicken," says Spider. "I raise them myself." He savors a bit, his eyes closing. "This was LeeAnne."

"Sorry, LeeAnne," I say.

"Thanks, LeeAnne," says Donna.

We drink from scavenged bottles of yellow wine that have been cooling over the side. The labels say 2000 RAMONET MONTRACHET. Whatever it is, it tastes *bright*, like laughter and sunshine, and suddenly things don't seem so bad.

We find ourselves telling stories. Captain wants to know how we got to Harlem, so we tell him about the Union, the library, Grand Central. The weird thing is that we find the whole thing funny, like it was just an amusing bunch of stuff that happened to us long ago, or happened to a completely different bunch of people. We don't talk about SeeThrough.

Captain tells us about skirmishes with the Uptowners and the Fishermen, river pirates and voodoo priests and wild dogs. How he got command of the *Annie* in what he calls a "cutting-out expedition."

"What do you know about the Old Man?" I ask. "I heard that kid back at the dock talking about him."

"Aw, he's out of his mind." He chews on some rice. "He said somebody he knew saw the Old Man. Said the Old Man cured some fool of the Sickness. Said the Old Man was an angel sent from the Lord to heal the righteous."

"Forget that," says Spider, cutting in. "The Old Man isn't an angel. Nothing like that. He's a dude the Sickness can't kill. He has, like, a mutation? An immunity. And there's these kids? They, like, worship him and do everything he says, because they think he's magic."

"Because they miss their parents," says Theo. "They'll follow anybody."

"There is no Old Man," says Kath. "People made him up. They like to think somebody knows what's going on. But nobody does. Because What Happened doesn't make any sense."

Captain sizes up Kath. "That's a pretty gloomy outlook." Kath just laughs.

"I know these folks are from downtown. What about you?" says Captain, looking at Kath. "Where are you from?"

Kath doesn't even pause. "Midtown," she says. Then, when it's clear that's not enough, she adds, "I've been hiding out on my own. Found a stockpile of canned food in an old restaurant."

I know she's lying, and I think the Harlem kids must know, too.

"Alone?" says Captain. He thinks it over. "Well. It's hard to be alone in this world."

"You think kids are doing the same thing all over?" says Peter. "I mean, Europe and China and everything?"

"Same thing," says Captain. "Tribes and loners and a lot of killing. People used to growing stuff or living hard are probably doing pretty good. Don't tell me those kids living off garbage dumps in the Philippines and whatever don't have it *better* than Before. But for people used to having things their way? That's a hard road, man."

"The meek shall inherit the earth," says Peter.

"I don't know about *meek*," says Captain. "The world's gonna belong to the ones who never had much." He smiles, without malice. "That's why Harlem's gonna take over."

Soon the wine is done. The plates get dunked over the side in a little cage. A black and silver cloud of mackerel nibble at the scraps. Peter asks what's for dessert, and he's obviously kidding, but then Theo brings up a sack, and inside it is a bunch of apples.

"From Solon's place," says Theo shyly. "I thought you might want them."

I pick one up. It's fat and firm, with a long stem and leaf still attached. The dusty skin takes on a keen shine when I rub it. It tastes even better than the wine. Sweet as honey. Crisp as daylight. We all sit together quietly, munching away and smiling.

The dark gathers around the ship, and Captain says it's time to get some sleep; he wants to move as early as possible in the morning.

"We'll keep watch fore and aft. Three hours each watch." Theo takes the first watch in the back of the ship. I take the first watch up front.

The bow is stepped up from the rest of the boat. You can lean into the apex of the rail and poke your head over the edge and watch the water slop around the hull. The big rope slacks and tenses with a creaking sound like a bullfrog.

It's still early, but after half an hour of staring at nothing happening, I'm getting sleepy. It feels as though this is the first time we've stopped struggling since we set off from the Square, and my brain is crying out like a pulled muscle. I can hear snoring from below: Captain or Spider.

There's a noise behind me, and I turn, gun at the ready. But it's just Donna, standing there awkwardly, clasping her hands in front of her.

"Are you busy?" she says, which is kind of odd. What I would be busy with is beyond me.

"No. I'm not very busy," I say.

"I thought maybe I would help you, like, watch," she says. "I can't sleep."

"Sure," I say.

She rests her arms over the edge of the rail like me, which is hard for her because she's so short. She looks like a skinny cat somebody's lifting by the armpits. We stare at the shore for a long while. Then:

"I wanted to say I'm sorry," she says.

"For what?"

"For...in the library? When you told me, you know, you like me?"

I frown. "I didn't tell you I *liked* you," I say.

"Okay...okay, when you told me you"—she clears her throat awkwardly—"*loved* me." Her eyes flick over at me, then back to the shore. "It was really sudden," she says. "I needed some time. To figure out how to respond."

"Nobody needs *time* for that kind of thing," I say. "It's easy. You either love somebody back, or you don't." Now I look over at her. "It's okay, Donna. Don't worry about it."

"No, it's not okay," she says, and then her words come out in sort of a syncopated rush. "It's not okay? Because I didn't know what to say because I was surprised and I hadn't *thought* of you that way I mean I knew I loved you like family? But this was different and like it took some time to adjust to like when your eyes are adjusting to the dark or something? You can't see stuff at first and I was worried? Because once Wash and I did stuff I don't even want to talk about that but you are so much more of a man than he ever was and I'm scared because what if you're not interested in me anymore if we really get to know each other I mean we know each other but not like that and did I mention I'm a virgin? And what if you're disappointed and then that Kath girl with the tits and everything you're obviously like besotted with her so why am I even saying this except that even though it's all peaceful now I have a bad feeling and I think we all might die really soon? So that kind of like focuses your mind and I figure what's the point in not saying anything and I love you, too, even if you don't love me anymore which probably you were just saying anyway because otherwise why would you go for Kath maybe because you were mad at me and I'm sorry I'm really sorry I love you and that's it I said it."

She's said all this while looking out at the water, and it takes me a while to piece it all together. While I'm doing that, she turns to look at me, kind of scared and sad. Then she says, "Okay, I better go."

And I take her hand and lean over and kiss her.

Her mouth is soft and sweet, still tasting of apples. She closes her eyes and reaches an arm around my neck, and at first it's gentle, but then we're holding each other and kissing hard, and it feels so *right* that I figure if I died just now it wouldn't be so bad. But then I pull away a little.

"Wait," I say.

"Wait for what?" she says.

"Just . . . *this*. I want to do this the right way."

"Meaning?"

"Meaning I have to...I don't know, tell Kath. *Break up* with her." It already sounds stupid as it comes out of my mouth.

"Are you serious?" says Donna. "It's the apocalypse. You've got, like, scruples?"

"I mean, it's not like we were boyfriend and girlfriend, or anything, and maybe she already broke up with me, I don't know...I mean, she—"

"Please stop talking about her," Donna says. She looks upset.

Then, with what looks like a serious expenditure of mental effort, she gets her head around it. "No," she says. "You're right. I mean, you're not right in my book, but you're right in yours. That's you. And you're...I love you, that's all. So, okay."

"I love you, too," I say, which may not be very original. We kiss again, not about-to-have-sex kissing, more hold-that-thought kissing.

We wait out the rest of the watch, Donna leaning into me, and for the first time I can remember, I'm happy.

Around us, in the quiet, it gets darker.

DONNA

OKAY. OKAY. OKAY.

Holy shit.

Like…

I'm in love. I mean, I *was* in love, but that was me on my own. But now I'm *in it*, *with him*. He's in love, with me. We're both in it together.

And suddenly I love everyone, even stupid McGee.

I even feel sort of sorry for her, although that makes me seem really conceited. But I do. I mean, I don't mean her any harm. Like, I didn't mean to hurt her when I talked to Jeff.

But I couldn't help it. Maybe it was the trip on the boat, like, I wouldn't exactly call it *romantic*, but for once we weren't getting shot at, or eaten, or otherwise traumatized. And something seemed—clean. Out on the water, it was almost totally free of the smell of rotting flesh. I don't know.

When we left Manhattan, I took a little nap, and I had a funny little dream; I was back in first grade and we're doing this play called *Rock*

Soup? Which is only amusing if you know where your next meal is coming from?

So when Jefferson brought it up out of the blue, I thought it was pretty freaky. I wondered if you could chart the thoughts of two people who knew each other, like, on a graph but in a zillion dimensions, because that's how complex thinking is. How many times would their thoughts snake around to cross at just the same point? And I felt crazy close to him, this image of a six-year-old Jefferson in my mind, this handsome young man there beside me, and suddenly the whole thing with Kath really didn't matter and whether or not it would be a smart thing to tell him how I felt didn't matter, either. Life was too short. *Really* too short. So I went up on deck after dinner, and I looked at him and said, "Jefferson, I know this isn't the right time, and I know these aren't the right circumstances, but I love you more than anything or anyone in the world."

Okay, I don't think I said it, like, exactly that way. Maybe it was a little less full-sentencey.

But anyway, damn, I guess sometimes things just work out. Like, how could I possibly stack up against the Blond Angel of Death? I thought the best thing that could happen was at least I would get it off my unimpressive chest. Sort of emotional barfing. Okay, that sounds terrible. But—well, it's been a pretty shitty couple of years, so I wasn't expecting too much. I thought I was basically charging a machine gun.

Is it wrong to be happy?

Screw it. I am. Nothing I can do about that.

Still—maybe he's not really into it the way I am. I keep on thinking stuff like that, like, maybe I'm too skinny. Maybe I'm too fat. Maybe he wouldn't like me naked. Maybe he wouldn't like me *psychologically* naked. That's just a sampler. But then I look at him; I *know* that he does love me. And that he always did.

The horrible thing is that the fricking boat is so crowded. This *huge thing* has happened, but nobody knows except me and him, and it's just *super* awkward not being able to be alone. I know that the world is ending and it shouldn't be a big deal to tell people we're, like, going out. But—I don't really know the protocol.

Note to self: The expression *going out* doesn't really fit a post-apocalyptic lifestyle.

Then again, it's kind of weirdly delicious, him and me having this big secret. Our eyes keep meeting, and it's like there's this sort of invisible love-beam passing between them, while everybody else is busy pumping the bilge, whatever that is, or feeding the engines with diesel.

Peter can tell something's going on. He's always had an amazing sense for gossip, and his antennas are totally buzzing. At one point, he intercepts one of my looks and triangulates between me, Jefferson, and Kath. He comes up to me and says, "Girl, what's going on?"

"Nothing," I say, blushing and smiling my ass off. I go and pretend to coil some rope.

Kath, on the other hand, seems none the wiser. Which doesn't surprise me, given that she's pretty much impossible to read anyway. She just does as little work as she can and stares at the passing landscape.

Maybe she wouldn't even care. Maybe she was just using Jefferson for, like, rest and relaxation, or for a way out of Uptown, and now that she's free of Manhattan, she'll be moving on.

Which, go for it, honey. Don't let the door hit your perfect ass on the way out.

I don't know. Part of me wants to get someplace, get off the damn boat, get some time alone with Jefferson. But part of me doesn't want to leave this moment, ever, like this time is sacred, like this boat is a cramped pocket universe. As long as we stay afloat, everything is pure potential. As soon as we leave, time starts again.

We tootle up the river or the bay or whatever the hell it is. Around noon, a wind comes up, and snow-white little waves march toward us from the east. They're beautiful. But maybe I'm just a dizzy, lovestruck moron and everything is beautiful. I try that theory on for size, strolling around the boat and checking everything and everybody out.

Yep. I'm finding loveliness everywhere. The rust on the metal deck. The dried blood on my forearm. The scar on the back of Theo's neck. Brainbox's premature crow's-feet that he gets from squinting.

When I pass Kath by the rail, I say, "You know, you have beautiful eyes."

She looks at me like she thinks I'm high. Which I guess I am.

We keep heading east, and the shadows stretch longer and longer ahead of us as the sun dips behind. It's still light out when we round this kind of shoulder of land and we see a stubby little light-house that Captain says is called Orient Point, which, I think, is a beautiful name.

And behind it is Plum Island.

It's nothing but a green lump on the horizon, but it's hard not to get creeped out by it. On Captain's map, it's surrounded by a purple box with the words ACCESS RESTRICTED printed all around. And though it's only a rough triangle with a thin straight bit sticking out, to my eyes it looks like a rabbit leg that's been torn off and dropped onto the ground.

I go up to the front of the boat, where Jefferson is staring at the island. I lean over the rail.

My hand scrabbles along the metal hull and finds his.

Me: "There it is." Ugh. Obviously.

Jefferson: "Yep."

Me: "So…what if we took a personal day? I mean, what's the rush?"

Jefferson looks over and smiles sadly.

I look down at the blue green.

Me: "I figured."

Jeff: "Do you think I'm crazy?"

Me: "No. I mean—yes. Who else would do this? Who else would dream of it? But—it's good. I mean, it's the right thing to do. I think."

Jefferson: "What if it's just an abandoned island? With dusty labs and shredded files? No answers?"

"Then we tried," I say. "Anyway, we should be so lucky. The way things have been going for us, it'll be inhabited by giant man-eating cockroaches."

He smiles.

Me: "You know, we *could* just blow it off completely. Like, turn the boat around and head home."

Jefferson: "That wouldn't be very courageous."

Me: "It'd take more courage than going ahead just because we came this far."

Jefferson: "What about Spider and Theo and Captain? They're supposed to kill us if we don't figure it out."

Me: "Do you buy that? I mean, now that you know them a little?"

Jefferson: (Shakes his head.) "No. But what if there is an answer? What if we could do something about it? Wouldn't you want a future, if you could have it?"

Me: "I *have* a future. I *like* my future now. I'd rather have a thousand days *with* you than a hundred thousand *without* you." It's weird, but when you fall in love, you find yourself saying goofy shit like that. At least, I do.

Jeff: "I'm not going anywhere. Not yet."

Back in the wheelhouse, Captain goes over the map. There's not much detail to the island, just a few wiry roads and a little dot he says is a helicopter pad.

On the west face of the island—the edge where the rabbit's leg would've been joined to its body—is a circular symbol with rays coming out of it, like a red eye from too much caffeine.

Captain: "That's another lighthouse. You can just about make it out from here. See? Southeast of that is a breakwater. We should be able to moor the ship in there, if the channel to the harbor isn't blocked."

Jefferson: "I think you and Spider should stay with the boat. Theo can come with us."

Captain: "Theo does what *I* say." It's been such a smooth trip that I've forgotten how uneasy we were with each other less than two days ago. "Anyway, nobody's doing anything today. I'm not gonna risk being stuck there overnight if I can help it. Not until I know what's up. We'll take a look around tomorrow morning."

So we get a break after all. Nobody seems too excited about actually getting there anyway, except for Brainbox. He keeps peering at the island through binoculars, whispering to himself. He's been doing that more and more since SeeThrough died.

We drop anchor in the channel between Orient Point and Plum Island.

Rummaging around among the mildewed cushions and greasy rags downstairs, I've discovered an ancient, pebble-sized bar of soap and a clean if God-knows-what-this-was-used-for towel. My plan is to take a bath so that, if we *do* get killed by mutant cockroaches, at least Jefferson will remember me not smelling like a goat. I slip over the side in my undies when nobody's looking, and, once I get used to the ovary-shriveling cold, luxuriate in the embrace of the water, sloughing off dirt and mud and tears.

That's when I see Jefferson breaking it to Kath. At least, that's what I think it is, because they're on their own at the back of the ship, and Jefferson is wearing a really serious look on his face, explaining something quietly and deliberately.

As for Kath, she seems to take it well, judging from the fact that after a particularly long speech from Jefferson, she just shrugs. Jefferson's eyebrows crinkle together, like he's not sure she's really gotten it into her brainpan or something.

She walks over to the rail, pulling at her shirt. Once she's wrestled that off, she calmly undoes her bra and drops it with the shirt in a little pile by her feet. The pile gets bigger when she pulls off her pants. Finally, stark naked, she executes this, like, Olympic-caliber dive off the side into the water.

I'm half hoping that she never surfaces, that this is kind of like some grand suicidal gesture. But no such luck. She pops up, spits out a little stream of water, smiles a toothpaste-commercial smile, and stretches out to float flat on her back.

This routine has pretty much gotten everybody's attention. The boys don't know what to do—they stare for a moment and then look up pensively at the clouds or wander over to the other side of the boat, though I can tell they're kind of unwilling to lose the view. As for me, I feel a little stupid. Stupid to be the priss in her underwear, like—what was the big deal? Stupid to have taken the time to feel sorry for her. She does a—frankly a kind of obscene—flip backward and underwater, and surfaces again.

Kath: "Oh, hey." Like she's noticing me for the first time, or pretending to. "What's up?"

Me: "Uh, nothing. What's up with you?"

Kath: "Oh, Jefferson just *broke up* with me. Which was kind of funny. I thought we were just fucking."

Ow.

I mean, I don't know why it should bother me. Like, it'd hardly be better if she was all heartbroken or something, but it felt like she was saying, *Yeah, whatever, I'm above the little dramas of you losers.*

It's really hard to think of good comebacks when you're swimming in your underwear.

Me: "Oh. Okay. Well, I'll let you, uh, use the…water."

I make my way to the side of the ship where an old tire hangs over the edge. I try to hoist myself up as elegantly as possible, but it's slippery and I end up looking like a baby monkey crawling on a kid's swing.

On deck, Jefferson is still loitering by the back. He casts me a look and, just by instinct I guess, I cover myself up with my arms. It's, you know, cold. And…we don't know each other that well. Yet. I don't know. Things seem insanely awkward all of a sudden.

You've got to hand it to the girl; she knows how to screw things up.

There's fresh mackerel fried in cornmeal for dinner, with sweet onions and strawberries on the side. More of that white wine. Damn.

Tonight it's less chatty. There's a sense that we're on the edge of something, the eve of something, even though we don't know what. I look over at Jefferson and read apology in his face. I smile and shake my head—no worries.

Of course Peter clocks all this. I'm in my new spot hanging over the front of the ship when he looms up behind me.

Me: "Peter, the most amazing thing—"

Peter: "I'm in love!"

Wait, what?

Peter: "Theo's *super* cute, isn't he? All, like, strong and silent and sweet."

Me: "Yeah, but he's—I mean, he seems *straight* to me."

Peter: "Do you think? When Crazylegs went over the side, with her coochie all over the place? Theo totally looked away and went over to the other side, like—'uccch.' "

Me: "He went 'uccch'?"

Peter: "Well, no. But that's what it was *like*."

Me: "I think that's just being polite. Like, looking away out of decency."

Peter: "Whatever, bitch, don't bring me down with your decency theory."

Me: "Sorry. I'm excited for you. I am."

Peter: "Thanks. Speaking of which. Have you and Jefferson got busy yet? Did I call that or what? Is he totally hung like a mule?"

I kind of wanted to have a different conversation about me and Jeff, like, a girlie, sighing, hugging, when-is-the-wedding kind of conversation.

Me: "Dude! We haven't, like, *done* anything."

Peter: "Why not?"

Me: "Because?" I gesture toward the tiny confines of the ship. "Besides. It's not like that." Then, off his exaggerated look of disdain, "I mean, it *is* like that. Like, I want to. But not, like, all rushed."

Peter: "Hello? Are you going to do it *before* you die of a painful disease or get murdered? In case you haven't noticed, time is a-wasting."

Me: "So go, like, mack out on Theo, then. Only…"

Peter: "I know. Don't get gay-bashed. Don't worry, I'll suss it all out. Like, ask him what his favorite club track is first."

Me: "I hope it works, Peter."

Peter: "I hope it works for you, Donna."

We hug.

Peter: "It'll be okay, Donna."

Me: "It will?"

Peter: "Sure. We'll get to the island, and Brainbox will cure the Sickness, and in a couple of days, we'll be bringing the good news back home. You and Jefferson will have ten Eurasian babies. Me and Theo will adopt half of them. I'll host a TV show called *Apocalypse Wow*."

Me: "Yeah. Maybe."

We look at the island. I don't want to get there. I want to stay here, for once. Here and now. The past is gone. The island is the future.

Night lowers all softly. Kath and Spider are on first watch, leaving me, Brainbox, Peter, and Jefferson in the wheelhouse to sleep.

As we settle down into our sleeping bags, Peter gets up. He stretches with feigned nonchalance.

Peter: "Hey, Brainbox? I always wanted to figure out which constellation is which. Will you come out on deck and point them out to me?"

Brainbox: "What constellations do you have in mind?"

Peter: "Uh, I don't know. Like, the major ones?"

Brainbox: (Shrugs.) "Not really interested."

Peter tries again. "Well—what about the mechanical winch? Could you show that to me and kind of explain how it works?"

Brainbox: "I don't see why you suddenly care about winches."

Peter: (Sighs.) "Brainbox, I want us to leave Jefferson and Donna alone so that they can mess around."

Brainbox: "Oh." He looks at us. "Okay."

Peter and Brainbox get up and leave. It's nice of them and all, but kind of a lot of pressure?

I guess you always think, like, *I want the first time to be special. I want it to be with someone I love.*

So this is, like, almost too much of a good thing.

Jefferson must see that I'm kind of freaked out.

He smiles. "I'm just glad to be here with you," he says.

I unzip my sleeping bag and hold it open for him. He slides over and in, and zips it up behind him. It's a tight fit, but it's warm and it feels good. My heart is at, like, rave music speed, like two hundred beats per minute. He kisses my lips, my eyes, my ears, my neck. Everywhere his mouth touches I'm bursting.

Jefferson: "Is this okay?"

Me: "Yes."

"Is this okay?"

"Yes."

"Is this okay?"

"Shut up."

So he does.

Is this okay?

Yes.

Dream of Charlie and Mom and Dad and the world Before. Everything is only a story and in this one, which is real, we are all together and Charlie is laughing on a swing, and I turn to Jefferson, and I say, *Look, the Hundred Acre Wood*, and he says, *Don't you know that's where we'll live?* But the rabbit has been caught by the hunter—pulling, pulling on the leg—

JEFFERSON

I OPEN MY eyes and there's a knife at my chest, the point drawing blood. For a crazy moment, I think it's Kath in a jealous rage, but it isn't; it's a kid, maybe fourteen, with mad eyes and wild hair, dripping salt water.

Donna is sitting up, looking at two more smiling children who have their guns to her head.

"Don't hurt her," I say.

One of them hits me in the face with the butt of his pistol. There's a crackling sound and a ringing in my ears, and my vision goes out for a second.

There's a thud from outside and three shots. A scream. Kath's voice.

They tie our hands up behind our backs with wet rope that tears at my wrists. They push us out of the wheelhouse and onto the deck.

They have Peter and Brainbox, too, and Kath is being dragged from the front of the boat. In the stern, I can see them punching and kicking at Theo, who's disarmed and down on the deck. Theo can barely protect himself. There must be six or seven of the skinny, wild-eyed kids beating on him. Another kid is sprawled lifeless against the rail. Maybe Theo killed him.

I'm wondering why we didn't get alerted by the watch when I slip on something wet. It's blood. Spider's body is laid out, arms above his head.

They dump Spider over the side, and he sinks out of sight. They do the same thing to their own.

In the predawn, I can see that they're young—probably not one of them is older than fourteen. Ragged, possibly drugged, judging by their ticky movements and the little scratches they keep worrying at. More and more climb on board, seeming to appear out of the water itself. I twist my neck and see a couple of flat-bottomed boats nestled up to the *Annie*'s hull.

Some of the children have knives, some bats, some machetes; some are even carrying assault rifles that look much too big for them. One of them taps a little packet on his hand and comes up with a cigarette. He lights it expertly, and it juts from his lips obscenely.

I keep thinking I've seen this before somewhere, and then I realize that they look like those pictures of child soldiers from the Congo and Burma and other places, before What Happened. They handle the weapons like toys, dangling rifles over their shoulders by their fingers, leaning back to support the metallic burden of a machine gun like they're holding a baby brother. They have terrifying dead-calm expressions, freezing eyes.

I ask them what they want. I get a slap across the face from a skinny blue-eyed boy with beads in his hair.

I ask him what his name is. Slap.

I tell him mine. He puts the hot snout of his pistol to my eye. I have no doubt at all that he's going to shoot.

Then more of them come from below. Captain, his right eye swollen over, is dragged up after them. His arm looks broken.

I think, *All this way, through everything we have suffered, and it ends with the island in sight.*

But that's not how it ends.

After grabbing our gear and weapons and some tools from the ship, they force us down into their boats. There are six or seven boats, all of them white-hulled shells, blue on the inside, that look like upturned box tops. We crowd into them, and they push off from the tug with paddles. They must have slipped up quietly from the side, saving the outboard engines, which now thrum to life as they abandon caution.

The little ships swivel nimbly and head in a flock toward Plum Island.

Behind us the *Annie* goes up in flames. I catch sight of Captain and see tears streaking his face. And a look of murder.

Dawn hits fast, and the sun is sitting on the horizon when we get to the breakwater. Still not a word from our captors. I keep trying to find Donna, who's on one of the other boats. I want to reassure her somehow. But I don't know if seeing my bleeding face would do her much good. When I do see her, I'm frightened by how pale and small she looks. But she's alive.

Inside the breakwater, a little harbor. They pull up to a rotting dock and heave us out, kicking and punching us when we don't move fast enough.

I try to understand what's happening. My guess is that this is an entire school grade—they must have been around twelve when the Sickness hit. Barely old enough to survive. How did they make it through what followed? These kids aren't shy and fearful like the Moles. They're bold. Beyond that. Fearless.

At the edge of the water there's an old cube truck covered in amateurish graffiti. They herd us into the back. Some of them follow us in, and the rest climb up onto the roof or hang precariously from the open gate.

The truck spasms to life, and we rattle along a dusty road past acres of overgrown grass and reeds. I can make out a blocky old lighthouse. A kid with a long rifle perches at the top.

We take a left at a fork in the road, and out of the back of the truck I can see a big, well-tended field, a variety of crops growing.

There's a traffic circle in front of a complex of four or five buildings. The main one is three stories high and about a block wide, with dead windows set into a reddish face. The truck stops, and we are gestured out.

A sign reads PLUM ISLAND ANIMAL DISEASE CENTER.

My arms burn; my head buzzes. We are getting to the heart of it.

Through the doors, a bland, abandoned atrium. Past that, a corridor with big rooms off both sides.

One room seems to be a dormitory. Mattresses are scattered around. A girl, maybe thirteen, thin as a corpse or a runway model, looks up from a mirror set in a cheap plastic housing. She's applying lipstick the color of running blood.

From the other side, the sound of muffled gunfire. I catch a glimpse of a big flat-screen TV. On it, a first-person shooter—*Call of Duty*, I think—with more feral teens like the ones who've taken us prisoner grouped around it, transfixed. A fug of smoke with a chemical tang that isn't tobacco hangs in the air.

I keep expecting to see clear Plexiglas, computer terminals, high-tech ID systems. But the farther back we go, the dirtier it gets. Gray concrete painted in government beige, scuffed with shoe rubber and chipped by rolling carts.

Finally, we come to a door like a bank vault, with a thick, little webbed-glass window and a circular metal handle. In front of it lies a dead body, pale and bleeding from the nose, face slack from muscles exhausted by agony. A recent victim of the Sickness. But years too young for it.

The child soldiers don't spare him a glance. One of them

knocks on the vault door with the edge of his machete. The tinny sound echoes somewhere beyond.

The round handle of the door spins smoothly and the door floats open.

A girl with blond braids, impossibly innocent-looking and wearing a daisy chain like a crown, is revealed. Below a charm necklace, a medical scrub folded over to fit her, crusted with dried blood.

She smiles, turns around, and guides us past a series of empty pens, cages, and metal doors set in the wall. I can hear a song playing—a pleasant riff with a plaintive voice that jars with the blood and the gray.

The farther we go, the louder the music gets until it is blasting, piercing. I can't think straight for it. Then, at the end of the corridor, in a big room past a long row of tables cluttered with little machines and racks of test tubes, I see someone bent over a table.

He's nodding to the music. Encapsulated in a suit of stout blue rubber with a boxy pouch at the back.

Whoever is in the suit stops nodding and looks up from his work as if he has a sense that he's being watched. The music stops, leaving an electric hush.

I can't help but back away as, slowly and deliberately, he turns to look at us.

Obscuring his face is a pitted, scratched square glass plate set in the rubber suit. The light from bulbs hanging from twisted wires above glances off it so that I can't see who's inside.

He stands and reaches up to unfasten the helmet, fingering a zipper out of a nested rubber seam.

And I am suddenly afraid that whatever is inside that suit will rush out and contaminate us.

With a hiss, he skins his head free of the helmet. And I see him.

Thin yellow hair, straight nose, eyes empty of color. A Galapagos of blotches over thin, almost transparent skin. Spiky bristles unevenly shaved.

An impossible face.

The face of a man forty years old, or more.

The face of the Old Man.

I hear Donna gasp. I reach for her hand. Peter mutters and crosses himself.

The Old Man smiles. An uneven grimace, thin, blotchy lips over yellow teeth.

"Hello," he says. "You're just in time."

His voice is oddly pitched, too high for his frame.

It's a while before I can speak. In the meanwhile he gulps water from a big plastic bottle.

"Just in time for what?" I ask.

"Did we lose anyone?" says the Old Man to the kid who slapped me.

"Yeah. Kevin," says the kid, with no particular emphasis. But the Old Man starts in surprise. Shakes his head in confusion. His hands shake.

"They attacked us," I say. "They attacked our boat. Killed our friend."

"Never mind," the Old Man says. "Never mind. He won't have died in vain."

"Who are you?" says Donna. "How is this possible?"

"Better living through chemistry. I wish I could say that I've cured it. But the truth of it is, I've only made an accommodation with it." He takes another gulp of water.

"Is it you? In the city?"

He shrugs. "I do have to make the occasional visit. Supplies, technical equipment. But...you should settle in." The Old Man smiles. "Everything in due time."

Then they take us away, past the infected body at the door.

They put us in a big room penned off with metal bars that only go up to waist height. They must have been designed for sheep or pigs. We're shackled to the bars with thick chains. The bare walls are scuffed and peeling. There's a smell of ancient dung. The pigment of tons of animal shit has sunk onto the ground and slopped up against the walls. I notice, scratched into the walls in angular letters but clearly in different hands, one name after another. The walls are covered as high as a human can reach with testimonies. All that's left of the kids who were here before us.

I try not to show the fear this puts into me, but Donna is looking just where I am.

"We're going to die," she says.

"We're not going to die," I say.

"The way I see it," says Brainbox, "this is going as well as could be expected."

This takes a moment to sink in.

"How do you figure that?" says Donna.

Brainbox shrugs. "Seems like a working lab."

"A working lab where they're experimenting on *humans*!" says Peter.

Brainbox shrugs, as much as he can, given that one hand is cuffed and hanging above his shoulder.

"Human trials are always the final stage," he says. "That's good news."

"Dude," says Kath, "you are twisted."

"We've got to get the fuck out of here," says Captain. "Theo, you good?"

Theo's face is swollen, his mouth bloody. "I'm strong," he says.

"How are we supposed to get out of here? Those kids are armed to the teeth," says Kath. "And they're *all kinds* of crazy. Did you see their eyes?"

"Their pupils are dilated," says Brainbox. "He's got them on some kind of drug."

A key rattles in a lock and the blue-eyed kid with the beads appears, flanked by six more Islanders. They're sporting our stuff. T-shirts, guns, the teddy bear Donna took from the library. One of them has an iPhone, maybe Donna's, and he's making a video.

"I'm doing a show," says Blue-eyes. "It's called *Lab Rats*."

The Islanders titter as this sinks in.

"Who wants to be the first contestant?" says Blue-eyes.

Nobody answers.

"Aw, come on. Don't make me choose." He looks pretty happy to do it.

Before I have a chance to rethink it, I say, "Me. I'll go." Donna's head snaps toward me, and I look down.

"Don't," she says. "Don't!"

I manage a smile, though I'm terrified.

"I'll be fine."

"No! You can't go!"

I take her hand.

"I'll see you soon," I say.

In the back of my mind is the idea that I'll be able to speak to the Old Man. Maybe I can explain. Maybe I can win him over.

Because, really, who else is going to go? Who started this?

The Old Man waits for me in a new room, with a new smell that's more human than the odor of the pen.

Metal tables with chains bolted into them are spaced evenly

339

around the room. Some squat, going-to-college refrigerators against the wall. Piles of filthy little cages.

He's out of his hazmat suit, dressed in khaki pants and a collared shirt with a tattered tweed jacket, a scarf wrapped around his neck. He shivers even though it's warm and sticky inside. On the table next to his chair is a big water bottle with the label ripped off.

He coughs, a rich, phlegmy bark.

"How?" I ask.

"How?" he says. Again his voice is strangely high—like it's been Auto-Tuned.

"How are you alive?"

He fidgets, scratches, coughs. Takes a long drag of water.

"How am I alive? Some days," he says, "I think I can't *die*." He closes his eyes and intones, "*Yea, they have slain the servants with the edge of the sword; and I only am escaped alone to tell thee.*"

He looks at me hopefully. I don't say anything, even though I recognize the verse.

"No?" His face falls. "There is no one to talk to. No one." Then, like a schoolteacher, "The Book of Job. King James Version. *Beautiful* poetry."

"How?" I say.

"*How* did I survive? Well," he says, "my *scientific* explanation would have to do with hormones. Specifically, steroid hormone-binding proteins. No?" He looks at me searchingly

340

again, and I think he is checking to see if any part of my brain has lit up in response.

I shake my head. Brainbox would understand this, I think, but I don't tell him that. I don't want to give this strange creature anything to use.

"No one to talk to," he says again. "No one who understands."

"Try me," I say. "Explain it to me."

He seems intrigued. "I could...but...you'll probably die like the rest. I find it difficult to detach emotionally—can you understand? I have problems with anxiety. It's part of my condition."

"What condition?"

"The human condition?" He snorts. "No. Living with this illness. The bugs in my blood. If I make friends with them, give them the right proteins to keep them company, they will leave me alone. If not, they will eat me up. So I pretend to be friends, until I can kill them." He grimaces again, one of his smiles. "Don't worry, the bugs can't hear us."

"You're trying to find a cure."

"Of course." He picks at a scab on the side of his nose. "I know this may look very sinister, but I'm one of *the good guys*."

"That's a relief," I say.

"Don't take that tone with me. You don't have the right. It wasn't my *fault*," he says. "You probably think it is."

"I don't really know what happened," I say. "I need you to tell me." I feel sick to my stomach. "So many people..."

"You think I don't know that? *Nobody* understands as much

as I do!" He's suddenly angry. Spit flies from his thin, cracked lips. He takes another sip of water. "Do you think it's easy knowing how many people have died? Don't blame *me*. Blame the Chinese."

"What do the Chinese have to do with it?"

"We would never have *made* this bug if AFIT hadn't *known* for a certainty someone else was developing it. And who would think of such a thing? The Chinese, you see. They're *social engineers*."

"It's a weapon," I say.

"Of course it's a weapon. What else would it be? *Nature* couldn't manage something like this." He actually looks proud.

"But why?" I ask. "Why just the adults and the children? If you're making some kind of plague...why not kill *everyone*?"

" 'He alone who owns the youth gains the future.' Somebody has to work in the factories once you've taken over."

The Islanders at my side laugh. "Word," says Blue-eyes.

"So this was like...a neutron bomb or something? Get rid of the grown-ups and the little kids, leave the rest standing?" It's starting to make sense.

"Bingo. Oh, I know that young people like to *think* they're rebellious. In practice, this emotional impetus can easily be channeled." He turns to the children. "You're happy, aren't you? With your *stuff*—your music and your video games and your pornography and your clothes? Don't I make sure you're fed? Don't I make sure you're having *fun*?"

"That's right," says Blue-eyes. "Just give us everything we fucking want, and we're cool."

The Old Man goes on.

"Anyway. It was the storm. They thought we were safe here, with Block Island to the east, Montauk to the south. But the storm...well, you saw the news. Hundreds of thousands of people without electricity. The coastline flooded. Our containment systems were horribly outdated. Not enough funding. Blame the government. Blame global warming." He seems lost in his head, pursuing an old argument.

"It escaped?"

"Oh, yes," he said. "It happens every once in a while. Like the foot-and-mouth outbreak in '78. Can't be helped."

"Wexelblatt Effects," I say.

"Exactly!" he says, pleased. "Look at you. Gold star."

"And you didn't have an *antidote*?" I shout.

"Of course not!" he says, as though it were a ridiculous suggestion. "How could we have an antidote to a disease we had just invented? No, you reverse engineer that. Of course you do. There's no danger if..."

He trails off. Shakes his head. Looks at the floor.

"You can keep it at bay...steroids...of course...can't process sodium...all my cortisol is bound up...you have no idea how much stress..." He coughs. "Sometimes I wish I were dead," he mutters. Then he seems to shake it off. Fetches something from the metal tray at his side.

A syringe.

"Let's begin," he says.

I jump at him, hands grabbing for his throat.

He's much stronger than he looks. Stronger than I could have conceived. He grabs my face and holds me there, his grip like a vise, and I see the muscles bulge out of his neck. It feels as though he'll tear my face off with his bare fingers.

"I used to be weak—would you believe it?" he says. "Steroids have their beneficial side effects."

The Islanders take my arms, and he lets go of my face.

"I'll try to save you," he says. "I *will* save you. Won't I? All of you." He looks at the Islanders, who gaze back at him adoringly. "Daddy will give you life. But before you can get well, you have to get *sick*."

They hold me and hit me until I stop struggling, and he slips the needle into my vein.

DONNA

SO, NO MUTANT COCKROACHES. That's a plus.

Otherwise it's pretty much all awful all the time. After they take Jefferson away, they leave us in the pen for hours. And—it's so *boring* to be scared? Like, you can be in a panic for only so long, and then it just turns into depression or despair or whatever. So after a while, everybody finds the most comfortable position they can and just hangs out, being miserable.

Brainbox is the exception. The hard drive is definitely whirring in there. He stares at the wall in this creepy, absent way and occasionally asks a weird question like, "Did you see how much water the Old Man was drinking?"

This gets on Captain's nerves, and he starts cussing him out, blaming him for everything that's gone wrong. And I think for the hundredth time about my phone, whether I'll ever get it back and see Charlie's face again.

We hear music and video game gunfire from down the corridor. Tittering laughter from the tween soldiers.

They're definitely not right in the head. The Old Man has them under some kind of spell. Their eyes are dull, their mouths slack. They sway like there's some slow music going on that I can't hear. When they come in to throw stale granola on the floor or hose out the pen, they hardly give us a glance, no matter what we say.

I think I know what it was like to be some cow unlucky enough to find its way here. I'd rather end up as hamburger.

Which is to say, it's worse than being eaten, I guess. And strangely enough, I have the, like, analogy of the cannibals at the library to go on. To think that, objectively, it might have been better to end up as brunch is kind of a major bummer.

Well, at least I got to see the world a bit.

I think about how much better things might have been if we'd just stayed back in the Square. A little scavenging, a little shivering, warm beer, the occasional DVD. Would that have been so bad?

And then I think of the parallel me, in the universe where the Sickness never happened. Parties, SATs, four years at, like, Wesleyan? A semester abroad in Rome, losing it to some cute Italian guy I meet in a club who never calls back. Graduating to a crowded walk-up in Brooklyn, maybe a shitty job at a magazine or some Web design crap, nights out, abortive relationships with baffling dudes. Semi-ironic wedding, a kid in my late thirties, divorce, Pilates, Sunday New York Times, too much wine in front of the TV at night, the kids don't call, assisted living. Somewhere in the mix, I run into Jefferson; we're Christmas shopping in SoHo. There's a feeling there, something missing that we could give each other, but it's too late.

Then Jefferson's version of the future. We cure the Sickness; we save humanity. The world gets a second chance, and we begin a new era of low-carbon emissions, financial equality, and universal niceness.

Now the truth. Jefferson is probably dead. And we're next.

Around nightfall—I can't tell exactly because there're no windows—Peter budges me awake. The Islanders have come back, and they're going to throw us into separate cells. They must not have enough rooms to spare, because Kath and I end up together in a filthy little rectangle with no furniture and a thick metal door. In the corner there's a bunch of notches where somebody was counting the days they were stuck here. It ends at eight.

We sit in opposite corners, like boxers. Every once in a while, we'll find that we're looking at each other, but neither of us knows what to say. Then, after about an hour, she says, "So you must be pretty proud of yourself."

Me: "Excuse me?"

Her: "I mean, you got the guy."

I look around.

Me: "I don't have anybody."

Her: "Whatever. You won."

Me: "Yeah, I'm just winning all over." I let it rankle for a while, then: "That's all it is to girls like you, right? Winning. You don't care about *him* at all. He was just something you could use to, like, show yourself you could get him."

Her: "Girls like me?" She looks almost hurt. "You don't know anything about me."

Me: "I know you're a freaking psychopath. I know you *murdered* that dude."

She shrugs, then her face clenches up, like she's going to cry. She composes herself.

Her: "You'd have done the same thing. You're just lucky, that's all."

Me: "Whatever." Which is all I can think of saying. But then I think about what she said as she tries to control her expression.

Me: "You're right. I don't know anything about you. Seems like things were...*better* for us. Down at the Square."

Now she's the one to go silent. Then, quietly—

Kath: "I would have liked it down there."

She flashes me a look for about a nanosecond, like she regrets that she just said something that wasn't totally pissy and is worried I'll jump on her for it. I shrug.

Me: "Maybe we'll make it back."

Kath: "Doesn't look like it."

Me: "I can't disagree."

Kath: "You love him, don't you?"

I don't feel like showing myself. But what the hell. It's all over anyway.

Me: "Yeah, pretty much."

Kath: "Me too, I think."

Me: "So that's one thing we have in common."

I could swear she smiles at me, and I smile back.

Me: "Maybe in a better world, we could have been frenemies."

She laughs.

I curl up on the floor and close my eyes.

When I wake up, she's gone.

There's no way she could have escaped. They must have taken her away when I was asleep.

The next face I see is Brainbox's. I'm doing yoga—kind of a girlie version of the part in prison movies where the dude gets crazy buff doing push-ups, I guess—when I happen to look up and see him staring at me through the square plastic window in the cell door.

I can't figure out how he got loose.

I want to shout, but I'm afraid they'll catch him. "Brainbox!" I hiss. "Open the door!"

But he just blinks and, in a second, is gone.

Maybe I imagined him.

Time stretches. Actually, I'm stretching, not time. Time is just doing its thing. I'm the one whose mind is going thin, elastic, full of holes, ready to snap, like an overchewed piece of gum. The darkness takes on colors, swims like grains of sand in a violent wave. I fall out of sleep and try to find my way back in.

Somewhere in this I am visited by my mother and father. In the afterlife, they are together and all is forgiven. They apologize to me for having done a lousy job. And I see Charlie. He's a young man now, clear-eyed and straight-backed. He tells me that it's all for the best— we don't belong on the earth; it was a mistake. God *repented*; that's what he says. We couldn't be trusted. So he made another flood. *I wish Peter were here*, I think. *He could explain this to me.*

I open my eyes, and instead of the sun or the moon, there is only the sickly green rectangle lit up by the corridor outside. I stand up, my joints complaining about the hard floor and the damp.

I hear nothing but the distant laughter of the Islanders. I call out to my friends, but nobody answers.

Finally, though I'm ashamed, I call out to the Islanders. Anyone to talk to, anyone to recognize me as a fellow creature. Nobody comes.

JEFFERSON

SO THIS IS WHAT IT'S LIKE TO DIE, I guess.

Everyone takes this trip, but only once, and there is nobody to tell you what it'll be like. Of course, that hasn't kept people from writing speculative travelogues.

People think Buddhists don't go in for that stuff, but it's not true. Sure, the Buddha wasn't big on the afterlife. When he died, he attained nirvana, which isn't heaven but a state of nonbeing. By then, he wasn't attached to anything—not possessions, not friends, not family, not life itself. Having passed on his teachings to his disciples, thereby giving the gift of freedom from suffering, he had done his job and was finished with the work of being.

His disciples, of course, were majorly bummed, and the way they expressed it, when writing about the Buddha's death, was to say that the earth shook and the heavens trembled, the sort of stuff that the Bible says happened when Jesus was crucified.

And right there, you can already see a philosophy turning into a religion. The seduction of myth. They also transmuted mental suffering into "hell"—they have a bunch of hells, actually. The kind of hell you end up in depends on the kind of desires and attachments you have. Greedy people go to the hell realm of the hungry ghosts and whatnot. This is handy as a metaphor—if you're greedy, you *are* always hungry, in a way. But people tend to take these things literally, so there are entire schools of Buddhism that cultivated these dogmas, this whole cosmology that isn't that much different from Catholicism or Islam or whatever and that seems to be about punishing the bad and rewarding the good and what have you.

The school of Zen Buddhism my father followed rejected all that stuff. To them, it was just a load of hooey, mental *stuff*, cheap gaudy decorations that cluttered up a beautiful, sparse room.

Still—there's this idea in Tibetan Buddhism I always thought was interesting. It's called the bardo. It means the intermediate state between dying and living. The idea is that after your body dies, your spirit is kind of hanging around for a while before it gets reborn. And you go through all these ordeals, these terrifying hallucinations, and basically the way you handle them determines the way you are reborn, or even if you are reborn at all. So you have to have your shit together or you could be catapulted into some crappy incarnation. To prepare for this, you have to master the ability to meditate through the bardo. Which is a pretty tall order, given that your body has just died and you're kind of floating around like a ghost.

Maybe it's the martial arts aspect of this idea—like, you're training up so you don't get your ass kicked or whatever—that appealed to me. Anyway, as the Sickness infiltrates my bones and I lie here on the concrete floor shivering, I get ready for spiritual combat.

The first thing to do is to let go. Like, basically, to give up.

This may sound like a totally loser thing to do, and I guess if this were a movie or something, I would look like a pretty crappy hero. In movies you're not supposed to give up. But looking at my situation, it seems kind of like the smart choice. Exhibit one: Nobody has survived the Sickness. Well, it looks like the Old Man did, but he's one in—what—seven billion? Anyway, whatever he did to survive it, or whatever he was in the first place, he seems to have gone totally nuts. And he clearly hasn't found a cure. Given that, it's pretty unlikely that he's going to cure *me*. Which means that I'm going to die.

This sounds terrible until you realize that we're all going to die anyway. I mean, if it isn't now, then someday I'll find myself realizing that it's today, or soon. And sure, under different circumstances, I'd have more time to do stuff. But really, who ends up thinking he's had enough time?

Then why did I want to cure the Sickness in the first place?

I guess I don't need to be all modest when I'm dying anyway. I didn't just do it for me. I wanted *everyone* to live. I didn't want people to suffer anymore. I thought maybe we could start again.

Maybe do better than the last time.

As for myself, did I want to live? Sure. That's human nature.

Still. I have to let go. I have to realize that I'm going to die. That I won't see the sun, and I won't taste food, and I won't feel anything or hear anything or even think anything.

When my father was dying—this was before the Sickness; I'm glad he didn't have to die from that—he fought. He was always a fighter, you see. The war never really ended for him. He had taken on the Germans, and now he was taking on death, and he wasn't going to surrender. In those last days, I saw all his Zen go out the window. Not because he was weak. Because he was strong. He loved life and he loved us, and he refused to let go.

So he scrapped and he fought and he went to the canvas, and in the end, he was beaten. And I kissed his cold forehead, and I told him that he didn't need to fight anymore. And I told myself that I would give up when my time came. I wouldn't have to be torn away from life. And I would enter the bardo with a clear mind.

But as this disease finds its way into every pocket of me and the fever runs, I find that I can't let go. And it's not the kiss of the sunshine or the taste of the air or the touch of music.

It's you, Donna. It's you that makes them drag me into the middle realm calling out.

The space between life and death is filled with voices and static, beeps and hoots that roll from one to the other like stations on a radio.

I break the surface, back in life like I'm coming up sputtering from underwater. Brainbox is looking at me curiously.

I'm at the business end of a syringe, which he pulls out of me. I'm just back from the bardo. At least that's what I'm thinking, so it takes me a while to say, "What are you doing?"

"I just injected you with adrenaline," he says.

Which explains why I feel the way I do, as if my veins are pumping liquid metal.

"How?"

"Oh," says Brainbox. "How did I get here? I made a deal."

I sit up. I'm agitated, angry. I can tell it's partly the drug, but that doesn't change it.

"What?"

"I made a deal with the Old Man."

"You made a *deal*? You made a deal with that—thing?"

"Yes—my life in exchange for my assistance."

"*Your* life?" I say. "What about *ours*?"

Brainbox looks away. "I couldn't do that. Without you, there wouldn't be anybody we could experiment on. The subjects need to be old enough to be losing steroid hormone-binding proteins. So…you understand."

"No, I *don't* understand. All of a sudden you're, like, working for *him*?"

Brainbox shrugs. "I'm not working for him. I'm working for us. For our *idea*. That's bigger than me or you, isn't it? If you could die to save humanity, wouldn't you?"

"I don't know, Brainbox. I'd rather save it without dying, given the choice."

"Well…" He shrugs. "I'm kind of the only one who's not expendable. You see, I think I've *figured it out*."

"Great—so let's get out of here."

"No, Jefferson. We need to conduct more tests." His eyes are hard.

"You're conducting tests on your *friends*!" I try to get up, but then I realize that I'm shackled to the wall.

"It'll be all right. You'll see," says Brainbox. "I can do this." He seems to be trying to convince himself.

"You don't need to do this. Please. Help us."

"But I *am* helping you," he says. "I'm helping all of us."

"Is this because of SeeThrough?" I'm desperate. Trying to push any button I can.

He stops fussing with equipment for a second.

"Her name was Chu Hua," he says. "It means 'chrysanthemum.' When they moved here, they called her Jenny, because people couldn't be bothered to remember her *real* name. But nobody even called her that."

He's looking into the middle distance now. I realize that he's broken.

"Brainbox—*Andrew*," I say, using his real name, "don't do

356

this. Help us. Help us escape. We'll figure this out. All of us. Nobody has to die." I'm definitely not ready for the bardo anymore. A few sips of air, a little hope, have done that for me. Screw nonbeing.

"You're wrong," he says. "People do have to die. Some people have to die so that other people can live." He takes another syringe out of a plastic sack. Jumbled in the sack, next to a bunch of vials, is Brainbox's useless crank radio. I'm thinking about the voices and the sounds I heard when he leans in with the needle.

"What is that?" I ask.

"It's something I'm working on. Well, something *we're* working on. He was close," he says. "We just needed the right cocktail of hormones. It'll change some things in your system. Make you more like the Old Man." He leans toward me.

"More like *him*?" I reach out for him, grabbing hold of his shirt before he can pull away. He sticks his foot in my gut and kicks, then calls for help.

The Islanders come and hold me down.

Time passes over me, hoisting me up and lowering me down on its swells. I hear sounds from down the corridor, chatter, the phlegmy, throaty sound of adult voices that must be coming from the video games they endlessly play. Sometimes I hear coughing, screaming, blows.

After many wakings from the dark, I begin to get the sense that my body belongs to me again. First I can move my fingers, then my arms, and at last I can stand up. The fever that possessed me is gone.

I see Brainbox's eyes peep through the door; they narrow as he sees me standing there instead of laid out on the floor. The anger of the adrenaline has burned itself off, and I feel only sorrow.

Five minutes later, he is back with some of the Islanders.

"You'll come peacefully?" he says after they've heaved the door open.

"Where?"

"The Old Man wants to see you."

I walk with Brainbox, my eyes filming and searing in the half-light. Again the little blond girl opens the door of the Old Man's laboratory. He's at his table, injecting himself. The helmet of his rubber suit hangs down his back, like the flayed head of an animal. When he sees me, he puts down the syringe and smiles.

"I don't believe it," he says. He turns to Brainbox. "Andrew, well done. *Mine* is crashing, as per usual."

"You were heading in the right direction," says Brainbox. "You just needed fresh eyes."

The Old Man walks up and grasps Brainbox by the hand, then hugs him. Brainbox gets a happy look. It's strange on his face.

Then Brainbox looks at me again. At a glance, the Islanders

have a dozen hands on me, and they force my naked arm out so that the Old Man can stick me with another needle.

"Don't struggle, Jefferson," says Brainbox.

"You're not dying—you're giving life," says the Old Man.

This time the Old Man doesn't inject me. He fills tube after plastic tube with the blood that he draws from my arm, until I'm too weak to struggle against the children. I sink down to the ground, and finally the Old Man pulls the needle out of me and they let me collapse.

Blood in hand, the Old Man leads Brainbox away to a table where a bunch of machines are whirring away and starts to question him.

That's when I see Kath. She's laid out on a table, barely covered with a sheet. Her body is pale and still, and at first I think she's dead.

The Islanders don't seem too worried about me; they lean against the wall, squat on the ground, and start messing with the impotent cell phones they all seem to have. I drag myself over to Kath, my head ringing.

There's a trail of dried blood out of both corners of her mouth. Her eyes, when they open, are rimmed with red.

"Jefferson," she says. Then, "You look good."

"So do you," I say.

"No, I don't," says Kath. Her face spasms and pink tears roll from her eyes. "I look awful. I look like I'm dying." She lifts her hand toward her face but doesn't have the strength to reach it.

I wipe the tears from her eyes.

"You're not going to—"

"Don't," she says. "Don't. I know it. I know I'm dying." Her cheek falls on my hand. I keep it there.

"Donna..." she says.

"What about Donna?"

"She thinks I don't love you. That I was just...that it was just..."

"It's okay," I say. "It's okay."

She doesn't seem to hear me. "But look—look what I did. They came, and they asked for one of us. And she was asleep."

"You volunteered? For her?"

"Not for *her*, for us," she says. "Here *we* are, together. And you love her, don't you? Well, maybe you'll both make it through. Hold my hand."

"Kath..."

"Do something for me?"

"Anything."

"Tell me you love me," she says. "And sound like you mean it. Nobody has ever done that. They said it, but they never really *meant* it. I could tell." Another tear leaks out. "Tell me you love me and sound like you mean it."

It's not even a decision.

I say, "I love you."

She grips my hand tightly.

"I knew you did," she says.

And she goes out of focus.

"Bring him over," says the Old Man to the Islanders. Not wanting their hands on me again, I walk over on my own.

"Amazing," says the Old Man, looking at me with a smile. "Like new."

"Congratulations," says Brainbox. "You're going to live."

He means me.

"You are going to live a very long life," says the Old Man.

"Well," Brainbox says, "we need a few weeks' course, to eliminate the virus. After that..."

I point to Kath. "Her. Give her the vaccine."

"It's not a vaccine—" says Brainbox.

"Give it to her," I say.

"She's too far gone," says the Old Man.

"She's ready for the junk pile," says Brainbox.

The Old Man laughs—a quickly restrained little explosion of breath.

I don't understand what's become of Brainbox. I don't know how he could say something like that. But the Old Man looks at him with affection and trust.

"That's a bit harsh, Andrew. But"—he turns to me—"essentially he's right. Her treatment was not effective."

"I've prepared your steroid dose," Brainbox says, handing him a hypodermic.

361

"Thank you," says the Old Man.

"I'll get the next subject," says Brainbox.

"Maybe that's best," says the Old Man. "Your friend needs a little time to calm down. You'll be all right?"

Brainbox nods and hefts a squat black device in his hand—a Taser, I think. He and Blue-eyes head toward the cells. Then Brainbox turns around and looks back at me.

"Remember, Jefferson," he says, "*some people have to die.*"

A little smile flickers on his face, and then he turns and leaves.

"Sit." The Old Man gestures toward a metal folding chair.

I shake my head.

"Oh, come on. You look like you're going to fall over."

I make my way through the thick air and fall into the chair.

"Do you know what a historic moment this is?" asks the Old Man.

No.

"This is the beginning of the way back. When we duplicate these results—*your* results—humanity will be saved."

I have nothing to say.

"Not to mention the fact that you will live a natural life."

"Natural life?" I ask.

"Yes," says the Old Man. "We've saved you. You might at least say thank you."

I look over at Kath. "It wasn't worth it."

"Oh, don't," says the Old Man. "*So many* have died. Don't be sentimental. Believe me, if I had been unable to overcome my emotions…" He looks away now, lost in thought. He comes back. "I would not be here today."

He takes a long drink of water, then picks up the syringe Brainbox gave him. I start involuntarily, but he holds it up to his own arm and smiles.

"Andrew's a thoughtful soul. Thanks to your friend, I will soon be able to dispense with daily injections."

"I don't understand," I say. "How did you survive in the first place?"

"I have what they call a *rare condition*. Partial androgen insensitivity syndrome. One in fifty thousand. In almost all respects, it is a terrible affliction to suffer. Not only the physical symptoms…"

Again his mind seems to wander. Somewhere in the past, he is being attacked. "Do you know what it's like, to be different that way? Do you know how people treat you?

"At any rate," he says, "it was natural that I would pursue research in the field of hormones. And, as it turns out, it was natural that I would be resistant to the…the bug. Even so, I have to pump myself full of steroids to survive." He holds up the syringe that Brainbox prepared for him. "The effect, as you can see, is physically unpleasant." He gestures at the blotchy, paper-thin skin of his face. "Not to mention the fact that I have a difficult time processing cortisol. Stress hormones. I'm a nervous wreck." He takes a swig of water. "Some days I don't want to go on. But I do. For humanity. And thank God for that. If it were not for my survival…the world would end."

He stares at me, wanting me to agree.

"I want to go home," I say.

"Oh," says the Old Man, "there's no question of that. You have to stay here. You're too important."

"I want to go home."

"This is your home now."

He slips the needle into his vein and presses the plunger.

DONNA

I'M GOING FULL-ON Green Mile up in this bitch. Like, my new best friend is an ant.

I met her—I think it was yesterday? She was crawling along the seam of the floor and the wall opposite my cell door. She looked kind of busy, but I was like, "Whoa, girlfriend! Hang out for a while! Have a drop of water. Try a piece of protein bar. Tell me what's doing back at the anthill."

But after a while, she moved on. Not many visitors since. Just the swimming darkness and thousands of seconds on my hands.

Then the door swings open. The blond kid is there, and Brainbox is with him. It's confusing because Brainbox is totally free? Like not tied up.

Blond Kid: "It's time to get ill." He taps a sawed-off bat against the wall.

Then Brainbox holds a Taser up to the kid's neck and zaps him.

How did Brainbox get a Taser? Why didn't the kid suspect him? What the hell is going on?

The kid is down on the floor, spasming, retching, and wetting himself all at once. Brainbox zaps him again.

Brainbox: "Come on. We need to get out of here. Something big is happening soon."

Me: "What's happening?"

Brainbox: "You'll see."

Me: "How do you know?"

Brainbox: "I heard it on my radio."

Me: "Dude, there's nobody on the radio."

Brainbox: "Yes, there is."

Me: "*What?!*" Like, what?!

Brainbox gives me a look that says *There's no time to explain now.*

"Come on," he says. "It's over."

JEFFERSON

"**THIS IS YOUR** home now."

The Old Man smiles.

Then a drop of blood oozes out of his nose. He wipes at it and looks at the red smear on his hand. He looks at the syringe Brainbox gave him. The syringe he just emptied into his veins.

His body tightens, as though his brain has ordered his entire body to clench every muscle at once.

I stand up. He tries to stand up, too, but he can't.

DONNA

QUICKLY NOW, all ninja and stuff, we lock the door behind the kid spasming. Brainbox has his club and his keys.

Across the corridor is another cell. We open it and find Peter in there, half asleep against the far wall.

Brainbox: "Be quiet."

Peter gets up quietly, squinting in the light of the corridor. Down the way, the video games and music are still going.

Peter: "Theo and Captain?"

Brainbox: "Past the games room."

But at that moment, two of the Islanders come out. They stare, amazed, and duck back, raising the alarm.

Peter: "I've got this. Go find Jefferson and Kath."

He charges toward the Islanders as they pour out of the games room.

JEFFERSON

I LEAN OVER and grab his throat.

His neck is like a tree trunk. I worry that my hands might lose their purchase, but the ridges and valleys of his screaming tendons and the absolute dryness of his skin mean that they don't slip.

His strength is terrible. He tears at my arms, scoring deep scratches that run with blood.

But, as the seconds go by, the air leaves him.

And finally he stops moving.

When I look up, Brainbox is at the door, with Donna at his side.

My first thought is to go to her and take her in my arms. But my hands are still frozen into claws; my blood and his blood are all over.

Peter bursts into the doorway, bruised and bloody himself. Captain and Theo trail behind him. They just have time to swing the metal door shut before the Islanders can get in.

DONNA

JEFFERSON IS ALIVE. I had prayed for this, to whoever was or wasn't out there. I had bargained and negotiated and promised anything in return.

Guess I'll be going to church. Guess I'll cultivate a better attitude.

He's leaning over the Old Man, who is very dead, his eyes all bulging. Judging by how Jefferson looks, he's the one who did it.

Brainbox goes over to a table where Kath is lying.

Brainbox: "She's gone," he says. "I'm sorry."

Jefferson straightens up and closes his eyes like he's about to cry.

Kath, you bitch. You always have to steal the scene.

Peter is trying to keep the round handle of the big vault door from spinning. The Islanders are trying to turn it on the other side.

We all go to help him, grunting as we grab onto the handle with slippery hands.

No way out. No weapons.

This is the end.

JEFFERSON

FOR A WHILE, there's nothing but the sound of breathing as we struggle to keep the door locked.

Then, quietly at first, I begin to hear a regular, mechanical drumbeat: *whup whup whup.*

The handle of the door turns for us as the resistance drops off on the other side.

I risk a glance through the glass—and I see the Islanders turning away from the door.

The sound gets louder. *WHUP WHUP WHUP.*

And I realize that it's the air being cleaved by blades.

That can't be possible.

We let go, looking up to try to catch the noise—

WHUP WHUP WHUP WHUP.

"I need to tell you," says Brainbox. "They're coming. I heard it on the radio."

"The radio's dead," I say.

"No. Shortwave. Long distance. The signal bounces off the ionosphere."

"I don't believe you," I say.

"Go and see," says Brainbox.

So we open the door. The sound is louder now, deafening; you can't speak over it. So we stop trying to.

By now the corridor is abandoned.

And in the forecourt of the building, the Islanders are standing, looking up at the heavens, their hair blown back.

I follow their eyes. This is not possible. Not unless everything we thought we knew was wrong.

Not unless something has been hidden from us.

Then, in a moment, I see it all, and the truth takes my breath away. Brainbox fiddling with his radio. In the middle of the night, alone in his library, he switches to shortwave and hears the voices of the world that has survived skipping off the top of the sky. Alone, he listens. And keeps the secret.

I look over at Brainbox. "Why didn't you tell us?"

"You wouldn't understand," he says. He looks up at the sky.

He looks up and doesn't seem surprised at all by what he sees.

It's a helicopter. A swirling halo of black blades above a gray underbelly.

On the belly, a white star in a blue circle. A word: NAVY.

Leaning over the edge, a man—a *man*—thirty, forty years

old? Who can tell anymore? A face in a thick, sealed helmet. He gestures for us to get out of the way.

I reach out and take Donna's hand. She looks into my eyes, unsure.

Nearby on the ground, a teddy bear somebody dropped.

We stand together and look up at the old world as it arrives.

The grown-ups are back.

ACKNOWLEDGMENTS

I am grateful to Professor James Giordano, director of the Center for Neurotechnology Studies and Regents' Fellow of the Potomac Institute for Policy Studies, for his advice on bioweapons and his patience with my slow understanding. Thanks also to the Science & Entertainment Exchange, a program of the National Academy of Sciences, for introducing me to Dr. Giordano. It needs to be stated that I took tremendous liberties with his good ideas and am entirely to blame for the resulting inaccuracies and inadequacies. My gratitude also goes to Alvina Ling, my editor at Little, Brown; and Suzanne Gluck, my book agent at William Morris Endeavor, for their kind guidance. Certain ideas regarding money, culture, and economics in David Graeber's book *Debt: The First 5,000 Years* were very inspiring. I also wish to thank Mr. Reif Anderson, formerly of the Allen-Stevenson School, for insisting that his students write stories daily. Thank you to Ms. Genny Thomas and Ms. Leila Thomas for their assistance and encouragement. Lastly, I would like to thank the populace of Black Rock City, Nevada, for their stirring example of how life might be lived.